P9-CMV-813

Hark! The Herald Angels Sing

ALSO BY DONNA ANDREWS

Toucan Keep a Secret

How the Finch Stole Christmas!

Gone Gull

Die Like an Eagle

The Lord of the Wings

The Nightingale Before Christmas

The Good, the Bad, and the Emus

Duck the Halls

The Hen of the Baskervilles

Some Like it Hawk

The Real Macaw

Stork Raving Mad

Swan for the Money

Six Geese A-Slaying

Cockatiels at Seven

The Penguin Who Knew Too Much

No Nest for the Wicket

Owls Well That Ends Well

We'll Always Have Parrots

Crouching Buzzard, Leaping Loon

Revenge of the Wrought-Iron Flamingos

Murder with Puffins

Murder with Peacocks

Lark! The Herald Angels Sing

A Meg Langslow Mystery

Donna Andrews

Minotaur Books

A Thomas Dunne Book
New York

This is a work of fiction. All of the characters, organizations, and events portrayed in this novel are either products of the author's imagination or are used fictitiously.

A THOMAS DUNNE BOOK FOR MINOTAUR BOOKS.
AN IMPRINT OF ST. MARTIN'S PRESS.

For information, address St. Martin's Press, 175 Fifth Avenue, New York, N.Y. 10010.

www.thomasdunnebooks.com
www.minotaurbooks.com

Library of Congress Cataloging-in-Publication Data

Names: Andrews, Donna, author.
Title: Lark! the herald angels sing : a Meg Langslow mystery / Donna Andrews.
Description: First edition. | New York : Minotaur Books, 2018.
Identifiers: LCCN 2018025710| ISBN 9781250192943 (hardcover) | ISBN 9781250192967 (ebook)
Subjects: LCSH: Langslow, Meg (Fictitious character)—Fiction. | Women detectives—Fiction. | Christmas stories. | GSAFD: Mystery fiction. | Humorous fiction.
Classification: LCC PS3551.N4165 L37 2018 | DDC 813/.54—dc23
LC record available at https://lccn.loc.gov/2018025710

First Edition: October 2018

10 9 8 7 6 5 4 3 2 1

Acknowledgments

The fabulous crew at St. Martins/Minotaur continues to be wonderful to work with—including (but not limited to) Joe Brosnan, Hector DeJean, Jennifer Donovan, Meryl Gross, Paul Hochman, Andrew Martin, Sarah Melnyk, Kelley Ragland, and especially my editor, Pete Wolverton. And once again I am spoiled by David Rotstein and the Art Department with another beautiful cover.

More thanks to my agent, Ellen Geiger, Matt McGowan, and the staff at the Frances Goldin Literary Agency for handling the business side of writing so brilliantly and letting me concentrate on the fun part.

Many thanks to the friends—writers and readers alike—who brainstorm and critique with me, give me good ideas, or help keep me sane while I'm writing: Stuart, Aidan, and Liam Andrews, Chris Cowan, Ellen Crosby, Kathy Deligianis, Margery Flax, John Gilstrap, Barb Goffman, David Niemi, Alan Orloff, Art Taylor, Robin Templeton, and Dina Willner. Thanks for all kinds of moral support and practical help to my blog sisters and brother at the Femmes Fatales: Alexia Gordon, Dean James, Toni L. P. Kelner, Catriona McPherson, Kris Neri, Hank Phillippi Ryan, Joanna Campbell Slan, Marcia Talley, and Elaine Viets. And thanks to all the TeaBuds for two decades of friendship.

Suzanne Frisbee and Joni Langevoort remain my stalwart experts in all things Episcopalian, so if the Reverend

Robyn and Trinity are doing anything inappropriate, it's obviously something I failed to ask them about.

Thanks to Janet Caverly and her family, who made a generous donation at the Malice auction in return for having her name used for one of the characters in this book. Anything positive that my fictional Janet does was obviously inspired by her namesake, and anything negative was obviously the character, not the real person.

And above all, thanks to the readers who continue to enjoy Meg's adventures!

Hark! The Herald Angels Sing

Chapter 1

"Melchior! Give Caspar back the frankincense! And Balthazar, if you don't stop throwing myrrh at the shepherds, I'm demoting you to junior sheep!"

I gazed sternly at the three middle-schoolers who were playing the wise men in this year's church Christmas pageant. Wise persons, actually, since we'd given the role of Caspar to one of the girls. Melchior and Balthazar assumed implausible expressions of innocence, and Caspar wisely postponed any vengeance she'd been planning against her rowdy fellow Magi.

I turned my gaze on the shepherds, who quickly pretended that they hadn't been about to start yet another fencing match with their crooks. And then on the Virgin Mary, who was chewing gum again. Her jaw froze, and then she swallowed hard.

"We only have three more rehearsals left." I spoke calmly, but with the precise enunciation that should warn any child who was even halfway paying attention that they were all on very thin ice. "If anyone has decided that appearing in the Christmas pageant is too much work, just speak up and I'll find someone to replace you."

The faces of the younger cast members—the ones playing sheep, assistant shepherds, or junior angels—took on an eager, hopeful look as they glanced around to see if any of the older children with larger roles were having second thoughts. The older children all assumed expressions of injured dignity.

Well, except for my own twin eleven-year-old sons. Both of them regularly appeared in children's roles in local theater productions and prided themselves on being young professionals in the dramatic arts, well on the way to following in their father's footsteps. Josh, who played Joseph, was doing a fair imitation of my stern parental manner. Jamie, the angel Gabriel, was contemplating his fellow cast members with an expression that tempered melancholy disappointment with celestial forgiveness.

I stared at the cast for a few more moments, letting my words sink in. Then I gave them a brief, approving smile and clapped my hands.

"Places, everyone!"

The children swarmed to take their starting positions. The sheep and shepherds milled stage right. Joseph, Mary, and the angel Gabriel formed a semicircle around the manger. The wise persons clustered stage left, followed by the half-dozen children who'd be playing their camels. The camels had been behaving quite angelically ever since I explained to them that the three best-behaved among them would get to wear the camel heads while the remaining three would play the camels' rear ends. I needed to find similar leverage over the rest of the cast. Since my notebook-that-tells-me-when-to-breathe, as I call my giant to-do list, wasn't within reach, I made a mental note to brainstorm on the matter.

Mary knelt beside the straw-filled manger and bent tenderly over it. Then she snapped her head up and shuffled backward a foot or so, still kneeling.

"Baby Jesus needs a new diaper," she said, wrinkling her pert, freckled nose.

Josh bent over, sniffed, and nodded.

"We don't need Baby Jesus," I said. Several shepherds tittered. "I mean, we don't need to have him lying in the manger this early in the rehearsal. We don't want him getting tired and cranky."

The central role of Baby Jesus was to be played by four-month-old Noah, the son of the Reverend Robyn Smith, Trinity Episcopal's rector. At least that was Robyn's idea. I was more of a pragmatist when it came to children. Noah might be cherubic-looking, but he was also colicky. I didn't think the congregation was ready for the spectacle of a red-faced infant Messiah shrieking loud enough to drown out the choir. I planned to make sure we didn't lose track of Noah's understudy, a highly realistic life-sized baby doll.

And since Noah had neither lines nor blocking to learn, we certainly didn't need him at rehearsal.

"Robyn?" I turned and scanned the sanctuary. "Has anyone seen Reverend Robyn?"

"Right here." Robyn bustled in through a side door. "Do you need Noah now?"

"We don't need him at all today," I said. "Could you take him back to your office?"

"Of course." She turned to leave.

"Robyn, wait."

I was about to ask why she was leaving without Noah. Then I realized—she was holding Noah. And bouncing him up and down while he uttered a few of the choking noises that usually signaled his intention to begin howling like a banshee.

I turned back to the stage. If Robyn was holding Noah—

"That's not Noah," Jamie said, shaking his head hard enough to make his halo bounce.

"What child is this?" Josh proclaimed dramatically.

I could see the shepherds and wise men starting to inch closer to get a better look.

"Everybody, stay where you are," I ordered.

I hopped up onto the stage and swept aside the thick

tangle of straw to peer down at the infant. Definitely not Noah—this child was blond. Although I estimated he was probably about the same age, four months, give or take a little. He, or more probably she, was wearing a pink onesie. Not that the color necessarily meant anything. When Josh and Jamie were infants, Michael and I had received a few pink and purple hand-me-downs. Michael had initially turned up his nose at these, but the week both boys came down with a stomach bug—and shared it with us—even he had given up his objections to the girly clothes when we'd run out of more masculine outfits.

I could figure out the baby's gender when I did the diaper change, which was definitely needed. Though the child was happy at the moment, smiling angelically, the way many infants do once they've accomplished a particularly smelly bowel movement.

Unlike Noah, who could be heard out in the hall, screaming his lungs out.

"Look." Jamie, who was leaning over the back of the manger, pointed to something—a note attached to the baby's clothing with a large safety pin. It was folded once, and there was nothing written on the outside, but presumably there was a message inside.

I lifted up the top flap of the note with the edge of my finger, something I realized I'd picked up from my cousin Horace, a trained crime scene investigator. Probably overkill in this situation, but still.

I read the note and froze.

Chapter 2

I let the note fall closed again and looked up at Josh and Jamie.

"What does it say?" Jamie asked.

Josh was busy frowning at Mary, who was lying back on one of the decorative hay bales gagging and breathing heavily, as if to suggest that the mere smell of the infant's diaper had triggered a life-threatening illness.

"I'll tell you later." I flicked my eyes around as if to suggest that the note's contents were a secret for their ears alone. Both boys got the point immediately.

"Stand back, everyone," Josh shouted. "The kid needs air."

"He might be contagious," Jamie added—in a tone that was softer, but still designed to carry.

The other children, who had been inching closer, jumped back. No one wanted to catch anything less than a week before Christmas.

"Josh, Jamie," I said in an undertone. "Look around to see if you can spot anyone who might have dropped off this baby. Josh, you check the grounds. Jamie, search inside the church."

Their faces lit up and they dashed out.

"Kirstie, can you take charge while we break?" Kirstie was the Virgin Mary's real name—unless I'd been calling her by the wrong name since the first rehearsal. She didn't always respond to it.

But she did this time. Her respiratory problem disappeared immediately as she stood up and gazed around, checking to see if anyone was doing anything wrong that she could pounce on.

"Take the children to the back of the sanctuary," I told her. "Don't let anyone go near the manger. Run lines with them if you like. I'll be back as soon as possible." I picked up the infant and headed for Robyn's office, through a foyer littered with the snow boots everyone had taken off on arrival. At least the snow itself had stopped for the time being.

Robyn was already in her office, pacing up and down while bouncing Noah vigorously on her shoulder. The bouncing didn't look like anything a baby would enjoy, but Noah did, and she'd figured out it was the only thing that placated him.

"We have a problem," I said as I entered.

"You know where the diapers are." Robyn pointed to the changing station she'd set up on her credenza.

"A bigger problem," I said as I laid the newcomer on the plastic mat that now covered the credenza. "I'll explain in a minute."

"Whose baby is it?" Robyn asked. "I don't recognize her. Or him."

"That's part of the problem. Someone just left the poor thing in the manger."

"Oh, dear," Robyn murmured. She tucked her white clerical collar back where it belonged, only to have it pop out immediately. And her black clerical vestments were spattered with blobs of what I hoped was merely baby food. She looked frazzled already. "Perhaps it's just a practical joke. Or perhaps someone in the congregation resents our using Noah in the pageant and wanted to suggest that her baby would be a better choice."

As if protesting this, Noah let out an unusually loud shriek.

"They could have a point," Robyn added with a sigh.

"Do we have anyone else in the parish with a three- or four-month-old baby?" I asked.

"Not that I'm aware," Robyn admitted. "And I think I'd have remembered if I'd seen a baby that adorable anywhere around town."

"Then I think Noah's role is safe, provided he can learn not to have temper tantrums during the Adoration of the Magi."

"Hmm." Robyn sounded dubious. Maybe I was starting to get through to her.

I turned my attention to the unknown baby. Who did, indeed, need a change of diaper. Badly. She could also have used a bath, but I made the best of it with a small mountain of diaper wipes.

"We should alert Chief Burke," I said when I had the diaper situation under control. "I already sent Josh and Jamie to scout around, in the hope that they could spot whoever dropped the kid off. And—"

"But Meg," Robyn said, gently. "If some poor unfortunate woman came to the realization that she was unable to care for her child and thought Trinity would be a safe refuge in which to leave the poor innocent lamb, we don't want to undermine our reputation as a sanctuary. In fact—"

"If that's what had happened, I'd agree," I said. "But I don't think so. She had this pinned to her."

Using a tissue so I wouldn't leave fingerprints on the note, I gently tore it off the safety pin and held it up for Robyn to read. Its block-printed contents were already engraved on my memory:

Rob—

I can't afford to take care of her, but from what I hear about Mutant Wizards I guess you can, so she's yours now. Don't blow it this time!

The note was unsigned. It was written on a scrap of pale blue paper about four by five inches, that looked as if it had been rather carelessly cut from a larger sheet.

"Oh, dear." Robyn shook her head. "I see what you mean about a problem. Are we sure she means your brother, Rob?"

"Why else would she mention Mutant Wizards?" There were probably other men named Rob working at my brother's highly successful software company, but Rob, as its CEO, was the one who was well known as a financial success. And, I had to admit, something of a ladies' man—though less so in the last two years, when to everyone's surprise—and Mother's relief—he'd found a steady girlfriend.

"And there's no signature," Robyn added.

"If what she says is true, Rob should have at least a vague idea who she might be without any signature. And if it's not true—well, she definitely wouldn't sign the note in that case. There's probably some kind of a law against making false paternity accusations."

"So you think . . ." Robyn's voice trailed off.

"We won't know till we ask him." I picked up the infant and set her in the portable crib Robyn kept in her office. It wasn't as if Noah was going to calm down and want to sleep in it anytime soon. "So as soon as I've notified Chief Burke, I'm going to call Rob."

"Oh, dear. I wonder how Delaney will take this," Robyn said softly.

I could have said "badly," but I figured Robyn already knew that. Delaney McKenna was Rob's girlfriend. She was smart, creative, personable, beautiful, and already a favorite with the entire family. Rob had sworn me to secrecy before confiding that he was planning to ask her to marry him sometime over the holidays and enlisting my help in figuring out the optimally romantic setting. I didn't tell him that pretty much everyone we knew had already figured out the way things were heading. I was expecting general rejoicing when he shared the news of their engagement.

But even Delaney had a few faults—a temper that matched her fiery red hair and a jealous streak a mile wide. As I dialed 911, I found myself looking down at the little blond stranger, already fast asleep in the portable crib, wondering if she was going to derail all of Rob's plans.

Chapter 3

"Nine-one-one, what's your emergency, Meg?"

The joy of living in a small town, where everyone knows your name. Even Debbie Ann, the emergency dispatcher. In fact, in my case, especially Debbie Ann.

"Someone abandoned an infant at Trinity Episcopal," I said. "Not sure that quite counts as an emergency, but it is time-sensitive, since I figure whoever did it can't have gone far."

"Do you have a description?"

I glanced down at the infant.

"She's blond, blue eyes, about two feet tall, thirteen or fourteen pounds—"

"I meant a description of the person who abandoned her."

"I figured that," I said. "But as far as I know, no one saw the drop-off. We just have the baby."

"Chief's on his way," she said after a moment. "And several deputies to help with the search. Can you give me any more details?"

As I told Debbie Ann about the unexpected drama during rehearsal, I noticed that Robyn had gotten out her first-aid kit. I looked down at the baby. Had Robyn seen some injury I'd missed?

Robyn rummaged in the kit, took out a pair of tweezers, and used them to pick up the note from where I'd left it on her desk. I breathed a sigh of relief.

"By the way," I said to Debbie Ann. "I suppose we should

also notify social services that we'll need a place for Jane Doe to stay."

"Lark," Robyn said. Or maybe it was "Hark!" Neither made much sense.

"Hang on, Debbie Ann," I said into the phone. "What was that, Robyn?"

"Her name is Lark," Robyn said. She held up tweezers to show me the note. And yes, scrawled on the back in large, loopy, untidy cursive letters was the word "Lark."

"Apparently her name is Lark," I told Debbie Ann.

"Excellent. Not a very common name—it could help us identify her. And speaking of identification, Horace will be there soon. I'll tell him to do a DNA swab."

"We will eagerly await his arrival," I said. "And we'll call if anything else comes up."

"Roger."

I disconnected the call and stared down at the baby. Lark, as I supposed we should start calling her.

"Can you hold that thing up again?" I pointed to the note.

Robyn obliged, and I used my cell phone to take pictures of both sides of the note.

"Is Debbie Ann sending someone?" Robyn asked.

"The chief and several deputies. Look, the chief will probably want to talk to me, but I don't want to leave the kids unsupervised for too much longer. I left Kirstie in charge, but I'm not sure how long she can keep them in line. The last time I had to leave rehearsal for this long I came back to find the wise guys playing poker with Melchior's gold and shepherds running chariot races by hitching the sheep to the costume storage boxes."

"You go on," Robyn said. "I can watch both babies."

"Until both of them need something at once. I can't do that to you."

Robyn looked relieved. After all, she was still a fairly new mother—and hadn't had my experience of managing infants in pairs. If Noah wasn't so single-mindedly attached to her, I'd volunteer to watch both infants. In fact, I realized with a sigh, I probably should anyway. Robyn could handle the pageant cast. And—

"Meg? What's going on?" Michael stepped into the office, looking both elegant and professorial in gray flannel pants and a tweed jacket—he must have come straight from some end-of-semester meeting at the college. The fact that he was in his sock feet was a little incongruous, but presumably he'd left his snow boots with all the rest in the foyer. "I found Josh wandering around the graveyard, peering into the shrubbery and digging into snow drifts. He claimed he was on a secret mission from you."

"He is," I said, and quickly explained about the foundling.

"What a cutie," he said, softly, as he peered down at the sleeping Lark. "So what can I do to help?"

"Can you take over the rehearsal?" I asked.

"While you talk to the chief?" he said. "Can do."

"And treat the manger as a crime scene," I said. "Keep the kids away from it."

"Roger."

He strode out. A few minutes later I heard his resonant voice from the sanctuary.

"Thank goodness," Robyn breathed. "Michael is so good with the children."

"And any changes he makes to my blocking are bound to be improvements," I said. "And the kids might be a little more willing to take orders from someone who is both a professional actor and a college drama professor."

"I'm sure they're delighted to be working with you," Robyn protested.

"Anyway, I have one more call to make before the chief gets here." I pulled out my phone, took a deep breath, and punched the shortcut button to call Rob.

Chapter 4

"Hey, Meg," Rob said. "What's up?"

"Long story," I said. "And I think I should tell you in person. Can you come over to Trinity?"

"You mean now? It's the middle of the workday."

"You're the boss," I pointed out. "You can set your own hours."

"But it's up to me to set a good example," he said. "And we're going to have a really interesting discussion on the new virtual reality game in a few minutes, and then—"

"Rob—remember the discussion we had the night before last?"

A pause, while Rob searched his memory. The discussion in question had been about the relative merits of surprising Delaney with an engagement ring versus letting her pick out her own.

"Yea-ah," he said, slowly.

"If you want that project to keep moving forward, get over here ASAP."

I cut the connection. And when Rob tried to call me back, I ignored him. If he complained, I'd explain that I had to talk to Chief Burke.

It wouldn't be entirely a lie. While I was ignoring Rob's attempts to return my call, the chief strode into Robyn's office, his round brown face creased in a slight scowl.

"So you've found an abandoned baby?" he asked. "What happened?"

I pointed at the portable crib, and explained, while the

chief stared down at Lark. The sight of her brought a quick smile to his face, in spite of the seriousness of the situation. On cue, Robyn held up the tweezers to display the note.

"And no one noticed who left the poor little cherub?" he asked when I'd finished.

"I'd have had my back to the manger and was busy trying to keep order." I explained about the rowdy wise persons and the dueling shepherds. "Normally I run a pretty efficient rehearsal, but the kids were just wild today."

"Not surprising," he said. "After all, they only had a half day of school today, and they're all pumped up about the start of their winter vacation." The chief and his wife were raising three of their grandchildren, so he was equally au courant with the school situation.

"Not to mention the fact that I don't think a single class did a lick of real work today," I grumbled. "Apparently they all watched *Mr. Magoo's Christmas Carol* and *How the Grinch Stole Christmas* and ate Christmas candy. I know scientists claim there's really no such thing as a sugar high, but I'm not convinced."

"Neither am I," he said. "And to top it all off, most of them can't wait to go out and play in the snow."

"Yeah. I keep telling them it's not going anywhere for the next few days," I said. "So since I was wrangling the wild bunch, King Kong could have walked through the room and I wouldn't have noticed. And if any of the kids had seen anything I'm sure they'd have found it much more interesting than the rehearsal, and they'd have made a big fuss. But I didn't ask them—I didn't want to contaminate any potential witnesses with my amateur interrogation efforts."

"I think after more than a decade of motherhood you've forfeited your amateur status when it comes to interrogation," the chief said with a smile. "But I appreciate your restraint. And here's Horace."

My cousin Horace Hollingsworth had halted in the doorway of Robyn's office, his stocky frame radiating uncertainty. I could see the very moment when Horace, the parishioner who didn't often show up for Sunday services, gave way to Horace, the seasoned crime scene specialist. His shoulders straightened, and he stepped inside more confidently. I wondered if I should tell him that one of his socks had a hole in the heel.

"We need DNA on the baby." The chief indicated the crib. "And Meg has a piece of evidence for you."

"Chief," Robyn said. "I have to protest—you're treating this as if it's a crime. What if some poor woman felt she had to give up her child for the child's own good? And saw Trinity as a safe, loving place to do so? And—"

"If that turns out to be the case, I can't imagine the town attorney would want to press any kind of charges." The chief sounded perfectly calm, but I noticed with interest that he was clenching his sock-clad toes impatiently. "But whoever left this baby made an accusation of paternity—if that's true, the biological father would have both a financial responsibility for the child and potentially a legal claim for her custody. We need the DNA to settle that."

"I see." Robyn still didn't look overjoyed, but she understood the chief's point.

"Besides—we got an Amber Alert yesterday. Missing baby in Suffolk. Believed to be custodial interference on the part of the father—"

"Does the baby look like Lark?" Robyn asked.

"Hard to say. The only picture they had was badly out of focus and several months old—taken right after the birth, and I have to admit that one chubby red-faced newborn looks a lot like every other to me."

"And that's the only picture they have of their baby?" Robyn sounded incredulous. She had a good point. She and Matt had already taken hundreds of pictures of little Noah. Michael and I probably had hundreds of thousands of our two. What kind of parent wouldn't have at least a few recent photos of a beautiful baby like Lark?

"Maybe the father stole the baby pictures along with the baby." The chief shrugged. "Lark's the right race, gender, and approximate age—that's about all you can tell from the hospital photo. I rather doubt that the father abducted the child only to abandon her here, but we'll need to rule out the possibility that this baby is the one missing from Suffolk. Horace, when you're finished here, join me in the sanctuary."

Horace nodded, and set his forensic kit down on Robyn's desk. The chief strode out.

"So what's the evidence?" Horace said. "Probably a good idea to secure that first. The kid's DNA isn't going anywhere."

Robyn held up her tweezers. Horace read the note, and his eyes grew wide.

"Is this for real?" he asked.

"Your guess is as good as mine," I said. "However, your expert DNA analysis will be worth more than all of our guesses put together."

"What does Rob say?" Horace reached into his kit and took out a brown paper envelope.

"I haven't told him yet."

"He's on his way over," Robyn added. Horace was holding the envelope open. After a gesture from him, Robyn dropped the note into it.

"I want to break the news to him in person," I said.

"You mean you want to see his face when you tell him." Horace was sealing up the envelope.

"That too."

Robyn was still holding the tweezers, looking as if she missed the fun of being able to show the note to any new arrivals. Then Noah uttered a few piercing shrieks, suggesting he was revving up for another grand scale performance.

"Just call if you need me," she said as she hurried toward the door. "I need to take Noah someplace where he won't deafen everyone."

"China, perhaps?" Horace said under his breath when she was safely out the door.

"I'm sure he'll be a wonderful addition to the choir when he's a little older," I said.

Horace nodded. He'd finished writing whatever it was he had to write on the brown paper envelope and tucked it into his kit. Then he took out a small package marked DNA COLLECTION KIT.

"I see you use the swab variety of DNA test," I said.

"Works better for our purposes than the kind where you spit in a test tube." He looked surprised at the question. "Some of our subjects aren't exactly cooperative, and it can be hard enough to get them to hold still to be swabbed. When did you become such a connoisseur of DNA tests?"

"Since Grandfather started taking an interest in it, and bought a rapid DNA testing machine for the lab at his foundation."

"He has?" Horace looked interested. "Is Dr. Blake thinking of getting his lab certified so we could use it for DNA testing?"

"You'd have to ask him," I said. "He's mostly interested in animal DNA, of course." Grandfather was a zoologist and environmentalist and had founded the J. Montgomery Blake Foundation to further his work with animals. "But while the lab's coming up to speed, he's gotten interested in comparing the accuracy of the results they can achieve with what the various commercial testing services provide. He calls it using humans as the guinea pigs for a change. So most of us have gone through several rounds of spitting into test tubes and having the inside of our cheeks swabbed."

"See if you can talk him into getting it certified," Horace said. "Not that we have to do DNA testing all that often, but when we do, it's a real pain to have to send the samples down to Richmond."

Lark barely stirred as he gently inserted the swab into her half-open mouth and rubbed it against the inside of her cheek. But as he was removing it she opened her eyes and reached out with one tiny, plump hand to grab his gloved index finger.

Horace froze and stared at her for a few moments. Then he carefully disentangled his finger.

"Striking blue eyes," he said.

Yes, they were striking. Was he merely struck by them, or was he reminding me that Rob, like Lark, had very blue eyes?

"Indeed," I said aloud. "Of course, a lot of Caucasian babies are born with blue eyes. Too early to tell if hers will stay blue."

"When do babies' eyes change?" Horace tore his gaze away from the baby and focused on putting the swab in the sterile container and labeling it.

"It varies," I said. "Dad always says you have no way of knowing the eye color for sure before the kid's first birthday."

"Any idea when Rob's getting here?" Horace was tucking the DNA kit into his bag. "I need to swab him, too."

"Grandfather should have his DNA profile on file," I reminded him.

"Grandfather's files don't have a proper legal chain of custody," Horace said. "I hope we don't end up needing that, but just in case . . ."

I nodded.

"So when Rob gets here—" Horace began.

"I'm here! I'm here!" Rob burst into the office. "The suspense is killing me! What happens when I get here?"

Horace was reaching into his bag and suddenly froze. I turned to see what he was looking at.

Delaney had come along with Rob.

Chapter 5

"So what's the big emergency?" Rob asked.

"I'm dying of curiosity," Delaney added. I noticed that they were wearing matching blue socks with pink flamingos on them. At any other time that would have made me chuckle. Now—

My phone rang. It was Debbie Ann, from the police station.

"Hey, Debbie Ann," I said. "Horace is here, and Rob and Delaney just arrived." I hoped she'd read between the lines that unless she was calling me about something earth-shattering, she should probably let me get back to figuring out how to brief Rob on what was happening without sending Delaney into orbit.

"I won't keep you then," she said. "Just wanted to let you know that your dad's heading over to the church to check out the baby, and Meredith Flugleman should be there any time now."

"Meredith Flugleman? Why—Oh, of course." Meredith Flugleman was from Child Protective Services. For that matter she was also from Adult Protective Services. At the moment, she was Caerphilly's only official social worker. And while she was probably as well-meaning and good-hearted as anyone I'd ever met, she was also so relentlessly upbeat, so cluelessly literal, and so monumentally annoying that the mere prospect of her arrival made me long to be back in the sanctuary dealing with the Christmas candy–hyped pageant cast.

First I had to brief Rob and Delaney on what was happening—preferably in a way that wouldn't set off Delaney's temper.

"Great," I said. "I'll keep you posted. Gotta go."

But I'd lost precious time. Delaney had drifted over to the crib.

"Aww," she cooed. "Is this Robyn's kid?"

"I could have sworn Noah had brown hair," Rob said.

"He does," Horace said.

"Then who's this?"

"Her name's Lark," I said.

"Pretty name." Delaney reached out a finger and laughed as Lark grabbed it. "Whose is she?"

"Long story," I said.

"We don't know yet," Horace said.

"What do you mean you don't know yet?" Rob asked. "Who left her here?"

"Mr. Langslow." The chief appeared in the doorway. And from his angle he probably only saw Rob. The door blocked his view of Delaney. "Good. After Horace takes your DNA, may I talk to you for a minute?"

"DNA?" Rob sounded puzzled.

"DNA?" Delaney didn't sound puzzled. She glanced from blond, blue-eyed Rob to blond, blue-eyed Lark. And then at Horace, who was clutching his forensic kit protectively to his chest as if arming himself against the outburst that was obviously coming. "She's yours then? Is that what they're saying?"

"Mine? Can't be," Rob said.

"Oh, sure," Delaney said. "Then why are the police here to take your DNA? Do you take me for an idiot?"

"I mean it." Rob was shaking his head. "The kid can't be mine."

"Delaney," I said. "Someone dropped off the baby here at Trinity with a note that seemed to implicate Rob. But so far that's just an anonymous accusation. Rob's DNA can disprove it."

Or prove it, if the anonymous accuser was telling the truth. Best not to bring that up right now.

Not that Delaney was listening anyway. She turned on her heels and headed for the door.

"Ms. Langslow is correct," the chief was saying. "You'd think that the availability of DNA testing would discourage false paternity accusations but in fact—"

He was talking to Delaney's back as she pushed past him into the hall.

"Delaney!" Rob started after her. "Wait!"

"Go to hell!" she called back.

Rob started to follow her. Horace and I both grabbed him. The two of us together would have had a hard time holding him if he'd made a serious attempt to escape, but he was visibly shaken and didn't fight us.

"This will just take a few seconds," Horace said, pulling out the swab from a second DNA collection kit.

Rob stood, hopping from foot to foot, while Horace poked around the inside of his mouth with the swab. The second Horace was finished, Rob took off as if I'd fired a starter's pistol.

"Sorry," the chief said. "I didn't see her. The girlfriend, I gather."

"Yes," I said. "At least she was, up until a few minutes ago. All bets are off at the moment."

Vern Shiffley, one of the chief's deputies, strolled in and leaned his long, angular form against the door jamb, scratching the sole of one grayish-white sock-clad foot against the toe of the other.

"Word's out," he said. "Diverting resources here."

"Search parties to see if we can spot the person who dropped off the baby," the chief said, in answer to my unspoken question.

"Sorry we didn't manage to detect whoever did it," I said. "I know that would have made things easier. Now you have to track him or her down when your department is already overworked, what with all the tourists coming to town for the Christmas in Caerphilly festival."

"To say nothing of the search for Pemberly, Mrs. Thistlethwaite's ginger striped tomcat, who disappears so regularly that he ought to be classified as a migratory species. And all of it with half a foot of snow on the ground and more on the way." Fortunately he looked more amused than annoyed. Then his face fell slightly "And then there's the latest Hatfield and McCoy nonsense from Clay County."

"Latest Hatfield and McCoy nonsense?" I echoed.

"Someone who works for the Dingles shot a Whicker," the chief said. "Or maybe it was the other way around."

"I thought the Plunkets were involved," Vern put in.

"Instead of the Whickers or instead of the Dingles?"

Vern shrugged.

"You could be right." The chief sighed. "I know I wasn't born here, but you'd think I'd have learned to keep them straight by now."

"I *was* born here, and I can't keep them straight half the time," Vern said.

Not surprising, since Dingles, Whickers, Plunkets, and Peebleses made up nearly two thirds of Clay County's phone book.

"They don't exactly take kindly to outsiders," I remarked. "So they've had another murder in Clay County?"

"Not yet," the chief said. "Victim's still alive—for the moment."

From the grim set of his jaw, I deduced the prognosis wasn't good.

"So how does this attempted murder complicate our lives here in Caerphilly?" I asked.

"They've asked us to keep an eye out for the alleged

shooter," the chief said. "Who took off into the woods and might be headed in our direction. Man by the name of Mark Caverly. Not native to Clay County, apparently."

"I'd have guessed that from the last name," I said. "Who is he, then, and what's he doing in Clay County?"

"From what I heard, he's an accountant that Mayor Dingle hired to straighten out the county's books," Vern said. "Guess they finally realized doing that takes someone who can actually count."

The chief chuckled. Just then his phone rang, and with a nod to us he stepped a few paces away to answer it.

"Are you really looking for this Caverly guy?" I asked Vern, low enough to make sure the chief didn't hear.

"The chief had me round up some of our best family trackers," Vern said. "They're out combing the woods for him now. At least they were until I called them off that and sicced them on looking for whoever abandoned the kid."

"Probably just as well to call them off," I said. "If they find Caverly, they're just going to hand him over to Clay County?"

"He might turn out to be a murderer," Vern pointed out.

"Even a murderer deserves a fair trial," I said. "Do you really think an outsider who killed a Plunket or a Dingle would get a fair trial in Clay County?"

"He'd be lucky if he lived to get a trial at all," Vern said. "Odds are before long we'd hear he'd either hanged himself in his cell or got shot trying to escape. It's happened before. That's why we set a bunch of my cousins to looking for this Caverly guy, instead of sworn officers. If they find him, they're going to watch him bash a few mailboxes—federal crime—and then help him turn himself in to the Feds somewhere else. Maybe Goochland County—they know all about Sheriff Dingle over there. Or maybe they'll encourage him to cross the state border and find an FBI office in North Carolina. Anything to keep him out of Clay

County for long enough to let them simmer down. Of course you didn't hear any of that."

"And I very much approve of everything I just didn't hear," I said.

"If you ask me, I think the chief's a little relieved to have this missing baby thing pop up," Vern said. "Gives him a much more solid reason not to have the whole force out looking for Clay County's fugitive."

"Good point, but we've got the baby—it's her parents who are missing."

"Same diff, really. She's missing from wherever she should be and whoever she should be with. And we aim to fix that."

He paused for a few moments, then levered himself off the door frame and strolled over to peer into the crib. Lark gurgled and waved her arms and legs at him.

"Cute little tyke," he said as he strode off.

"Little do you know how much trouble you're causing," I said to the baby as I took a seat at Robyn's desk where I could keep an eye on her. She crowed and chirped as if delighted to have someone talk to her.

"Where's my patient?"

Chapter 6

I glanced up to see Dad barging in, carrying what looked like a battered old-fashioned black doctor's bag but actually contained a very modern high-tech portable medical kit.

"Not sure she counts as a patient," I said. "There doesn't seem to be anything wrong with her."

"Then why call a doctor?" My grandfather trailed in after Dad, looking more like a scarecrow than usual. Dad was also wearing old, disheveled clothes—in fact, they both looked as if they'd been dragged through a hedge backward—but somehow the disarray looked less startling on Dad's shorter, plumper form.

Grandfather frowned down at Lark. "Looks perfectly healthy to me." He had large holes in the big toes of both his socks, and the toes themselves were wiggling vigorously, as if reveling in their freedom from both boots and socks.

"I'm sure the chief just wants to make sure she's as healthy as she looks," I said. "Before we turn her over to Child Protective Services."

"Oh, so Meredith's coming?" Dad, now standing by the crib, rummaged hurriedly in his bag. "I'll make this quick, then, and get out of your hair."

Leaving me to cope with Meredith by myself. Well, I could understand how he felt.

"So whose baby is this anyway?" Grandfather asked. "And why are you turning it over to Child Protective Services."

"We have no idea whose baby she is," I said. "And that's

why the chief called Child Protective Services. We found her lying in the manger."

"Wrapped in swaddling clothes, I assume." Grandfather looked pleased with himself for coming up with this biblical allusion.

"In a pink onesie, which I suppose is the modern equivalent," I said. "And—"

"Meg, you've got to do something!" Rob burst back into the room, looking wild-eyed. "She won't speak to me!"

"I'll talk to her," I said. "But I think you should give her some time to calm down."

"Give who time to calm down?" Grandfather asked.

"Delaney," Rob and I said in unison.

"What have you done now?" Grandfather scowled at Rob. I deduced that he must approve of Delaney.

"Nothing," Rob said. "Meg, I don't think she's going to calm down."

"She has to calm down eventually. And it might be just as well to wait until we can tell her the results of the DNA tests."

"DNA tests?" Grandfather peered down at Lark with greater interest. "So this is potentially a new great-grandchild?"

"No!" Rob shouted. "Absolutely not!"

"Calm down," I said. "We believe you."

"At the moment you're the only ones, then," Rob said. "Look—whoever had this kid would have gotten pregnant about a year ago, right?"

"Correct," Dad said, looking up from his examination. "She appears to be a normal, healthy baby of approximately four months of age. So allowing a wide margin of error—say two to six months—she would have been conceived between fifteen and eleven months ago."

"Then no way she's my kid," Rob said. "Because a year and a half ago was when Delaney and I started getting really serious. And I haven't cheated on her. Not back then and not since. So this kid can't possibly be mine."

"A pity," Grandfather said. "A likely looking specimen if you ask me."

"Aargh!" Rob threw himself down on Robyn's settee and glared at Grandfather. Which showed how very upset he was—normally he was charmed by almost anything Grandfather did, no matter how annoying. "Me-eg!"

"Rob, I'll talk to her when I get a chance," I said. "And I will suggest to your grandfather that in the interest of family harmony he might want to refrain from saying things that will only add to his unjustly accused grandson's suffering."

I frowned at Grandfather as I said it.

"Just trying to keep up with what's going on," he said. "So what are you calling it?"

"It?"

He gestured toward the crib.

"*Her* name is Lark," I said.

"Odd sort of name," he said, with a harrumph. "How'd you pick that?"

"I didn't," I said. "Whoever dumped her here did."

"Given the circumstances, I'd have gone for something like Cuckoo."

"Cuckoo?" I echoed. "Are you seriously suggesting we name her Cuckoo?"

"The cuckoo is an obligate brood parasite," Grandfather began.

"A what?" Rob asked, sounding interested in spite of himself.

"An obligate brood parasite," Grandfather repeated.

"It means they lay their eggs in other birds' nests," I translated.

"Precisely." Grandfather beamed at me. "Non-obligate brood parasites lay eggs in the nests of other birds of the same species, but also make their own nests and lay eggs there. Bank Swallows and African Weavers are some of the most common species that do this. It's a way of helping ensure that their genes survive—if their own nest is destroyed or raided, they still have some young in another nest who might survive. But obligate brood parasites have completely lost the instinct or ability to build nests and incubate their young. They're totally dependent on other birds for the continuation of the species."

"Is all this leading up to some practical suggestion to solve my problem?" Rob asked. "Because if it isn't, I'd just as soon postpone the ornithology lesson."

"Just suggesting that Lark isn't a very relevant name for our little intruder," Grandfather said. "I'd have to look it up to be sure, but I don't think larks are known for practicing brood parasitism."

"We're not renaming her Cuckoo," I said.

"Although curiously enough, cowbirds are among the most common brood parasites," Grandfather continued.

"Cowbird would be even worse," I said. "Let's just stick with Lark, shall we?"

Grandfather shrugged as if to suggest that if we failed to take advantage of his superior knowledge of ornithology it was our loss.

"As far as I can tell, she's just fine," Dad said, tucking his stethoscope back into his bag. "Ask Meredith to let me know who ends up fostering her, and I can drop by in a day or so to check on her."

"Can do," I said.

"Let's go see if Horace is still around," Grandfather said. "I could borrow a DNA collection kit from him and have my lab techs run their own test. Most police labs are so backed up that it could take weeks or even months to get the official results. But I can have my technicians fast-track it. Do something useful with that fancy new rapid DNA machine I just bought them. And give Rob the proof he needs a lot sooner."

"Great idea," I said. "Rob, could I ask you something?" He'd been at the door, about to dash out in search of Horace, but he paused and let Dad and Grandfather go by.

"She ran out without even putting her boots on," he said. "Just grabbed them and ran out into the snow."

"She was pretty quick to assume the worst," I said. "Any reason why?"

"Things have been a little weird lately," he said. "I figured maybe it was just because we both knew we were on the brink of something pretty major, you know? Working through last minute doubts and all that. Bound to put stress on a relationship."

I was impressed—Rob wasn't generally quite so attuned to such things.

"Seems logical," I said aloud.

"Yeah, that's what I thought when Michael suggested it," he said. "And then there's the ex-girlfriends showing up."

"Ex-girlfriends?" I echoed. "Plural?"

"Only two of them," he said. "And one was just a bit of drunken flirting at the office Christmas party."

"And the other?"

"The other had herself delivered to my office after hours in a big Christmas present, and then jumped out of the box wearing nothing but a few strategically placed sequins. Took a while to convince Delaney that I hadn't given her any encouragement. And just when we'd got past that . . ."

He sighed and shook his head.

"Go find her," I said. "I can help if necessary, but I think you need to at least try to talk to her. After all, if you get married, you'll have disagreements from time to time. You need to figure out how to solve them without big sister's help."

"This is a pretty big disagreement."

"So I'll help if you need me," I said. "But you try, too."

He nodded and ran out.

"My goodness! Where's the fire?"

Meredith Flugleman had arrived, looking trim and formal in a pin-striped skirted suit. She'd even put on little crocheted slippers after taking off her snow boots, to protect her pantyhose from runs. After blinking slightly at the haste with which Rob had left, she strode briskly over to me and held out her hand.

"Meredith Flugleman, Child Protective Services," she said, unnecessarily, during our brief, businesslike handshake. Did she think I'd forgotten her since yesterday's town and county staff holiday party?

"Child in need of your services," I said, pointing to the crib. "Did Debbie Ann explain how she arrived?"

"She did." Meredith's face wore an all-too familiar expression—a frown that combined puzzlement with just a hint of disapproval. "But I suppose she must have gotten it wrong. How could the baby just appear in the manger during the Christmas pageant rehearsal without anyone noticing it?"

"Early dismissal from school today," I reminded her. "Which meant that the children arrived bouncing off the ceiling. I had my hands full keeping order, and would have had my back to the manger. The chief's trying to find out if any of the kids saw anything, but I doubt it."

"Well, let's hope he succeeds," Meredith said. "And quickly. Because I'm going to have a hard time placing the infant, even for the short term. Right now nearly all of our resources are already fully deployed."

I assumed this was bureaucratese for "nearly all of our foster families already have as many children as they can handle."

Meredith pulled her cell phone out of her purse, gave it

a stern glance as if willing it to behave properly, and pressed a few buttons. Then her frown vanished.

"But this voicemail could be good news. Excuse me." She pressed more buttons, turned her back, and walked a few steps away, patting at her hair as if checking to make sure no invisible strands had escaped the tight knot at the back of her head.

She hadn't yet taken more than a cursory look at Lark, I realized. Every other person who'd been in the office had. Robyn found her adorable. Michael called her a cutie. Even Grandfather, who didn't have a sentimental bone in his body, pronounced her a likely looking specimen. But to Meredith, she was merely a problem in logistics. Not for the first time, I wondered how in the world she had ended up in social work. Had she stuck a pin at random in a list of respectable careers for the modern professional woman?

And what happened if she had no resources to allocate to Lark? Would she start looking for a foster family in other counties? How long would that take, and where would Lark end up while it was going on? Surely not with Meredith. I remembered once when I'd been at the women's shelter Robyn ran, doing a few repairs, Meredith had dropped by to extract some bureaucratic paperwork from one of the residents. The young woman had given her infant to Meredith to hold while she filled out the forms. Meredith had quickly revealed that childcare was not her strong suit.

"My goodness," Robyn had said in an undertone from where we were watching. "You'd think she was holding ten pounds of dynamite wrapped in paper-thin glass."

"While roller-skating across a minefield," I'd added. "Maybe I should go over and offer to help."

"Let's give her a moment," Robyn had replied. "She's got to learn eventually."

But Meredith had handed off the infant as soon as she

could that day, and I suspected she'd done all she could to avoid repeating the experience.

"Well," Meredith said as she thrust her phone into her handbag. "That was not the news I was hoping for. Mrs. Shiffley is in the hospital."

"Which Mrs. Shiffley?" I asked.

"Mrs. Bertha Shiffley." Meredith sounded slightly surprised that I had to ask. "She's the only Mrs. Shiffley on our foster parent rolls."

Though not, of course, the only Mrs. Shiffley in the county. In fact, there might be as many as a hundred other Mrs. Shiffleys in Caerphilly. Was Bertha the only one civic-minded enough to volunteer to foster, or merely the only one who'd manage to pass whatever persnickety screening process Meredith used to vet candidates? I had my suspicions.

"What's she in the hospital for?" I asked aloud.

"She fell off the roof while installing Christmas decorations," Meredith said. "Rabbi and Mrs. Grossman have agreed to take the two children who were staying with Mrs. Shiffley. But that brings them up to their maximum of four, and leaves us with only one couple who have already been vetted and approved as foster parents." Quite possibly, from her tone, a couple of whom she did not altogether approve.

"Who's that?" I felt a little anxious about where Lark would end up. Of course, whatever was making Meredith uncomfortable probably wouldn't bother me. It might even be something I approved of. Maybe they were artists. Freethinkers. Unreconstructed hippies. Still. The unknown mother may have intended for Lark to end up with Rob, but either accidentally or on purpose, she'd left her in my care. I felt responsible.

"Well . . . you and Mr. Waterston. You are eligible foster parents."

Chapter 7

"Michael and I are eligible foster parents? That's a surprise." I wasn't lying. Michael and I had applied a couple of years ago, when Meredith had begun showing up to make lengthy fact-filled presentations at joint town and county meetings about the need for more foster parents. We weren't inspired by civic zeal so much as the pragmatic realization that Meredith would keep returning again and again to repeat her earnest PowerPoint presentation until she had recruited enough potential fosters to meet some arbitrary quota and keep her happy. Others had volunteered, possibly for the same reason, and mercifully the torture by PowerPoint had ended. Although, since Meredith had never formally notified Michael and me that we were on the list, I had assumed we had somehow fallen short of the required level of perfection.

And she didn't look particularly delighted at welcoming us to the ranks of foster parenthood. "Of course, I can see how awkward that could be given . . . well, the circumstances," she said.

"You mean the fact that my brother is accused of being the father? It's not as if Michael or I would hold that against the poor kid." The mother, yes, if Chief Burke managed to track her down. But Lark was certainly an innocent.

"If there were any other option available, I wouldn't ask you to do this. Although I suppose it might be just as well to have her with your family in the event there turns out to be a connection." Meredith brightened at the thought, as if it made everything so much tidier.

"Not that it will turn out that way." Clearly Meredith didn't believe Rob. Perhaps I was foolish for doing so, but I did. "Just let me check with Michael."

I dashed out of the office before she could object and headed for the sanctuary. But I saw the chief standing just outside the door.

"If you're looking for your rehearsal, I sent it down to the parish hall," he said. "We're treating this as a crime scene."

"Did any of the kids see who left the baby?"

"One of the shepherds asserts that two ninjas rappelled down from the ceiling with the baby hanging from a rope sling between them," the chief said. "The girl wise man is positive that her fellow magi must have snuck it in as a joke, though she has no idea how. And a kindergartener explained to me with great earnestness that you can't see the stork when he brings you babies because he's invisible, and it doesn't even matter if you don't have a chimney."

"I think he's confusing the stork and St. Nick."

"Probably. So unless I want to put out a BOLO on storks and ninjas, the children's eyewitness testimony gives me nothing to work on. Any idea where Ms. Flugleman's going to place the baby?"

"Probably with us, if Michael has no objection," I said.

"That's good," he said. "Though I didn't know you were approved foster parents."

"Neither did we. I suspect we're on the secret list of people Meredith prefers not to entrust a child to unless she has no other options."

The chief chuckled, and I proceeded down to the parish hall. As I approached I could hear the children singing "Silent Night." Reassuring. Most of the pageant consisted of the various cast members posing, pantomiming, or delivering very short lines to the accompaniment of Christmas carols sung by the children, with or without the choir.

When I peered into the parish hall, I saw Michael standing on a chair with a copy of my script. The sheep and shepherds on one side and the wise men and camel parts on the other were either singing or pretending to, watching as Mary, Joseph, and the angel beamed down at the cardboard box that was representing the manger.

Michael spotted me and waved.

"Take five," he said to the children when the carol had ended. "You want your director's seat back?" he added, turning to me.

"Any chance you could take over as assistant director for the rest of the rehearsal?" I explained about our newfound foster parent status. "So I should round up what we need to keep her for what I hope is a very short time—unless you think we should find some reason to weasel out."

"No, it'll be great," he said. "It's not as if we don't have plenty of room—and plenty of hands to help us out with her, with so many relatives coming to town for the holidays. It'll be fun!"

As I made my way back to Robyn's office, I made a mental note to remind him of that the first time Lark woke us up for a midnight feeding.

I could hear her crying now—not an impressive Noah-style wail, but she definitely wasn't happy about something. I found Meredith standing over the crib, wild-eyed, wringing her hands. When she saw me walk in, she backed against the wall on the opposite side of the room and seemed to breathe a sigh of relief.

"I was about to call your father," she said. "It—the infant—she seems to be unwell."

"She's probably hungry." I checked Lark's diaper, just in

case, then picked her up and set her against my shoulder. "Or bored and wants attention."

Lark calmed a little when I picked her up, but was still fussing quietly. I checked the small fridge, in which Robyn usually kept a bottle or two of formula ready so whoever was keeping an eye on Noah would have something to give him if he howled bloody murder during the Sunday service or a meeting she couldn't easily interrupt. I stuck the bottle in the microwave for what I recalled as the optimal number of seconds, tested the temperature on my wrist, and offered it to Lark. She began sucking greedily.

"Well," Meredith exclaimed. "You don't seem to have lost the knack."

She didn't have to sound so surprised. Maybe I wasn't on her short list for parent of the year, but I happened to think Michael and I were managing to raise two pretty nice kids—in spite of whatever shortcomings she might see in how we went about it.

"I'll drop by later with the orientation kit," Meredith said.

"Orientation kit?"

"A list of the major dos and don'ts," she said. "Child welfare rules and regulations. Copies of several relevant parts of the Virginia code. Some nutritional guidelines. And—well, there has been a lot of new research in early development lately. I'm sure you'll find it all very useful."

She favored me with another brittle, professional smile, picked up her purse, and trotted out.

I waited, a little tensely—Meredith was famous for appearing to leave, then darting back in with one more question or bit of what she thought was useful advice. Rather like Lieutenant Columbo, except that his "one more thing" usually elicited an important clue. All Meredith ever seemed to accomplish was embarrassing people whose reaction to her apparent departure was to remark how glad they were she was gone.

I didn't relax my guard until I saw her car drive out of the parking lot. Then I breathed the traditional sigh of relief.

"I'll probably have to read her ridiculous orientation kit," I told Lark. "Always possible that it was written by someone other than Meredith. Someone who's actually fed or changed an infant at some point in her life—or at least picked one up. But I think Uncle Michael and I have a pretty good idea what you need."

Though I mentally marshaled my defenses against any Meredithian interference. My cousin Rose Noire, who occupied one of our many spare bedrooms, was currently off in the mountains on some kind of winter solstice retreat with a group of fellow New Age herbalists. But she'd be back tomorrow, and I could put her in charge of Lark's nutrition and of making sure her stay with us was a wholly positive, organic, enlightened experience. I could get Dad to drop in daily to monitor her health and well-being. Meredith might try to boss Michael and me around, but she'd have a harder time doing so if we were backed by Caerphilly's eminent natural food and wellness expert and its most beloved physician.

"So the boys want to meet our new temporary family member," Michael said, strolling into the office with Josh and Jamie behind him.

"Couldn't we have a new brother instead?" Josh asked. "That would be more fun."

"It's okay," Jamie said. "We can still teach a little sister to play baseball. Look at Great-Grandma Cordelia." Cordelia, who had played in the All-American Girls Professional Baseball League as a young woman, was the unofficial but highly effective batting coach for the Caerphilly Eagles, the boys' Summerball team.

"Lark's only staying with us until we find her real parents," I explained. "I doubt if she'll stay around long enough to learn to play catch."

"What if her real parents don't want her?" Josh countered. "After all, they dumped her on us."

"Then Child Protective Services will find someone to adopt her," Michael said. "Someone who wants a baby very much but doesn't have one."

"But we don't have a little sister," Jamie protested, assuming an expression designed to show that he was suffering mightily from this cruel deprivation.

"I think we'll survive," Josh replied.

"I gather rehearsal is over," I said.

"And the boys and I are going Christmas shopping," Michael said.

"You're not invited," Josh added.

"Because you're the one we're shopping for," Jamie explained.

"Good," I said. "Someone needs to wait with the kids until their parents can collect them."

"Robyn's handling that," Michael said.

"Then I will take Lark back to our house and get her settled in. I'll text you if I think of anything she needs."

"Good idea. Laters!" Michael gave me a quick kiss and headed out, with the boys following.

Lark had fallen asleep still holding the nearly empty bottle, so I tucked her back in the crib. Then I pulled out my trusty notebook and began making a list of things we'd need to care for an infant, even temporarily.

"Coast clear?"

Dad and Grandfather had returned.

"Meredith's gone, if that's what you mean," I told them. "And Lark's coming home with us for the time being—apparently Michael and I are the only available foster parents in the county."

"Good! That will make it much easier to keep an eye on her." Dad beamed at the prospect of adding another patient to his roster.

"Any chance you could help me haul a few things to my car?"

Dad and I left Grandfather in charge of Lark—after all, how hard could it be with her fast asleep?—and went to the overflow room, the church's general-purpose storage and filing room. Robyn had installed a couple of cabinets there, in which she collected clothes and household items to be donated to the poor or to women passing through the Caerphilly Women's Shelter. Michael and I had long since handed down the baby gear we'd used with the boys—much of it to this very collection—so I didn't think Robyn would mind if we borrowed a few items for the short term.

We loaded the car with a portable crib, a folding playpen, some bottles, a few items of clothing, and half a dozen diapers scrounged from Robyn's ample supply. It would normally have been a very quick task, but we spent at least fifteen minutes searching the vast herd of snow boots to find Dad's. A few parents had arrived to pick up their kids after the rehearsal and were doing the same frustrating task. I couldn't help gloating over the fact that my boots—like Michael's and the boys'—were relatively easy to find, since I'd attached brightly colored sleigh bells to the laces. Although, to my dismay, I noticed at least one other pair of boots whose owner had done the same thing. If my bells became a fad, I'd have to think of something else to make our boots easily findable.

When we stepped out into the parking lot, we both had to stop for a moment to let our eyes adjust to the glare. Some of the children were running up and down one end of the parking lot, yelling excitedly as they threw snowballs at each other, while a couple of the parents were plying snow shovels at the other end, removing some of the mounds of snow the plow had left behind. A pity their efforts were about to be undermined by the next round of snow.

"What a beautiful winter day!" Dad exclaimed.

"It'll cloud over later," I reminded him.

"Bringing us even more snow!" he exclaimed, and then burst into song. *"I'm dreaming of a white Christmas!"*

I decided not to point out we already had more than enough snow to ensure a very white Christmas indeed. Instead, as we crunched over the parking lot to my car, I breathed in the cold, crisp air, listened to the happy shouts of the snowballers, and made a conscious effort to match my mood to his buoyant good spirits.

"Need anything else?" Dad said when we'd finished loading my car. "Because unless you do, I should go and change."

"I'm fine," I said. "What are you changing for?"

But he'd already dashed back into the church.

No doubt he'd tell me when he felt like it.

Chapter 8

I went back inside and shed my snow boots, being careful to remember where I'd left them, exchanging greetings with the various parents who were rummaging for their children's boots. Then I returned to Robyn's office to find that she had taken over the job of watching Lark. Grandfather, who was probably grateful to be off the hook, had disappeared.

"Oh, good," Robyn said. "There you are. You found everything you needed for Lark, then? She'll be such a big hit at the party."

"Party? What party?" Not that I had anything against parties, but I had a lot to do to get ready for taking care of Lark, and I had been planning to go straight home. But I put on a cheerful face. No matter how loudly all the tasks in my notebook-that-tells-me-when-to-breathe were calling to me, I didn't want to spoil Robyn's excitement over the latest entry in Caerphilly's packed calendar of holiday events.

"The Christmas party at the women's shelter," she said. "And in honor of the occasion, we're relaxing the rules and allowing a man to visit."

"A man? Who?" Both for practical safety reasons and for the peace of mind of the women who stayed there, Robyn had made it a rule that no men were allowed at the shelter. As a result, I was there a lot—if the place needed any repairs, they usually fell either to me or to one of the two young Shiffley women, Amber and Brianna, who'd defied old-fashioned gender stereotypes and gone into the building trades like at least half of the men in their family. As far as I knew, only one man was ever welcomed or even tolerated at the shelter—Dad, who provided free medical care to the women and children who stayed there.

"Well, who do you think would visit this time of the year?" Robyn asked.

Possibly a repairman for the furnace, I mused, if it was acting up again, although I'd thought that it was working reasonably well now, thanks to the repairs Brianna and I had done. But neither of us were furnace experts.

Robyn was humming something. Trying to give me a clue, no doubt. But while Robyn had many excellent qualities, being able to carry a tune wasn't one of them. She seemed to be humming either "The Itsy Bitsy Spider" or "Ding Dong! The Witch Is Dead," neither of which suggested any visitor who would be particularly welcome at the shelter.

"Oh, for goodness' sake—Santa!" she finally exclaimed. "'Santa Claus is comin' to town,'" she warbled, in several randomly chosen keys.

So that was what she'd been trying to hum. I'd never have guessed.

"Nice," I said aloud. "The kids will love that. Not, I suppose, with the reindeer and sleigh, though."

"No—actually, we did think of that. A horse-drawn sleigh, at least—it was a tempting idea. But then we realized all the tourists would think it was part of the Christmas in Caerphilly festival, and follow it to the shelter, and that would draw too much attention. So he's just going to ride over there with me—I can drop him at the door, so he doesn't have carry the presents very far."

"And who do we have playing Santa?"

"Ho, ho, ho! Merry Christmas!"

Of course. I turned to find Dad, resplendent in red

velveteen and white fake fur. He hadn't put on the boots yet, and the beard was askew, but still, even partly costumed he made a decent St. Nick.

"Can one of you fix this?" he asked, pointing to the beard. "And help me with these blasted boots? I can't bend over properly in this costume."

I directed Dad to sit on Robyn's sofa and got to work with the spirit gum to attach the fluffy white beard. Robyn handed Noah to Dad, and bent down to help him with the boots. To our astonishment Noah, who had been fussing persistently in what was, for him, a relatively low level of volume—not much louder than a jet engine—gurgled a few times before falling fast asleep in Dad's lap.

"You're hired." Robyn seemed awestruck. "I've never seen him do that."

We were almost sorry when our work with beard and boots was done and Dad had to give up Noah to pick up the sack of presents. But Dad's calming effect seemed to linger on, even after Robyn had tucked the little noise machine back in his carrier.

"Wait—wasn't Grandfather with you?" I asked Dad as we all marched out to the foyer. "What's he going to do while we go to the party—because we can't take him to the shelter, you know."

"He understands about not being able to come with us." Dad had picked up a pair of boots that was obviously several sizes too small to be his and was studying them with a puzzled expression—apparently having forgotten that he was already wearing boots. "He's going to get some reading done in the parish hall, and one of us can pick him up after the party."

"Great." I retrieved the boots Dad was holding and put them down in what I hoped was their original location. Thank goodness the parents had now collected most of my pageant participants, so there were only twenty or so pairs of boots left in the foyer.

Robyn and I took off to make our separate ways to the shelter. Well, not exactly to the shelter but to one of the places nearby where those of us who helped at the shelter tended to park so no one who knew of our involvement would spot all our cars in one place. As I made my way through the crowded streets of the town, I wondered if the shelter's location was really such a big secret anymore, but I wasn't going to be the one to give up the cloak-and-dagger precautions we all took.

The impending snow didn't seem to have daunted the tourists. They were out in force, and with them the locals who were pitching in to make Christmas in Caerphilly a success. Parties of carolers and small groups of musicians, all in Victorian costume, were stationed every few blocks in the central part of town. Most of the churches had set up food stands in or around the town square, with costumed parishioners doing a brisk business in coffee, hot tea, hot chocolate, hot spiced cider, brownies, gingerbread men and women, shortbread, sugar cookies, rock candy, funnel cakes, cotton candy, taffy, fruitcake slices, roast chestnuts, miniature apple or pumpkin pies, and tiny plum puddings. As long as you weren't trying too hard to watch your diet, you could fill up on these, which was a good thing, since every restaurant that took reservations had been booked up weeks in advance, and those that didn't had lines out the door.

Of course, as long as the weather didn't get too cold, most tourists didn't mind the wait. In addition to the omnipresent musicians and carolers, Michael had convinced the town to hire several dozen of his perennially impoverished drama students to provide what he called "street theater." Students small enough to pass as urchins picked the pockets of portly Victorian gentlemen, only to be apprehended by kindly bobbies in mutton chops. Apple-cheeked nannies in outfits reminiscent of Mary Poppins gossiped loudly and amusingly as they wheeled prams along the sidewalks. A tall figure in a deerstalker hat prowled the streets, occasionally whipping out a magnifying glass to study a boot print or a bit of trash and then muttering, "Aha! The game is afoot!" before striding off purposefully, with his stout companion trailing along behind him. And an elderly gentleman in a shabby greatcoat and tall hat stalked the streets, dismissing beggars, carolers, and the occasional bold tourist with a grating "Bah, humbug!" Although the whole thing had started off as simply a random series of vignettes, the drama students had been gradually improvising an overall plot, so anyone who spent enough time in town would ultimately figure out that the urchins were actually in league with Professor Moriarty, who was planning to kidnap Scrooge, but would be foiled late in the day by Holmes and his secret allies, the nannies. At least, that was what was going on a few days ago, when I'd had time to roam the town and observe. Knowing the drama students, by now the whole thing could have mutated into something completely different. No matter—it kept the tourists happy. And happy tourists meant happy restaurant owners and shopkeepers.

I managed to make it to the shelter first, and entered my pass code in the digital lock on the gate. I smiled up at where I had deduced the security camera was hidden. Just then Robyn pulled up to drop off Dad.

"Should we wait for her?" Dad asked, as he joined me in the front yard.

I glanced across the door of the house—a three-story white-frame Victorian with soaring ceilings, several cupolas or turrets, and, most important, enough rooms to easily handle fifteen or twenty residents. The door now bore a festive wreath trimmed with a red flocked bow. Beside the door was a small curtained window. Opening the gate set off a chime in the house, so by the time you made it into the yard and approached the door, someone was almost always at the window, peering out. When I visited, I usually saw anxious faces, until they confirmed that I wasn't whoever they were hiding from. Then the anxious looks disappeared, maybe even replaced by a smile if it was someone who'd met me before and knew I was coming to fix things up.

The curtain was pulled back wider than usual, and I could see three faces. A young woman and two children, girl and boy, both around five or six. The children's faces were wide with wonder. For that matter, the young woman, who looked as if she might still be in her teens, seemed a little awestruck.

"I think we should go on in," I said. "Your public is waiting."

Dad snapped into character. Although come to think of it, he was almost always in a jovial mood, especially this close to Christmas. So he was mostly just being Dad, only a little noisier. And without his usual tendency to announce that anything out of the ordinary must be a clue to an as-yet undetected murder.

"Ho, ho, ho!" he boomed as he shouldered his present sack. "What a heavy bag! Let's go deliver some presents and make it easier to carry."

The door swung open, and we could see a cluster of eager faces in the entry.

Dad was always a hit as Santa. He'd made his debut appearance in the role about a decade earlier, when someone had knocked off the rather unpleasant local who'd traditionally played the role in the annual town Christmas parade. Lately Dad had expanded his holiday-time Santa mission, making appearances at a staggering number of children's hospitals and pediatric wards in addition to the annual parade.

But the shelter children probably wouldn't have had a chance to see him in the parade—it didn't pass down this quiet residential street, and Robyn tried to limit the residents' time outside the shelter, for safety reasons. A good thing the shelter's backyard was much larger than the front, filled with trees, and surrounded by an eight-foot privacy fence, so the kids weren't stuck indoors all the time.

Josefina, a fifty-something Mexican-American woman who'd arrived at the shelter as a resident a decade ago and stayed on to become its cook, housekeeper, and den mother, took an immediate fancy to Lark, and kept her occupied while Dad distributed the presents and Robyn and I circulated with juice and cookies.

"Your mother has outdone herself again," Robyn murmured. "The new decorations are fabulous."

The new decorations weren't actually new. Quite a few of them were ones Mother had been using for the last few years at our house or at what she and Dad called their farmhouse. Perfectly lovely decorations, of course, that she'd merely grown tired of seeing. I'd successfully protested the extravagance of buying new decorations until this year, when Robyn had sent out word that the shelter could use something better than the sparse collection of shabby hand-me-down decorations they'd been making do with.

Technically, the shelter's new decorations were still hand-me-downs, but no one could have guessed it. Mother had done a fabulous job of taking the very random-looking collection of decorations donated by at least a dozen families and figuring out a way to use all of them in a well-coordinated design. Well, most of them. A couple of families had donated items she considered bland, too cutesy, or downright tasteless, like the blown-glass skunk ornament, the yodeling pickle, the twerking Naughty Reindeer, and the plush Pull My Finger Farting Santa doll. After opening the box that had contained the last two items, Mother had been forced to retire to her bed with a cool cloth over her forehead for several hours. Fortunately she'd found a way to not use them.

"Wonderful news!" she'd subsequently announced at a meeting of St. Clotilda's Guild, Trinity's organization for ladies who wanted to do good works, which had taken on the shelter Christmas decoration project. "We had so many donations that I was able to sell some of the more coveted items to buy a stand for the Christmas tree!"

Luckily, she'd managed to pull it off, so anyone who didn't see her donations festooning the shelter would assume they were among the "coveted items" whose sale had helped fund the tree stand. Actually, she'd bought the spurned donations herself for an extravagant price, and sent them to a cousin in California with orders to donate them to a thrift shop there, just to make sure the donors didn't run across their items. Except for the twerking reindeer and the farting Santa. She'd sworn me to secrecy and enlisted my help to burn those.

Although I didn't break my word and reveal how Santa and the naughty reindeer had met their demise, I did take pictures of all the worst ornaments so Michael could see them. I was a little worried that he might be planning to give Mother a few tasteless ornaments as a gag gift. Although surely anything he came up with would be tame beside what we'd already seen—wouldn't it?

I shoved the farting Santa and the twerking reindeer out of my mind and concentrated on the lovely decorations that had found their way to the shelter. Battery-operated candles graced all the windows, the kind whose bulbs flickered slightly to increase the illusion that they were real. The tree that brushed the ceiling and the yards and yards of evergreen garlands had been provided by some of the Shiffley woodsmen. The tree was thick with ornaments—Mother had wisely resisted doing anything artsy, like a theme or a restricted color scheme, and just gone in for a good old-fashioned eclectic tree. I recognized some of the ornaments—the tiny gold musicians that had once decorated a small tree in our house. I think Mother had replaced them with glitter-dusted red and purple velvet fruit. A large flock of brightly colored felt elves that Mother had found adorable, until it became clear that Thurston and Bruce-Partington, Mother and Dad's cats, found them both irresistible and indigestible. Presumably the elves were safe here, since Robyn kept the shelter itself pet-free in case of allergies—with Clarence Rutledge, the local vet, providing a temporary refuge for any livestock the residents might bring with them. Yes, the tree was a hit; all the decorations were.

"It's like living at the North Pole," one of the children had said when we'd finished decking the shelter's halls.

And today it was even more like the North Pole, with Santa Dad distributing presents. I could see Josefina's broad face beaming as the women and children opened their gifts—she'd been our secret weapon, our spy who reported back what each of them wanted or needed most. Everyone seemed to be having a wonderful time.

Well, almost everyone.

I noticed one girl, a little older than the rest, who didn't seem to be enjoying Santa's visit. In fact, she seemed to be leaning against the wall that was farthest away from Dad and peering suspiciously at him.

I went over and offered her a cup of hot cider.

"You okay?" I leaned against the wall beside her.

She nodded and looked up at me over the top of the cup, studying me coolly, as if assessing my suitability for some important mission.

"He looks familiar," she said finally, nodding in Dad's direction.

"You mean Santa?" I asked.

"He looks like the doctor who visits here sometimes."

"Dr. Langslow?"

She nodded.

Clearly she was approaching the Age of Doubt, as Dad used to call it.

"You know who Clark Kent and Superman are?" I asked.

She frowned and nodded.

"Batman and Bruce Wayne?"

Another nod.

I put my finger to my lips and gave her a sidelong look, as if letting her in on a secret.

She studied me for a few more moments. Then she turned those very alert eyes on Dad for a while.

"Hmm."

I wasn't sure whether she'd bought the theory that Santa whiled away the time between sleigh rides as a small-town general practitioner, or if she'd just decided to humor me. But she sipped her cider and seemed to relax a little.

I found myself liking her. I could think of some kids who would have rushed to spill the beans and spoiled everyone's fun.

When all the presents had been distributed, Robyn slipped away to fetch her car. A few minutes later Dad glanced at the wall clock and pretended to be startled.

"Look at the time!" he exclaimed. "I must fly! I'm due in Tokyo in half an hour!"

He made his exit, tossing handfuls of wrapped candies after him. The residents followed him out into the yard and waved good-bye as he hopped into Robyn's car. I think the children might have tried to follow him down the street, but at just the right moment, Josefina distracted them.

"Who's ready for cake and ice cream?" she asked.

While the children swarmed the dining room, Josefina collected Lark and returned her to me.

"*Preciosa,*" she cooed. "Any time you want a break, you drop her off here. We haven't had nearly enough babies around here lately."

"I just may take you up on that," I said. "Especially if she's still with us when all my visiting relatives go home and Michael's new semester starts. And—sorry. I should get this."

My phone was ringing, and I could see that it was Dad.

"Could you pick up your grandfather?" he asked. "Robyn and I are going over to the hospital to cheer up the kids there, but he's getting impatient."

"No problem." It wasn't as if any part of my day was going to turn out the way I'd planned, thanks to Lark's arrival. Spending time with Grandfather might be nice.

Chapter 9

I bid farewell to Josefina and headed back to Trinity. When I got there, I found Grandfather pacing up and down in the vestibule, occasionally stopping to glare through the doorway into the sanctuary.

"I thought a church would be a nice peaceful place to do a little reading," he said in lieu of hello. "But then they started in on that infernal caterwauling. There they go again."

The choir had begun a rousing chorus of "Joy to the World."

"Not a moment of peace," he fretted. "Can you give me a ride to your house?"

"Sure." Although I wondered why he wanted to go to our house instead of Mother and Dad's farm, where he was staying. Still, I didn't want to ask in case he found the question inhospitable. So I waited while he called Dad to fuss about being left behind and arranged to be picked up later in the evening. Then I hoisted Lark's carrier again and we headed for home.

Part of Grandfather's reason for accompanying me became clear about halfway through our journey.

"Speaking of obligate brood parasites," he began.

We hadn't been, but I knew it would make him cranky if I pointed that out.

"Do you want to know the most fascinating thing about them?" Grandfather asked.

I sensed that answering "no" wouldn't be good for family harmony so I put on my polite face.

"What's that?" I asked.

"You'd think the host birds would figure out what was happening and retaliate, wouldn't you? Break the unfamiliar eggs. Kill the alien fledglings, or at least evict them from the nest."

"Do the host birds even notice?" I asked. "I mean, the term 'bird brain' does apply here."

"Well, in some cases it's hard for them to notice. Over time, the cuckoo, for example, has evolved to lay eggs that are remarkably similar to the host birds'. Meadow buntings lay white eggs with black speckles, so the cuckoos that prey on them lay white eggs with black speckles. The streaked laughing thrush lays a pale blue egg, and so does the cuckoo that targets them. Ornithologists sometimes have to use genetic markers to tell the eggs apart. Really a fascinating adaptation!"

"I'm starting to get the idea that cuckoos are really creepy birds," I said.

"They're positively diabolical." From Grandfather's tone, I got the feeling he rather admired the cuckoos' ingenious if underhanded tactics. It figured. While in theory he loved all of nature, he had a sneaking fondness for anything fierce or dangerous. Brood parasitism probably put cuckoos and cowbirds into this category. "And there's a growing body of research that suggests both cuckoos and cowbirds engage in retaliatory mafia behavior."

"Retaliatory mafia behavior?" I tried to picture it. Fedora-clad cuckoos with miniature sawed-off shotguns under their wings. A stout cowbird with a Don Corleone wheeze making the host birds an offer they couldn't refuse.

"It seems that after laying their eggs, the parasite birds hang around to observe the behavior of the host birds," Grandfather explained. "If the host birds destroy the cuckoo's eggs, the cuckoo will come back and destroy the hosts' eggs. Once the eggs hatch, if the host birds kill or evict the fledglings, the cuckoos retaliate by killing the hosts' fledglings. Same with cowbirds. So detecting and expelling intruder eggs actually has a negative effect on the host birds' ability to pass on their genes. Because of the cuckoo or cowbird predation, host birds who try to get rid of the intruders raise fifty to sixty percent fewer of their own offspring."

"So instead of being too stupid to tell their own eggs from a cuckoo's, the host birds are actually smart enough to realize that the cuckoos have them over a barrel, and the safest thing to do is suck it up and raise the alien offspring."

"Precisely!"

"If that's true," I said, "then cuckoos are quite possibly the creepiest birds on the planet. They make vultures seem cuddly. And what's this 'host bird' nonsense, anyway? Let's call it what it is—they're victims!"

"An accurate statement. But after all, 'Nature, red in tooth and claw,' you know." It was one of Grandfather's favorite quotes. Had it ever occurred to him that Tennyson wasn't paying Nature a compliment? "Interestingly, while there's considerable evidence of egg mimicry in the old world *Cuculus canorus,* from what I've read, our new world equivalents, the various cowbirds, show no signs of developing this tactic. Of course, there's a lot of work going on in this area, and I'm still catching up with the literature—mind if I use your library for a while? I need some peace and quiet."

He brandished an inch-thick wad of paper—a portion of the literature, I assumed, that the choir practice had distracted him from.

"Be my guest," I said as I pulled my car to a stop in our driveway. Frankly I was relieved to know he was seeking peace and quiet. I was more than half afraid he'd been planning to while away the afternoon making scientific observations of Lark and getting in the way of anything I needed to do to take care of her. "It should be quiet—school's out, so the boys won't be in there doing homework. In fact, they're off Christmas shopping with Michael."

"Maybe I'll take them on a nature walk when they get back," Grandfather said as he strode off toward the library. "Let me know when dinner's ready."

Yet another reason for his decision to accompany me.

I felt a small surge of envy. I'd have loved to spend the afternoon in our library. It had started life as a ballroom, built by a socially ambitious previous owner a century ago. For a while, when Caerphilly had lost access to its Carnegie library building, we'd housed much of the town's book collection. Now that the real library was open again, we still had the two-story-high Mission-style shelving, built by the Shiffley Construction Company at less than cost in return for our putting up with the public library for the duration. And in place of the library tables that had gone back to their original home, we had a few sturdy Mission-style oak tables that had become the boys' favorite place for doing homework, along with quite a few superbly comfortable easy chairs. Grandfather had long since claimed a particularly well-placed chair as his own. I'd have liked to park myself in a nearby chair and lose myself in the book I was reading, even at the risk of having him regale me at frequent intervals with odd bits of ornithological lore.

But I had too much on my plate—including Lark. Whose diapers wouldn't change themselves.

I was about to shove cuckoos, cowbirds, and obligate brood parasitism out of my mind when it occurred to me: cuckoos and cowbirds didn't just fly away after laying their eggs. They stayed around to keep an eye on the birds they'd drafted as foster parents.

Wouldn't Lark's mother make at least some effort to spy on us? Just to make sure her baby was in good hands? Mother or father or whoever had left her, but somehow I had a feeling it was the mother.

I pulled out my phone and called Randall Shiffley, who in addition to being Caerphilly's Mayor and County Manager was unofficial head of the Shiffley clan.

"So I have an idea," I said, after we'd exchanged greetings. "You know those family trackers you and Vern organized to look for the fugitive from Clay County?"

"Most of them are now focusing more on looking for whoever left that baby at your church," Randall said. "Which could be pretty useless. If we wanted to catch this Caverly guy, at least we'd have a chance—after all, we have a description of him and a driver's license photo. All we know about whoever left the baby is that he or she isn't carrying an infant. Lot of tourists fit that description."

"I thought the goal wasn't so much to catch Caverly as to help him get arrested someplace other than Clay County."

"More than ever, since we're starting to suspect that the poor guy's a fall guy rather than a killer," Randall said. "Rumor has it that the guy who was killed—Lucius Plunket—was either trying to horn in on the Dingles' moonshine business or planning to rat them out to the ATF."

"Moonshine business?" I echoed. "Is that still a thing or have the Dingles just not noticed that it's the twenty-first century?"

"It's very much still a thing, and not just with the Dingles. Of course, these days the small family moonshiners are kind of dying off. There's a craft distilling movement growing up, and distilling's legal in some states—though still illegal as far as the Feds are concerned. But there's also a growing problem with the old-fashioned moonshiners getting run out of business by the new wave of big operations run by hardcore criminals. And it's not a harmless family operation anymore—the same people are usually involved in drugs, and whatever else enterprising thugs find it profitable to buy and sell."

"You seem remarkably knowledgeable about modern moonshine operations."

"Not from the moonshiner's perspective, if that's what you're worried about." He chuckled. "And not usually from the consumer's perspective. Though I do have a great uncle who has been known to bring some mighty fine sippin' whiskey to family gatherings. We don't ask if he makes it himself, and he certainly isn't going to tell us."

"But does he bring it in those earthenware jugs you always see in the movies?"

"No, he brings it in cobalt blue bottles," Randall said. "He thinks something about the blue glass improves the flavor. Got the whole family saving blue bottles for him—mostly from fancy bottled water like Tŷ Nant and Saratoga Springs. But he doesn't sell his whiskey—only shares it with family. So even though it's technically illegal to distill it, no one's about to turn him in."

"Besides, you don't know for sure he's making the stuff," I said. "For all you know, he could be passing himself off as a big bold bootlegger when all he's doing is buying some kind of alcohol, steeping a few herbs in it, and pretending it's moonshine."

"I like the way you think," he said. "If I'm ever in the embarrassing position of having to take official notice of Uncle Hiram's blue bottles, I will swear up and down that that's what I thought was happening."

"Getting back to those trackers," I said. "Something Grandfather said gave me an idea." I explained about cuckoos and cowbirds being obligate brood parasites, and engaging in mafia retaliatory behavior to make sure the hosts didn't attack the alien eggs.

"You worried that whoever dumped the baby's going to

go after Josh and Jamie if they don't like the way you're treating their kid?"

"No, but if I were her I'd probably want to check in on the kid. Not sure I could leave town without doing that. So if you could get a few of the trackers in place where they could observe our ho[illegible]

"Brilliant idea! I[illegible] [illegible]et you know when the[illegible]

"Won't I [illegible]

"We [illegible] [illegible] she's already so[illegible] [illegible]ell them to ap- [illegible]are they're not spot- [illegible]y of them arriving, you [illegible] some remedial skulking

Chapter 10

I spent the next several hours happily getting things done. I set up a little temporary bedroom for Lark in the sitting room portion of Michael's and my bedroom. I put the baby bottles through the dishwasher and set aside a space for them on the counter, right between the refrigerator and the microwave. I texted Dad to find out what kind of baby formula he recommended, and then texted Michael a request that he bring home a supply of that, along with a package of suitably sized diapers.

Randall texted me within half an hour of our conversation to let me know that his cousins had arrived and taken up their observation posts around the house. I peered out of various windows from time to time, but never spotted anyone lurking. Unless one of them had disguised himself as a sheep to infiltrate our backyard. Always possible, but I was pretty sure the sheep was a real sheep, escaped from our neighbor Seth Early's pasture across the road to partake of the theoretically greener grass to be found wherever Michael and the boys had shoveled a path through the snow. It was certainly producing authentic-looking sheep droppings.

Dad showed up at around 5:00 P.M., so I fed him and Grandfather—and myself—by heating up a batch of lasagna Michael had made earlier in the day. Grandfather was full of new information about brood parasitism in insects and fish. I might have enjoyed my dinner more if it hadn't been accompanied by discussions of mouthbrooding cichlid fish, kleptoparasitism, and myrmecophiles, but at least it was an improvement over the autopsies and rare diseases that Dad so often considered suitable dinnertime conversation.

They eventually departed, still chatting excitedly about nest usurpation in the cuckoo bumblebee. Michael called to report that he and the boys had at least another hour of shopping, and then would I mind if he took them to one of the movies on their must-see list. Since our eleven-year-old boys' must-see list usually looked a lot like my hell-no list, I didn't mind at all. I made a fire in the living room, settled Lark in the portable crib nearby, put on a playlist of soothing carols, and got to work on wrapping presents. Starting, of course, with the presents for Michael and the boys, since this could be my last chance to wrap [illegible] them [illegible]. In fact, probably my last [illegible] thing without two dozen fam[illegible]

The dogs dozed nearby—[illegible] [illegible], and Spike, [illegible] deceptively cute eight-an[illegible] made himself the boy[illegible] first moment he'd see[illegible] the same protective [illegible] But I wasn't taking any chances yet[illegible]w, he could supervise her well-being from the flo[illegible]

When I'd wra[illegible] of Michael's and the boys' presents, I decided [illegible] a break. I made myself a cup of hot herbal tea, gr[illegible] a couple of Christmas cookies, and settled back [illegible] sofa by the fire. Spike, always on the lookout fo[illegible]portunity to sample forbidden food, joined me [illegible] couch and kept me under close observation unti[illegible]offed the last crumb. Then he shrugged and cu[illegible] to go to sleep.

The [illegible]ell rang. I reluctantly heaved myself off the sofa [illegible]swered the door.

"Hey, Meg." Horace. Still in his deputy's uniform, so either he was still on duty or had only just gotten off. And from the layers of snow-flecked wraps he shed in our foyer, the temperature was still dropping. "Sorry to bother you, but things were pretty chaotic before, and after you left I thought of a couple of things I should have done to help us identify Lark."

"Okay," I said. "What kind of things?"

"I want to get foot impressions," he said. "Most hospitals take those. They don't put them into a central database or anything, so they're of limited use for identifying an unknown infant, but if we hear of a missing infant who matches Lark's description, we might be able to confirm or eliminate the match with a footprint."

"Why footprints instead of fingerprints?" I asked.

"Babies' fingers are amazingly hard to read because they're so tiny. Footprints are a lot easier."

He had opened his kit, and I watched as he took impressions of both of Lark's feet. He examined each resulting print minutely, then filled out all the identification fields and tucked them back in his kit.

"Anything else?" I asked, as I watched him cleaning the ink off Lark's feet with baby wipes, to her giggling delight.

"Yeah. I want to do serology."

"Serology?" It took me a second. "That's blood typing, right? You want to take her blood? She won't like that."

"Yeah, I know. But we could use it for identification purposes. Determining blood type is a lot easier than running DNA. Quicker. And cheaper. It'll be quick."

I nodded, and he took out another of his little kits. I took a few steps away from the crib. I couldn't see what was going on—but more important, Lark couldn't see me. If drawing blood traumatized her, I wanted her to hate Horace, not me.

But Horace was good—he managed to get his sample

with only a brief, startled squawk from Lark. I hurried over to comfort her while Horace packed the sample away in his bag.

"So this will help sort out the paternity issue?"

"It might. Of course, it mostly gives us probabilities, not certainties, but it could save us from running expensive DNA tests on people who are statistically unlikely to be the father. It'll be a whole lot more useful if we find the mother, but I'm not holding my breath on that."

Just then his stomach growled.

"If you haven't eaten, there's lasagna in the fridge," I said.

"I'd love some," he said.

He followed me into the kitchen, and I nuked him a plate of the lasagna. While I was doing so, his phone rang, and he was soon deep in a conversation with someone about the technical side of serology and DNA testing. At least that's what I thought he was talking about. He was throwing around a lot of jargon, and I only understood about every other sentence. I decided to let his fellow criminalist amuse him while he ate, and made my way back to the living room.

I tried to get back into my zen wrapping mood, but the spell was broken. I pulled out my phone, called Delaney, and got her voice mail almost immediately. Rob's phone rang the customary four times before his voice mail kicked in. I couldn't think of anything that was likely to calm down Delaney or encourage Rob, so I just hung up. Maybe they were off somewhere sorting things out.

And maybe if I went to bed elves would show up to wrap the presents.

I was feeling discouraged. I believed Rob when he said he couldn't be Lark's father. With a few exceptions—mainly Samantha, an old girlfriend he'd narrowly escaped marrying shortly after he graduated from law school, and now

Delaney—his relationships were remarkable more for their intensity than their longevity. When he was besotted with one woman, he hardly noticed anyone else. And given how over the moon he'd been about Delaney right from the start—yeah. I believed him.

But could we convince Delaney? I leaned back to give the matter some thought. Thought quickly morphed into something more closely resembling a nap.

The doorbell rang again. I considered ignoring it. Maybe Horace would answer it, if he heard it. I was much too comfortable by the fire, and if I got up, I'd not only awaken Lark, who had fallen asleep in my lap, I'd also disturb Spike, perched on the sofa beside me, and Tinkerbell, asleep at my feet—or at least between my feet and the fire. I suspected the fire was the real attraction. Still, she made a good foot warmer and—

The doorbell rang again. I realized the dogs were looking at me expectantly and a little puzzled. I wasn't exhibiting the proper, predictable, Pavlovian response a human is supposed to make to a ringing doorbell.

I sighed and got up. As I set Lark gently in the portable crib, the dogs, reassured that all was right with the world, bounded into the hallway to bark at the door.

The doorbell rang a third time, sending both dogs into frenzies of excitement.

"Coming." Not that the impatient person outside could hear me through our massive front door. I flung it open to see Meredith Flugleman standing just outside, frowning at her wristwatch.

"There you are," she said. "I hope I'm not interrupting anything. I was beginning to wonder if your doorbell actually worked."

"I was at the other end of the house." I decided that was less rude than saying, "When I heard the doorbell, I was afraid it would be someone I had no desire to see—and look! I was right."

"I brought Mrs. Peters." She stepped aside and gestured to a woman who'd been standing behind her. From the gesture, and her tone, one would assume Mrs. Peters was a fabulous personage whose mere arrival at my door should fill me with delight.

"Just Valerie," Mrs. Peters said. She was tiny—maybe five two—and almost painfully thin. Her pale, thin face was spotted with acne, and the end of her nose was red, suggesting she might be suffering from a cold. A few strands of light brown hair escaped from the brown knit hat she wore pulled down over her forehead. Her narrow shoulders were hunched, and her hands jammed in the pockets of a well-worn brown quilted jacket. At first, I'd have taken her for a fourteen-year-old, but on closer inspection I realized that in spite of her waif-like look she was at least in her twenties. Maybe even her thirties.

"Come in." I hoped it sounded sufficiently gracious. I stepped aside. Meredith tripped briskly inside and began methodically shedding her wraps and donning her little crocheted slippers. After looking up at the porch ceiling for a second, Valerie shrugged and followed her in. She made no motion to shed anything, and she didn't do a very good job at wiping her feet.

"What can I do for you?" I asked.

"This is Mrs. Peters," Meredith said, as if that explained it all. And then, when I didn't react. "The mother of the missing baby. From Suffolk. As soon as I heard about her missing daughter, I got in touch, and then I brought her up here so she can see if the baby you found is her daughter."

"Oh, right—I don't think anyone actually told me her name. Welcome."

Mrs. Peters—Valerie—didn't seem to have heard me. She was studying our front hall. Which I had to admit was worth studying. As usual, Mother had taken charge of putting up our Christmas decorations, and she'd outdone herself. She'd gone in for a traditional red, green, and gold color scheme and a "Twelve Days of Christmas" theme. Each of the twelve days was represented by a mobile made of gold tinsel, and each mobile fluttered in the gentle breeze of several little hidden fans. The partridge in the pear tree was nice. The two golden turtledoves circling each other were adorable. Each mobile was larger and more intricate than the last, and by the time she'd finished off with the asymmetrical three-level twelve drummers drumming, the entire upper portion of the hall was one shimmering mass of gold. Both of the tall, narrow (space-saving) trees were trimmed in red and gold, and the walls were decked with garlands of evergreen interwoven with gold tinsel, decked with a basketball-sized red velvet bow every few feet. When you added in the poinsettias, the Christmas cacti, the shiny golden bowls of cinnamon and spruce potpourri, the gold-painted nativity scene . . . it looked as if King Midas had come to spend the Yuletide with us.

Most people stared around, open-mouthed with wonder. Or exclaimed how lovely it all was. Valerie had a rather vague, sleepy expression, and her eyes wandered over the decorations as if she either didn't quite see them or couldn't be bothered.

"In here, Mrs. Peters." Meredith's voice had a bit of an edge to it, as if it had been a rather long and trying ride up from Suffolk.

Clearly I was not having a positive first reaction to Valerie Peters. Could she possibly be beautiful little Lark's mother? I glanced down at Spike, who was glaring at both of the new arrivals. The more mellow Tinkerbell had already ambled back into the living room.

Valerie stopped staring at the decorations. She pulled her hands out of her coat pockets. I realized she was holding a pack of cigarettes in one and a lighter in the other.

"If you need to smoke, could you do it on the porch?" I asked. "My husband's allergic."

Actually, Michael wasn't technically allergic. He just loathed cigarette smoke. As did I. Not to mention the fact that we didn't want the boys exposed to the fumes. What kind of mother was she, anyway?

Spike chose this moment to start growling at Valerie. Growling, and stalking slowly toward her, as if planning to attack.

Chapter 11

"No!" I shouted to Spike. "Bad dog!"

He didn't pay any attention. Luckily he was so intent on growling at Valerie and creeping in her direction that I was able to grab him and shove him into the hall closet without taking any damage. Shoving Spike into the closet was what we usually did when he took it into his head to dislike one of our visitors, but usually he managed to bite me in the process. This time he was so intently focused on Valerie that he barely noticed me. From inside the closet he continued to growl, and then he escalated to barking and hurling himself against the door.

"Sorry," I said. "He's badly trained, but he makes a good watchdog."

Meredith shuddered. Valerie didn't seem to have noticed the danger she'd been in. She was still holding her cigarettes and lighter. Then she sighed in the overly dramatic manner I'd have expected from a teenager and stuck them back in her pocket.

"Where's the baby?" Meredith was using her annoying perky voice. "We don't want to waste any more time reuniting mother and child, now do we?" Yes, it had definitely been a long drive.

"If it is her baby," I said. "Let's not get her hopes up till we're sure."

"Of course, of course." Meredith sounded slightly irritated that I was interfering with her happy ending.

I led them into the living room. If I thought I was about

to be reunited with one of my boys, I'd have knocked Meredith down in my haste to reach the crib and pick him up again. Valerie slouched along behind us, studying her surroundings with sullen eyes.

"Here she is," Meredith trilled, gesturing dramatically toward the crib. Valerie shot her an annoyed glance—I warmed to Valerie, just a little, for that—and glanced casually down into the crib. Lark had awakened and was in a good mood. She smiled up at us and made gurgling noises as she waved her arms and legs.

Valerie's face didn't light up in recognition. She didn't utter any cries of joy. She didn't reach down to pick up Lark. She studied her for a few moments then nodded.

"You recognize her?" I asked.

"Yeah, pretty much."

"Pretty much?" I probably let my disbelief show.

"My ex has had her more'n me." She glanced at Lark again. "She's grown a lot."

At that point, Tinkerbell began growling—a deep bass sound you felt as much as heard.

"Shush, Tink," I said.

She shushed, but I could tell she didn't like it. She was staring intently at Valerie.

Hell, I didn't like it. Spike hated everybody—well, everybody but Josh and Jamie. Tink, on the other hand, was an excellent judge of character. She and I studied Valerie through narrowed eyes.

Meredith didn't seem to like how things were going.

"I'm sure Mrs. Peters is a little overwhelmed by all this," she said. "I'll go get the car seat and we'll take the baby off your hands."

What was wrong with Meredith? Normally she'd be the first to insist on paperwork in triplicate and every other formality she could think of. The only thing I could think of was that being in charge of Lark for five minutes had so traumatized her that she'd do anything to avoid repeating the experience.

"Surely we're not going to hand over Lark until we have positive proof that she actually *is* Mrs. Peters's baby," I said.

"Didn't I just say she was?" Valerie said.

"Meg, really," Meredith began.

"I know, I know," I said, shaking my head with mock regret. "It's terrible that we have to take care of all those formalities. But I'm sure Mrs. Peters will understand why we have to do it. I mean, what if some nut case had showed up and tried to claim the baby before she got here? You brought some kind of identification, right? A footprint, for example."

"Yeah, right." Valerie rolled her eyes.

"Meg," Meredith tried again. "The baby recognized her."

I considered pointing out that Lark was a very happy baby, and would probably have reacted much the same to anyone she saw. That, in fact, I would have expected a much stronger reaction if Valerie really were her mother. But I suspected Meredith wouldn't get it.

"It's a liability issue, you know," I said instead. "The county attorney will kill us if we don't dot every *i* and cross every *t*."

That got through to her. I could see the familiar everything-in-triplicate Meredith begin to reassert herself.

"Well, of course—but how can we possibly?" she spluttered. "I mean—it's not like the baby would have any kind of ID."

"She has the best kind of ID," I said. "Her DNA. We've already taken her DNA to see if it matches Rob's—we'll just get a DNA sample from Mrs. Peters, and I can get the test expedited."

Valerie looked blank, as if she hadn't understood a word of this. Meredith looked put-upon—clearly she'd been hoping to expedite Lark out of her jurisdiction as soon as possible—but she nodded.

"That's going to take time, though, isn't it?" she asked, through clenched teeth.

"Remember, Grandfather has that rapid DNA machine," I said. "The one that only takes a couple of hours to process a sample. And we should be able to get the DNA sample right away—last time I looked Horace was here taking his dinner break."

I pulled out my phone as I was speaking and called him.

"What's up, Meg?" he asked.

"Are you still here in our kitchen?"

"Finishing up that plate of lasagna," he said. "Excellent batch, by the way. You need anything?"

"Can you come out and take another DNA sample?" I asked. "In fact, two—one for official processing, and one for Grandfather to expedite through his lab."

"Another paternity candidate?"

"Maternity this time," I said. "But we need confirmation."

"Roger," he said. "Where are you?"

"The living room."

I turned back to Meredith and Valerie.

"He'll be right out."

Meredith smiled the sort of brittle smile that let me know I was trying her patience. Valerie didn't appear to be listening. She'd discovered the cut-glass jar full of red-and-green-foil-wrapped Hershey Kisses that Mother had positioned on the coffee table as part of the décor, and had grabbed a handful. Clearly not her first candy binge—her teeth were yellow, and I could even see a couple of spots of decay. Was Meredith really going to turn over a helpless baby to a woman who apparently hadn't found her way to the dentist in a decade or two?

"Hey, Meg." Horace stepped through the archway between the hall and the living room. He was holding a pair of DNA collection kits in one hand and a pair of gloves in the other.

"Hey, Horace," I said. "You know Meredith Flugleman from Child Protective Services. This is—"

But before I could introduce Valerie, she spotted Horace. She dropped the candy jar—fortunately it landed on the sofa and didn't break, though the candies flew everywhere. She paused for a second, staring at Horace as if he were the Ghost of Christmas Yet-to-Come. Then she made a dash for the hall. She had to go past Horace to do so.

"Hey," he said, reaching out an arm as if to stop her.

She threw her purse at him, hitting him square in the face. Then she ran past him into the hall. I heard the front door open and slam shut.

"What has gotten into her?" Meredith said. "Horace, what did you say to her?"

"He didn't say anything," I pointed out. "Or we would have heard him."

"I think it was the uniform," Horace said.

"Arrest her," I said.

"On what grounds?" Meredith asked.

"Attempted kidnapping," I suggested. "I bet the DNA test will prove she's not really Lark's mother."

"That would work." Horace was pulling on his gloves. Why was he doing that instead of chasing Valerie? "Assaulting a police officer's good, too." He bent down to examine the contents of Valerie's purse, which now lay scattered on the floor around his feet. He picked up something and held it out to show us. A baggie full of dried plant matter. "Possession of marijuana's even better."

"Oh, dear." Meredith's face fell. "Are you sure? Perhaps it's just potpourri."

Horace held the baggie close to his nose, sniffed, and

shook his head. I refrained from rolling my eyes. I could smell the baggie from here. Perhaps Meredith had a cold. Or perhaps she'd led a sheltered life and didn't recognize the aroma.

"We'll need to send it in for testing to be sure," he said. "But if I had to put money on it, I'd bet anything it will turn out to be weed."

"Shouldn't you be chasing her?" Meredith sounded indignant.

"Need to secure the evidence first."

"And the Shiffleys are watching the house," I said. "In case the mother turns up to check on Lark. I'm sure they'll see which way she goes."

"Good to know." Horace was dropping the telltale baggie into a brown evidence envelope. "And from the look of her, I doubt if she'll be hard to catch. Does she have a vehicle?"

"She came with me." Meredith was working her way up from indignant to full-out righteous wrath. "She told the most barefaced lies imaginable, and got me to bring her out here in an attempt to kidnap the baby. Why on earth do you suppose she did it?"

"She's probably so out of it she didn't realize Lark wasn't her baby. I mean, assuming she really did have a baby kidnapped to begin with. Might be worth checking with the Suffolk PD in case it turned out to be a false report. Aha. Paraphernalia."

He tucked two more items from Valerie's purse into evidence envelopes. Then, while writing on the envelopes with one hand, he pulled out his phone with the other and punched some buttons.

"Hey, Debbie Ann," he said. "Can you put out a BOLO on a suspect? Her name is—" He looked questioningly at us.

"Valerie Peters," Meredith and I said in unison.

"Valerie Peters," Horace echoed. "About five-two, slender, probably in her twenties. Wearing a brown coat and a brown knit cap. Just fled the Waterstons' house on foot. Wanted for assaulting a police officer, suspected possession of marijuana, and attempted kidnapping. . . . Roger. No, we're fine here. I'm going to give pursuit, but if she doubles back, I think Meg could take her with one hand tied behind her back. And Meg says there's Shiffleys watching the house, so they've probably got eyes on. Okay—later."

He smiled at me as he shoved his phone in his pocket.

"I'll keep you posted," he said and hurried out to his car.

About thirty seconds later I heard his siren start up.

"My goodness." Meredith collapsed onto the couch, not even noticing that she had landed on some of the scattered chocolates.

I picked the rest up and put them back in the jar. Then I gave Tinkerbell a liver treat.

"Good dog," I said. "You know a phony when you see one."

I let Spike out and gave him a treat as well. He strutted proudly back to the hearth, as if he had single-handedly foiled the kidnapping attempt. Then he and Tink curled up, one on each side of the portable crib.

I strolled over to the tree—not one of the red-and-gold ones in the hall, but the main tree in the corner of the living room, the one that didn't have a theme, just all the ornaments Michael and I had picked up over the years. I sorted through the presents until I found a reasonably large one addressed to Dad from Michael and me. I began unwrapping it, working as carefully as possible, in the hope that I could reuse the paper.

"It's not Christmas yet." Meredith was looking shocked, as if she found the idea of opening a present on December twenty-first only slightly less heinous than trying to kidnap a baby. "It's not even Christmas Eve till Monday."

"I know," I said. "I just want to try out Dad's present. See if it works okay."

"So what is it, anyway?" she asked, when I pulled the paper off.

"A radio," I said. "One that gets the police channels. I thought we'd test it out by seeing if we can pick up what's happening with the search for Valerie."

I fixed us both cups of tea, and for a while we sat side by side on the sofa, listening as the chief and his officers tracked down and apprehended Valerie. Meredith wasn't all that bad company when she was stunned into silence. And Horace was right. Valerie didn't prove hard to catch, thanks to some help from the Shiffleys watching the perimeter.

"Well, I'm glad that's taken care of." As soon as word came over the radio that Valerie was on her way to the police station, Meredith chugged the last bit of her tea and stood up. "So sorry to have interrupted your day with this. Suffolk County should have done a much better job at vetting Mrs. Peters. I will be letting them know my thoughts on the subject. Meanwhile, I should be going. We could be having more snow any minute now."

Her expression suggested she was terrified of being stranded out here in the back of the beyond. Or maybe it was being stranded with my family that gave her pause. She collected her purse and coat, walked briskly to the door, and put on all her wraps as quickly as possible.

"Have a safe trip back," I said as I let her out. Yes, it did look like snow, and I shared Meredith's eagerness not to be snowbound together.

My cell phone rang as I was heading back to the couch. It was Chief Burke.

Chapter 12

"Good work on determining that Mrs. Peters was not our foundling's mother," he said. "I'll drop by later to get a statement from you. Or tomorrow, if tonight's not convenient."

"I'll be up for a while," I said. "Although tomorrow's fine if you're busy tonight. But would you mind telling me what the Dickens is going on? Meredith Flugleman shows up on my doorstep and tries to railroad me into giving Lark to a pothead who may not even be her mother—in what universe does that make sense?"

"Apparently Ms. Flugleman dashed down to Suffolk as soon as she heard about the kidnapping there, intent on reuniting Mrs. Peters with her missing baby. Without telling me or liaising with my counterpart down there. And for some reason, without her usual insistence on a foot-high stack of paperwork. Wretched woman." I suspected if the chief hadn't long ago given up cursing he'd have added a more pungent adjective or two. "And according to the Suffolk police, it wasn't a kidnapping after all—not surprisingly, the dad has custody, and the child was with him all the time. Mrs. Peters could be in some trouble for filing false charges against her ex—although I was pleased to hear that they hope to use that as leverage to get her into much-needed treatment."

"Let's hope Meredith has the good sense to stay away from Suffolk for a while," I said.

"Or that she carefully observes the speed limit if she does venture down there." The chief chuckled.

"So if the Suffolk father had the baby all along, why did Valerie identify Lark as hers?"

"She was probably too drugged to realize she was looking at the wrong infant," the chief said. "Cannabis doesn't enhance IQ. Or maybe she was afraid she'd get in trouble if she didn't claim the baby, after Ms. Flugleman had taken all the trouble to bring her up here. We may never know. Although I'll certainly be asking her once the public defender gets here and we start talking to her."

"As if you need another distraction."

"She probably won't be much of one," he said. "We'll be arraigning her here in the morning, and probably extraditing her back to Suffolk before tomorrow's over. Then we can get back to looking for Lark's real mother. And Clay County's attempted murder suspect."

"And Mrs. Thistlethwaite's cat."

"Oh, Pemberley's been found. Behind that new seafood restaurant on the town square. And Clarence Rutledge is arranging to attach a small tracking device to his collar—like the ones your grandfather uses for his zoo animals. Should make future cat hunts a little less stressful."

"At least something's going right then."

"I'll fill you in when I come out to take your statement about Mrs. Peters." With that he hung up.

I was just slipping the phone into my pocket when it rang again. Not a familiar number, but I answered anyway.

"Ms. Langslow? Um . . . it's Caleb Shiffley?" From the rising inflection, it almost sounded as if he was unsure of his own name. Probably just unsure of his reception.

"Hi, Caleb," I said. "What's up?"

"Um . . . Vern said to call you? I mean, if we found the suspect?"

"Suspect? Isn't she on her way down to the jail by now?"

"Not the lady Ms. Flugleman brought. The other lady. The one we caught trying to sneak into your yard just now."

My pulse quickened.

"Bring her in," I said. "You can use the back door if it's closer. And you might want to let Chief Burke know she's here. I think he wants to talk to her, too."

"Yes, ma'am."

I made sure Lark was soundly asleep with the dogs on either side and made my way quietly to the kitchen. I peered out the window over the sink. The first snowflakes were starting to fall, and it looked as if they were sticking to the ground on the shoveled paths. Normally our two younger llamas would have been frolicking in it, while the older two just stood around sticking out their tongues to catch snowflakes—had they picked that up from the boys?—but now all four of them were clustered just inside the fence along one side of their pen watching a small party of humans approaching on one of the paths. Caleb Shiffley was in the lead, and another Shiffley, whose name I didn't remember offhand, brought up the rear. Between them was the woman. They towered over her, but then they were Shiffleys. Shiffleys only came in two sizes: tall and taller. She probably wasn't more than two or three inches short of my five foot ten. She wasn't wearing a hat—just a silk scarf tied around her head in babushka style—and her coat didn't look nearly warm enough for the weather. When they climbed the back steps, I could see that she wasn't even wearing boots.

I opened the door and let the three of them in. The two Shiffleys began shaking off the snow and shedding their boots and coats in the utility room. The woman just stood looking anxious and shivering, with her shoulders hunched and her hands buried in her pockets. She had a nasty half-scabbed laceration on her cheek and several deep scratches on her hands. And she looked like someone who had been sleeping rough for the last few nights.

"Thanks, Caleb, and, um . . ."

"Wayne, ma'am," the second Shiffley supplied.

"And Wayne. Why don't you take our trespasser into the living room while I make you all some hot coffee?"

"You had no right to drag me in here this way," the woman said. "And you have no right to keep me here."

"Meg Langslow." I held out my hand, which she ignored. "I live here. You don't. You're trespassing. And I'd like to know why." She flinched slightly, and I felt slightly guilty. "You're also obviously freezing, you're clearly not dressed for how cold it is out there now, and the temperature's dropping further by the minute. Come in, warm up, and we'll sort this out." I turned back to Caleb and Wayne. "You hungry? I've got some of Michael's lasagna."

"Yes ma'am," Caleb said.

"Wouldn't say no," Wayne added with a grin.

"Let me get you settled in the living room and then I'll get the food started."

It had occurred to me that it could be interesting to see how the woman reacted when I led her into the living room where Lark was sleeping.

She noticed the crib right away, even though she pretended not to. She didn't take the seat closest to the crib, but she did position herself so she could see it. And then kept her head resolutely turned at an angle where she could pretend she wasn't looking at the crib but could still dart the occasional glance at Lark when she thought no one was looking.

I was very pleased that neither Caleb nor Wayne said anything about the baby—either they had uncommon good sense or they'd been briefed well and knew how to follow orders. As I returned to the kitchen I made a mental note to commend them the next time I was talking to Vern or Randall.

After starting the machine to brew a carafe of coffee, I got out the lasagna and was about to measure out three portions. Then I reminded myself that what seemed like reasonable portions to me would probably look like hors d'oeuvres to hungry young men who had been spending the day out in the freezing woods. And I was a bit peckish myself—I'd hardly eaten anything at dinner, thanks to Dad's and Grandfather's appetite-depressing conversation. Even our trespasser might be hungry. So I stuck the rest of the lasagna in the microwave and sent Michael a quick text suggesting that provisions were low and if he planned to bring the boys back with an appetite he might also want to bring back pizza. I grabbed a loaf of Rose Noire's whole-grain bread and put it on a tray with butter and two kinds of her homemade preserves. When the lasagna and the coffee were ready, I added them to the tray along with the cups, dishes, and silverware, and hauled it out to the living room.

The woman was still staring straight ahead, although I suspected she was watching Lark in her peripheral vision. Caleb and Wayne had taken out their smartphones and appeared lost in them—although I suspected one false move from the woman would prove they were only pretending not to be watching her. They both jumped up when they saw me and offered to take the tray.

"Set it on the coffee table," I said, handing it to Caleb. "And help yourself."

I fixed a plate and a cup of coffee for the woman and set them down in front of her. Her glance flicked down at them and then away again.

"Suit yourself," I said. "But if you're planning to make a

daring escape before the authorities get here, you might want to fuel up. And warm up."

She pursed her lips as if reluctantly acknowledging that I was right. Then she picked up the coffee and took a sip.

"And while I know you plan to make your visit a brief one, it would be nice if we knew what to call you while you're here."

She looked at me over the coffee cup.

"Janet," she said finally.

Chapter 13

I waited, hoping Janet would manage to drop a last name to go along with the first. She was looking into the coffee cup.

Baby steps.

"Eat up, Janet," I said. "Unless you're a vegetarian—I didn't think to ask. My cousin, who does much of the cooking, is a vegetarian. I'm sure we've got a tofu casserole in the fridge."

"No thanks." She wrinkled her nose slightly. "I'm not a big fan of tofu."

"You and me both." I dug into my lasagna. She could eat or not eat; I wasn't going to worry about her. It had been a long day.

She relented and took a tiny bite. I could tell she was trying to chew it slowly, but she was obviously starving. She looked up, saw me watching her, and smiled slightly. Then she dug in with as much enthusiasm as the two Shiffleys.

I followed their example.

"So," I said when we'd polished off the lasagna. "You want to tell me why you were sneaking around in the woods behind our house?"

She tensed again and shook her head slightly.

"Well, then I'll tell you. You're the one who left the baby in the manger at Trinity Episcopal Church earlier today, and you wanted to check to make sure she's all right before you head out for wherever you're planning to go without her."

Her shoulders slumped, and she closed her eyes as if acknowledging defeat.

"Yes," she said. "I'm sorry if I caused any trouble, but I had to find someplace safe to leave her. Because she's not safe at all with me."

"Why not?"

"Some bad people are looking for me," she said.

"What bad people?"

"You have to let me go." She was shaking her head. "If they catch up with me—"

Light dawned.

"You're on the run from Clay County." It was a statement, not a question—and her expression told me I'd gotten it right. "From Sheriff Dingle and all his merry but ever-so-corrupt men."

"I can't let them find me," she said. "They might kill me."

Caleb and Wayne had been silently watching our conversation. I saw their expressions change when I mentioned Clay County. And now Caleb spoke up.

"Ma'am, if it's those Clay County jerks who're after you, don't worry. No one here in Caerphilly's gonna help them catch you."

"And there's a dozen of our cousins still out there in the woods, guarding the perimeter," Wayne added. "On account of Mayor Shiffley told us to be sure not to let anything happen to Meg or the baby."

"Speaking of the baby, Mrs. Caverly," I said. "Wouldn't you like to hold her for a while?"

Instead of answering, she burst into tears. She did manage to nod, so I went over, picked up Lark, and handed her to her mother. Not that I planned to let her or anyone else take the baby until a DNA test confirmed my suspicions—and until both of them were out of danger. But from the expression on her face, I was pretty sure that yes, we'd reunited Lark and her mother.

"Caverly?" Caleb said. "Haven't I heard that name before?"

"Her husband's the one Clay County's looking for," I said, looking at Janet. "Isn't he?"

"I don't know where he is," she said sharply. "Even if I did know, I wouldn't tell you. But I don't."

"That's fine," I said. "When—"

Caleb and Wayne suddenly both straightened up and looked a lot more vigilant. Caleb put down his plate, walked out into the hall, and peered out of one of the windows there. Wayne merely looked alert and stuck his hand in his pocket. I wondered if the two of them were armed. Shiffleys often were, though usually with rifles. Or hunting knives.

Caleb had already relaxed by the time I heard the approaching car.

"Chief's here," he said.

Janet tensed again.

"Don't worry," I said. "He's been doing everything he can not to find your husband. Not officially, anyway, because he knows what could happen to someone locked up in the Clay County Jail."

Janet looked only slightly reassured.

"Let the chief in, will you," I told Caleb.

I could see through the front windows that the snow was coming down harder. Caleb opened the door and a blast of cold wind came in with the chief.

"Merry Christmas, Caleb," he said as he shed his wraps. "My compliments to your family on this."

"Thank you, sir."

"Well." The chief paused in the doorway and surveyed the room. "Merry Christmas, Meg. Good work, Wayne. Mrs. Caverly, I presume."

"You have to let me leave," she said. "They'll kill me if they catch me. Or worse, they'll torture me to tell them where Mark is. I don't know, but they won't believe me, and—"

"Relax." The chief took out his notebook and sat down in one of the comfortable armchairs. "You're perfectly safe here." I found his solid, reliable presence reassuring. Surely Janet was exaggerating the danger to her, and maybe even to her husband.

"What if Sheriff Dingle's officers show up and try to arrest me?" Janet didn't seem reassured.

"I will inform them that you are already in my custody, and that I will consider any request for extradition they may care to make once our charges against you have been dealt with."

"Charges? What charges?" Janet looked indignant.

"I'm sure we could prevail upon Meg to file trespassing charges," the chief said. "That should be sufficient to keep you out of their hands for the time being—especially if I drop a hint to the commonwealth attorney that here's no need to rush. If you were to resist arrest, that would give me additional grounds to detain you in the relative safety of Caerphilly. We can talk about it later. At the moment, I think it's much more urgent for you to tell me why you're on the run in the first place, so we can see what we can do to rescue your husband."

"Rescue him?" Janet sounded surprised. "You mean you believe our side of the story?"

"Since I haven't actually heard your side of the story yet, I can't say whether I believe it or not." The chief sounded slightly testy. I watched as he took a deep breath and let go of some of his irritation. "I can promise you that I will listen to it, and weigh it carefully."

"Oh, and you're going to take my word over the Clay County sheriff's." Janet sounded bitter.

I could see the chief was struggling for a way to convey his deep distrust of anything having to do with Clay County without saying anything directly critical of someone who was, after all, a fellow law enforcement officer, however unworthy. I decided to help him out.

"The chief's much too polite to say this," I said. "But Clay County and Caerphilly are like the Hatfields and the McCoys. The fact that they don't like you doesn't automatically mean we will, but it does make us just a little bit inclined to be biased in your favor."

"A little?" Caleb said softly, and he and Wayne laughed.

"Ms. Waterston is correct," the chief said. "There has always been a great deal of ill will between the counties. And while I myself am a relative newcomer to the area, and try to remain unbiased, I cannot deny that I have often had grave concerns over how Clay County conducts its affairs."

We all watched her consider it—even the chief.

"If you're honest, maybe you can help us," she said. "And if you're in league with them, I'm already dead, so what does it matter? So I might as well tell you."

"Good." The chief nodded. "Caleb, Wayne—can you go out and make sure no one barges in to interrupt us? Apart from my officers or any returning members of Ms. Langslow's family, of course."

"Yes, sir," they said in unison. They both picked up their plates, utensils, and coffee cups and carried them out to the kitchen. I nodded with approval. Somebody had raised them right.

"Could you use some coffee?" I asked the chief.

"I could indeed," he said. "It's a bitter night out there. And Mrs. Caverly might like a refill."

I took Janet's cup and went into the kitchen. Caleb and Wayne were just slipping out the back door. I locked up behind them, and poured the coffee.

I returned to the living room, resigned to the fact that the chief would probably chase me out when he started interviewing Janet. But to my surprise, he didn't.

"Thank you. And could you stay and take a few notes, just until one of my officers gets here? Assuming that's acceptable to you, Mrs. Caverly."

She nodded.

I was puzzled, but I made sure not to show it. Maybe the chief thought Janet would find my presence reassuring. Maybe he wanted a witness to whatever she said. After all, just because Clay County was after her didn't automatically make her innocent. Even Clay County occasionally caught a few real crooks. I took my notebook out of my tote bag and assumed what I hoped was a discreet and professional expression.

Chapter 14

"So, Mrs. Caverly," the chief began. "I assume you and your husband are relative newcomers to Clay County."

"Well, Mark is," she said. "He took a job there. Assistant treasurer. The pay wasn't that great, but we figured living in the country would be cheap, and it would be a nice, quiet, healthy place to bring up a family, and the title would look good on his résumé."

"When was this?"

"Mark started in July. I stayed back in Philadelphia with my parents. I wanted to have the baby there with the obstetrician I knew. So Mark came down here alone, and I was going to move down as soon as he found a place. And he wasn't having any luck—at least I thought that's what was happening. I should have realized it wasn't going well—I just thought he was sounding negative because he was lonely and the job was turning out to be harder than he expected and the housing market was impossible. But now I know he wanted us to stay with my parents. Where it was safe."

She stared into space for a few moments.

"What happened?" the chief prompted.

"Mark started acting really weird for a few weeks," she said. "And then he finally told me why, two weeks ago when I came down for a visit. When he was hired, Mayor Dingle told him the county finances were in bad shape, and they needed a whiz to straighten them out. It turns out what they wanted was someone to figure out how to launder the profits of their illegal moonshine and marijuana business."

The chief nodded slightly, as if this confirmed some suspicions of his own.

"He wanted to just quit, but they'd already sort of threatened him," she said. "Told him that he knew too much, and that if he changed his mind about working with them, it wouldn't be healthy. But we could already see that they would never totally trust him. At least I could. I told him that as soon as he set up the money laundering scheme for them, they'd decide they didn't need him anymore, and they'd get rid of him. And I don't mean by firing him."

"Did he consider going to the DEA or the ATF?" the chief asked.

She paused. I had the feeling she was deciding whether to trust us with something.

"He tried," she said finally. "I think the Dingles found out he'd done it. Maybe someone at one of the agencies was careless. Or maybe Mark wasn't as good an actor as he thought he was. Maybe they were just paranoid. Anyway, we were lucky. Someone we knew warned us that they were going to knock off someone the Dingles didn't like and frame Mark for murder."

"Who's they, the ones you suspect of planning the murder?" the chief asked. "And who warned you?"

"One of Sheriff Dingle's men committed the murder," she said. "Not sure who, and it doesn't really matter—he's behind it. And I'm not going to tell you who warned us." She set her jaw in a stubborn expression. "It's one thing for me to trust you with my life, but I don't know you well enough yet to give away someone else's secrets. Someone who was in a position to know. Let's leave it at that."

Maybe that was what she was hiding.

"Fair enough," the chief said. "So the plan was to murder Lucius Plunket and frame your husband for it."

"They called Mark and asked him—ordered him—to show up at a meeting at the courthouse," she said. "At eleven at night. I was visiting again. We had a bad feeling about it. I said we should just take off—go back to Philadelphia. Mark was afraid they'd hunt him down and kill us all. So he decided to take off—he was going to try to drive down to the DEA office in Richmond and turn himself in. Ask for protection as a whistleblower. But just in case, he told me to take Andrea back to Philadelphia and lie low until he was sure it was safe."

"Andrea?"

"Our daughter."

"We thought she was named Lark," the chief said.

"Lark? Why would you think that?" Her expression added, "What kind of crazy person names a baby Lark?"

"It was written on the back of your note."

She shook her head as if puzzled, so I pulled out my phone and called up the pictures I'd taken of the note. The front, with her note to Rob. And the back, with the handwritten name.

"Oh, that." She laughed and shook her head. "That's not Lark. I guess my handwriting's worse than I thought. It's Hark. As in 'Hark! The Herald Angels Sing.' Before everything went to hell, I was making a list of Christmas carols I wanted to add to the holiday playlist on my phone—well, not so much an organized list as just jotting the title down on the nearest piece of paper when I heard one I liked on the radio. It all seems so long ago. I guess I cut the note out of one of those pieces of paper. So you've been calling her Lark."

"And maybe we should keep on calling her that until any danger is past," I suggested. "I'm not sure even the Dingles are warped enough to hurt a four-month-old baby, but if they are, they'll be looking for an Andrea, not a Lark. Let's play it safe."

"Ms. Langslow makes a good point," the chief said.

Janet stiffened, and glanced involuntarily at the window before answering. Then she nodded.

"Lark it is," she said.

"I can accept that you have no idea where Mr. Caverly is hiding," the chief said. "But do you have any way of getting a message to him?"

"I could try to send him an email," she said. "Of course, I have no idea if he'd get it. And I wouldn't want to give away where I am or where I'm going. They might have hacked into his email."

"The Dingles? Are you kidding?" I said. "Or, for that matter, anyone in Clay County? Not bloody likely."

"Now, now," the chief said. "I'm sure there are a few technologically adept individuals in Clay County. Mrs. Caverly is wise to be circumspect."

"Yes, they could have hired someone," I said. "The way they hired poor Mr. Caverly."

"So you and Mr. Caverly fled separately," the chief said. "That would have been several days ago."

She nodded.

"What happened?"

"A friend managed to smuggle me out of Clay County," she said. "I was going to take the bus back to Philadelphia—but when I got to the bus station, I saw a car with Clay County tags nearby. I was pretty sure they had someone staking out the station. I found a place to hide and tried to get in touch with my friend. She hasn't gotten back to me—I'm worried that something has happened to her. So I decided to find a safe place to leave An—Lark. After all, they'd be looking for a woman and a baby. They might still be able to recognize me, but I figured to them one baby would look much like another. And once I got her to safety, I could figure out what to do myself. Maybe look for Mark. Maybe figure out a way to get out of town and contact the DEA myself. I hadn't figured it out yet."

"May I ask one question?" I looked at the chief for permission, and he nodded. "Why try to pin paternity on my brother, Rob?"

"Sorry," she said. "I wasn't trying to cause trouble for him or anyone. But I didn't want her to disappear into the foster system. I thought if everyone thought she might be the daughter of someone from Caerphilly—someone important—they'd keep her nearby."

"But you must have known eventually they would run a DNA test and prove she wasn't Rob's?"

"Yes, but that could take weeks," she said. "I figured by the time the results came back, either the danger would be past and Mark and I could come back to claim her, or we'd both be dead and at least she wouldn't be."

I nodded. She was right about the lag time the police had to put up with when they sent off DNA to a lab. She would have had no way of knowing that Grandfather's new toy had probably already churned out the results to prove that Rob and Lark were unrelated.

"But why Rob?" I asked.

"I didn't really know anyone in Caerphilly," she said. "And what if I picked a name at random and the guy turned out to be Asian or African-American so it was obviously a lie? But a couple of weeks ago Mark had shown me an article about Mutant Wizards. This was back when he first started realizing the job in Clay County wasn't all it was supposed to be, and he was looking around for other options. There was a picture of your brother in it. He was the right physical type to be Lark's father. And he was a bachelor; there wouldn't be any danger that I'd break up a marriage. And I thought maybe if they thought a prominent citizen was her father, they'd take even better care of her."

"I suppose that's logical." Maybe she should have thought

it through and realized that even a bachelor might have a relationship that could be damaged by a false paternity claim. But she'd been panicking about her daughter's safety. I could cut her some slack. As long as she helped fix the problems she'd caused.

"Mrs. Caverly," the chief said. "Is it possible that you have any other information about the illegal activities your husband discovered? I'll be getting in touch with the DEA and the ATF, and possibly other law enforcement agencies to deal with the problems in Clay County. Any bit of information you can provide would help."

He took her through what I'm sure she thought was an endless series of questions. She seemed to be trying. But I deduced that her husband had done his best to keep her ignorant of the details of what he'd discovered. He probably thought doing so would protect her. How could he have foreseen that by keeping her in the dark, he was making it almost impossible for her to protect him?

Meanwhile, I was taking notes. Not notes for the chief, but notes for what I thought we should do when he finished interrogating Janet.

Eventually the chief gave up trying to get information she clearly didn't have.

"Thank you, Mrs. Caverly," he said. "If you think of anything else that could possibly be of help, please let me know."

She nodded.

"And now I need to figure out what to do with you," he said.

"Why not leave her here for the time being?" I asked.

"Would you be okay with that?" He frowned slightly. "After all, while we don't think anyone from Clay County has followed her here, we have no way to be sure."

"I wouldn't be comfortable having her here indefinitely. No offense," I added, turning to Janet. "But secrets are hard to keep in a small town like this. And for that matter, we have a houseful of relatives arriving tomorrow, so we'll need all our guest rooms for them tomorrow night."

The chief nodded.

"But for tonight we could ask the Shiffleys to stay in place," I said. "I feel very safe with them guarding the perimeter. And even better—just in case anyone from Clay County saw her come in here, we can let them see her going away again. We get one of the Shiffleys to sneak in here—the shortest one they've got—and then he puts on her coat and scarf and we make it look as if you're taking her away in handcuffs."

"That would tend to throw any lurking Dingles off the scent," he said. "But that still leaves us with the worry that her presence here will eventually become known."

"So we call Robyn tonight and get her to set up a relocation for Janet and Lark," I said.

"Good idea," the chief said.

"The priest of the church where you left Lark runs a shelter for battered women," I explained to Janet. "And she has contacts in a sort of Underground Railroad to help women relocate safely. Once Mark is safe you can come back, or go back to Philadelphia or whatever you like."

"And if the Dingles succeed in killing him, at least Lark will be safe." She didn't sound very optimistic.

"And you," I pointed out.

She shrugged as if her safety were an unimportant detail.

"It's a plan, then." The chief stood up and tucked away his notebook. "If you and Mr. Waterston are okay with it, I see no reason why Mrs. Caverly shouldn't remain here overnight. And I'll know where to find her if I need to bring her in on those trespassing charges." He smiled to let her know he wasn't really serious.

"And besides, there are a couple of things we need her to do," I said.

"Such as?" Janet looked anxious.

"Well, first of all, you need to give us a DNA sample so we can have proof positive that you're Lark's mother," I said. "I think you are, but for her protection, let's prove it."

"Good idea," the chief said. "I'm a big believer in getting solid evidence. I'll make sure Horace is one of the deputies who comes out to arrest the fake Mrs. Caverly. He can take the sample."

"I'd love to get Dad in to check out those lacerations," I said. "But you know how he is about keeping secrets. Maybe we should wait until just before she leaves."

"Horace has a pretty deft hand with a first-aid kit," the chief said.

"And last but very much not least, she has to help my brother put his life back together."

"Put his life back together?" She frowned, obviously puzzled.

"I know the article you read described him as a bachelor," I said. "He is—but he was about to propose to his girlfriend over the holiday season. They've been together for nearly two years, so if he had been Lark's father, he'd have been cheating on her. She didn't take that notion very well. The DNA tests can prove that Rob isn't the father. But they can't prove he didn't have an affair with you—so you could honestly think that he was at least possibly the father."

"I can tell her it was an outright lie," she said. "That I picked him because he was rich and single and I didn't know anyone else in Caerphilly County to name. If that doesn't convince her, I'm not sure what else I can do."

"You might be the only person who can convince her," I said. "So I'd like to get her over here before you leave, swear her to secrecy, and give it a try."

"Okay." She nodded. "Can it wait until tomorrow, though? I'm almost asleep on my feet."

"I think we're in agreement here," the chief said. "I'll arrange for Horace and whoever else is available to come out here to do the fake arrest."

"And I'll arrange the decoy," I said.

Chapter 15

While the chief called the station to request that Horace and any other deputies available come out to the house, I pulled out my phone and opened up the text app.

"Caleb," I typed. "You there?"

"Yeah," he texted back. "What's up?"

"Can you have one of your cousins sneak in here? Whoever's the closest to Janet's size."

A pause. Then:

"K"

I assumed that meant OK. Why were kids his age so stingy with their letters?

I left Janet with the chief while I went upstairs to move my little makeshift nursery into one of the guest rooms. The one farthest from the stairs. I planned to post Tinkerbell outside the guest room door, just in case anyone tried to sneak in or out.

I made sure there were sheets on the bed and towels in the adjoining bath. Then I paused, looking out one of the windows. We were on the second story, and it was half again as high as your typical second story, thanks to the house's old-fashioned high ceilings. But still.

I texted Caleb again.

"I'm going to shine a light out one of the windows on the back of the house in a second," I said. "Can you tell the rest of your cousins to watch for it?"

"K," he texted back.

I waited a few moments, then turned on my phone's flashlight and waved it around in the window.

"Got it," Caleb texted back. "What about it?"

"Room where the lady you caught is staying tonight," I typed. "I think she's legit, but if you see anyone trying to get into or out of that window or one of the ones beside it . . ."

"Check."

I turned off the flashlight and headed for Michael's and my room to grab a nightgown and a bathrobe for Janet. And a sweatshirt and some sweatpants for the morning. They'd be a little long on her, but better than nothing.

I left the clothes on the bed in the guest room and went downstairs to find the living room full of people. Horace had arrived, along with Vern Shiffley and my friend Aida Butler, another of the chief's deputies. Caleb had brought in another of his cousins. The cousin was only around five ten, which made him almost a midget by Shiffley standards. Then again, he also looked very young. Perhaps he was still growing. He was wearing Janet's coat, and Aida was scolding him to stand still while she tied on the head scarf. Horace was swabbing Janet's mouth with another of his DNA kits. She was shivering slightly, probably because she was wearing only a t-shirt and jeans. Definitely not practical for tonight's weather. Of course, three days ago, when she'd first gone on the lam, we'd been having unseasonably warm weather.

"I've talked to Robyn, and she's going to arrange a safe house for Mrs. Caverly as soon as possible." The chief was tucking his cell phone in his pocket. "And she's going to come by before dawn tomorrow morning to move them both over to the women's shelter."

"We'll have her and Lark ready." I approved of the idea. The police kept a close eye on the women's shelter. And moving her out of here while it was still dark was wise. Still, dawn. I reminded myself that since today was the winter solstice, sunrise tomorrow would be about as late as it ever got. About seven-fifteen or so. Of course, what dawn tomorrow lacked in early it would make up for in cold. Plus who knows how much more snow.

"When young Ambrose is ready, Vern and Aida will escort him to Vern's cruiser," the chief added, looking at the young Shiffley who was going to impersonate Janet. He was probably hinting that it was past time for Ambrose to be ready. Ambrose straightened up, and the two deputies stood beside him for our inspection.

I nodded with approval. Aida was my height, and Vern was a Shiffley. They didn't tower over Ambrose, but they'd make his height less noticeable.

"I'll take Janet up to her room, then," I said.

Janet collected Lark from the crib and followed me upstairs. I stayed long enough to collect her clothes for washing, so she'd have her own things again, clean, in the morning. Then I shut the door and went back downstairs.

"Okay, that will work," Aida was saying. "Just don't flounce too much."

The chief and the three deputies were studying Ambrose, now not only clad in the coat and scarf but also holding a woman's handbag in front of his chest with both hands.

"The purse is a nice touch," I said.

"Belongs to Mrs. Burke," Aida said.

"Minerva asked me to pick it up," the chief said. "She left it behind at church this afternoon. I don't think she'll mind if we make use of it in a good cause, as long as she gets it home tonight as planned. Off you go, then."

We watched as the three of them made their way down our front walk to Vern's cruiser. Ambrose minced a little, but it probably looked okay to any Dingles lurking in the shrubbery. Vern taking his arm to help him over an icy spot was a nice touch. Horace and the chief and I, all three, breathed a sigh of relief once they drove off.

"I'll get one of these samples over to Dr. Blake's lab tonight," Horace said. I wondered if Grandfather had ordered his DNA technician to come back to the lab in the middle of the night.

"At this time of night?" The chief echoed my thoughts while glancing at the clock.

"The main DNA guy there's a total night owl," Horace said. "And I already made arrangements to drop off the fake mother's DNA tonight when I went off duty, so he's expecting me. And I'll check our official samples into evidence."

"Instead of sending them down to the Crime Lab in Richmond?" the chief asked.

"On a Friday evening?" Horace sounded incredulous. "Not to mention the fact that Monday's Christmas Eve and Tuesday's Christmas. Even if there was anyone there to receive our samples, the lab won't be open to process them until Wednesday. Of course, if there was anything really time-sensitive that depended on getting official DNA results over the weekend, I could call a guy I know at the lab and see if he could arrange it. But I don't think that's the case."

"You're right," the chief said. "I forgot about the season. A pity the bad guys never seem to take the holidays off. No, what Dr. Blake's lab can tell us will do for the time being. Go drop those samples off now. And then consider yourself off the clock. You've had a long day."

"Thanks." Horace headed for the front door. He stopped in the hall to don his coat, hat, and gloves and then strode out into the storm, letting in another blast of cold air as he went. I followed him so I could lock up. When I returned to the living room, the chief was standing there, holding his phone and looking thoughtful.

"More coffee?" I asked. "Regular or decaf, depending on whether the current county crime wave is going to keep you up all night."

"I would love another cup before I go," he said. "And let's play it safe and make it regular. My night's not over yet."

He followed me out to the kitchen and sat at the table while I started the coffee.

"She's hiding something," I said.

"Yes." He nodded slightly. "The name of the person who helped her escape Clay County, for starters. Let's hope that's the only thing."

"You look worried," I said.

"In other words, why am I not delighted to be so close to wrapping up the case of the abandoned baby?" He clenched his jaw and brooded for a few moments, staring at the table. Then he looked up.

"It's no big secret," he said. "Lucius Plunket died about an hour ago."

"The guy Mark Caverly is accused of killing?" He nodded. "Are you sure?"

"They'd brought him to the Caerphilly Hospital," he said, "there being nothing that even resembles an ICU in Clay County. So, yes, I'm sure. The hospital notified the next of kin and Sheriff Dingle. I'd have expected the sheriff to call by now and tell me their fugitive has been promoted from alleged attempted murderer to just plain alleged murderer. He's been calling pretty much on the hour for the past couple of days to demand that we scour the county to find him. But now, nothing."

"That does sound ominous."

"And the news from my sources in Clay County is unsettling."

"You actually have sources in Clay County? I'm impressed."

"Not very many," he admitted. "And I wouldn't bet my

life on any of them. But this time around I think they might be giving me the straight scoop. Word is that Sheriff Dingle's officers may have captured Mark Caverly."

"Oh, no." I glanced up involuntarily, as if Janet could have overheard. I was relieved to hear the shower start, which made it unlikely that she could have crept back down to eavesdrop.

"Exactly." The chief had also glanced upward. "So we're on a very short timer when it comes to bringing in state or federal resources to protect him."

"Do you really think they'll try to kill him?" It sounded over the top, even for Clay County.

"I certainly hope not," he said. "After all, it's not as if the entire county is populated with crooks and thugs."

"No," I said. "Although they're awfully good at finding the crooks and thugs they do have and electing them."

"True." He chuckled slightly. "Although I'm not completely discounting Mrs. Caverly's fears, I think a more likely scenario is that they'll keep him locked up over Christmas without bail, then railroad him into prison on bogus charges."

"Can they do that? Wouldn't the judge do something?"

"Judge Dingle?"

"Ah."

"It's happened before in his court. And obviously if that happens, Mr. Caverly would stand an excellent chance of having his conviction reversed on appeal, but in the meantime he'd be spending months or even years of his life in prison."

"Where the Dingles almost certainly have friends or allies."

"And even if they didn't, life in prison is neither safe nor pleasant for someone suspected of being a police informant. So my goal is to arrange for federal intervention before any of that happens. Maybe I should ask if you could put that coffee in a disposable cup. I should get back to the station to keep the pressure on."

"No problem." I poured his coffee into one of the dozen or so Caerphilly College travel mugs we happened to have, thanks to Michael's former dean, who considered them thoughtful Christmas gifts and used to give one annually to every member of his department, even if they had been on the faculty for thirty years and already had enough travel cups to caffeinate a small army.

"Thanks." He took the cup and stood up to leave. "Call if you notice anything out of the ordinary."

"Will do."

As we were heading for the front door, it flew open.

Chapter 16

I started, and even the chief looked momentarily concerned. Then we both relaxed as Josh and Jamie tumbled inside, shedding large amounts of both new and old snow.

"Mommy! Turn your back!" Josh ordered.

"Presents coming through!" Jamie elaborated.

"I don't think your mother has X-ray vision," Michael said. "So she can't very well see through the store bags."

"But she could guess from the size and shape of the bags!" Josh argued.

"Or from what store the bags come from," Jamie added, with greater logic.

"I will stay here while you take the bags upstairs." I ostentatiously turned my back. "Say goodnight to Chief Burke."

Michael and the boys exchanged greetings, Christmas wishes, and good-byes with the chief, accompanied with a few messages for Adam, his youngest grandson, who was one of the boys' best friends. Michael came over to join me.

"Any trouble here?" he asked softly.

"Trouble, no. Excitement, yes. Lark's mother has been found and is staying here tonight and leaving again with Robyn at dawn. I'll fill you in later."

"That's good," he said. "At least I assume it's good—is Rob off the hook?"

"According to the mother," I said.

"Then it's good."

"Assuming we can convince Delaney. Somehow I have to find the time tomorrow to track her down and get her in a room with Janet Caverly. On top of welcoming and feeding all our arriving house guests and running the Christmas pageant rehearsal."

"I have an idea," he said. "How about if I take over the rehearsal? Not that I'm trying to steal your directorial gig—"

"You're welcome to steal it," I said. "And I can use the time to hunt down Delaney."

"It's a plan, then." He yawned. "It's been a long day, and if we're getting up at dawn to see our guests off, we should probably hit the hay soon."

"We don't all have to see her off," I said.

"You can sleep in if you like," he said. "The boys and I are going to get in a bit of sledding before the rehearsal, so we'll be up in time to see her off."

"I won't be able to sleep." And I wouldn't. Michael was perfectly capable of getting breakfast for the boys, but I couldn't ask him to do that and feed the animals. And I had the feeling Janet would be more comfortable with me helping her pack up.

He went upstairs to supervise the boys' bedtime rituals. I went downstairs to the laundry room.

Janet's clothes wouldn't make anywhere near a full load, so I fished out some of the more critical items from the mountain of family laundry that had piled up over the last few busy days. I was tempted just to throw everything in, but I reminded myself what a bad idea that was. I'd ruined one of my favorite blouses not long ago by not fishing a magic marker out of someone's pockets. So I yawned my way through my usual laundry routine, making sure everything was right side out, zipping all the zippers, and emptying all the pockets. The boys' pockets yielded several tissues, a crumpled dollar bill, a wrapped peppermint, several paper clips, five movie ticket stubs, and a half-chewed piece of gum in the foil wrapper.

Janet's jeans pockets yielded a tightly folded piece of paper with two phone numbers written on it. One was preceded with the letter *R*. The other had no identifying initial beside it—just a careless slash of the pencil. But whoever had written it down had then drawn a line around it three times to form a rectangle, as if to emphasize it.

I pulled out my phone and snapped a picture of the phone numbers. I sent the picture to the chief, with a short email explaining what it was. Very short—I hate tapping out emails with my thumbs. And then, after studying the paper for a few more seconds, I folded it up again and inserted it back where I'd found it. It would probably stay put and survive the wash more or less intact.

Why not just leave it out and give it to her? Didn't I trust Janet?

Not a hundred percent. I still had the nagging feeling that she was holding something back. And I also got the definite impression that it went both ways—she didn't entirely trust us, either. I didn't want her to think I was prying. Under normal circumstances, anyone who'd ever opened up a washer to find little bits of tissue all over everything would understand how I'd come to find the paper. But circumstances weren't normal.

So I tossed the jeans into the washer and pressed the start button. Then I trudged back upstairs.

I paused outside our bedroom door. It occurred to me that I hadn't tried calling Delaney in the last hour or two. For that matter, I hadn't heard from Rob since I'd left Trinity.

Moving as quietly as possible, I climbed up to the third floor, where Rob and Rose Noire had their rooms. They'd both been living in our house almost as long as Michael and I had. Caerphilly's chronic housing shortage was partly to blame. But the arrangement seemed almost normal to Rob and me. We'd grown up in a household that nearly always contained a few relatives who helped out with childcare, housekeeping, cooking, or gardening in return for free room and board. Widowed aunts. Cousins negotiating difficult divorces. The occasional nieces or nephews taking time to find themselves, before or after college. Since Mother's approach to homemaking was strictly supervisory and Dad had no practical skills whatsoever, I'm not sure how we would have managed without this revolving crew of extra hands.

Michael and I were a lot more useful around the house, but I'd be the first to admit that we wouldn't have survived the boys' first few years without Rose Noire's help. Not with our sanity intact, anyway. Shortly after arriving, she'd begun planting organic herbs on a pasture adjoining our farm that belonged to Mother and Dad, and it had grown into highly successful business, so I was guardedly optimistic that she'd stick around awhile longer. With any luck, until the boys were in college.

Rob, on the other hand, could easily have afforded to buy any of the nice houses that occasionally went on sale in town, but then he'd either have had to do his own cooking, cleaning, and yard work or hire someone to do it for him. He found living with us much easier, and had arranged for his accountant to reimburse us generously for his share of the household expenses. I knew he'd probably want a place of his own when he got married, so I'd assumed once he had brought off his proposal to Delaney they would start house hunting.

As long as Janet hadn't torpedoed the whole thing.

Normally I didn't keep track of whether Rob came home or not. He had a day bed in his office at Mutant Wizards, and officially, at least as far as the boys were concerned, that's where he'd slept any time he stayed out all night.

But after what he'd been through today, I was worried about him.

As I walked down the third floor hall I pulled out my phone and tried his number. It went to voice mail immediately. So did Delaney's after four rings.

I checked his door. Open, as usual. I peered in. No Rob.

Although his spare laptop was sitting on the desk. Spare, because Rob liked traveling light; he usually left his work laptop at the office, but liked to have one to use at home. Mainly for games he couldn't play on his phone, but it was a full-fledged laptop.

I went over and started it up. I knew his screen lock password—he'd long ago given it to me, the better to enable me to perform small useful chores like finding a file he'd left on the home laptop and emailing it to him at work.

Or helping him find his iPhone. Rob misplaced his phone at least once a day. If he was near one or the other of his laptops, he'd use the "find my iPhone" feature to locate it. If he was anywhere else, he'd call and ask me to do it for him.

Feeling little guilty, I logged into the site that let me do it. I watched as a compass icon swung back and forth for a while. Then the screen resolved into a map of downtown Caerphilly. The little green dot representing his phone sat blinking at a location that I knew was the Mutant Wizards office.

Damn. I was half hoping to find that green dot on the other side of town, where Delaney lived.

I pulled out my own phone and called the Mutant Wizards security desk. The guard who answered was one I knew—a Caerphilly College student working the night shift.

"Hey, Paton," I said. "It's Meg. I was a little worried about Rob. Is he there?"

"Fast asleep in his office," Paton said. "No idea why—for once, there's no one here working on anything. He's been here all evening—shared a pizza with me a few hours ago. You need to talk to him?"

"No, it can wait till morning," I said. "I just wanted to make sure he hadn't got stuck in a snowdrift or anything."

"He's fine," Paton said. "I threw a blanket over him when I made my rounds an hour ago. And I can make sure the diner sends over a good hot breakfast in the morning."

"Thanks." I'd long ago decided that Paton would eventually make someone a wonderful father. "You haven't seen Delaney, have you?"

"Yeah, she stormed in here earlier."

"Stormed?"

"She didn't exactly say 'bah, humbug,' but I could tell she wasn't feeling much holiday cheer. Barely even looked at me when she stomped out again a few minutes later."

"Oh, dear. Do you know if she talked to Rob?"

"This was before he got here. She did seem kind of put out at not finding him."

"Thanks. And Merry Christmas."

Okay, maybe this was good news. Apparently Delaney had calmed down enough to try to contact Rob. I could help that out tomorrow. And at least Rob was safe and sound. And maybe it was a good thing he hadn't come home. Running into Janet wouldn't have improved his mood, given the complications she'd brought into his life.

I turned the laptop off and made my way quietly downstairs again, past Rose Noire's room and the several guest rooms awaiting the family members who'd be arriving later tomorrow. Or was it tomorrow already?

Michael was already not-quite-snoring, and I knew I'd follow his example as soon as my head hit the pillow, falling into a deep and dreamless sleep.

Chapter 17

"I don't care if it is six-thirty," I muttered as I grabbed the latest two slices of toast from the toaster. "It *feels* like the middle of the night."

The snow had stopped for the time being, after depositing a mere two additional inches. Still, I was glad Michael and the boys were feeding the llamas, the cow, the chickens, the ducks, the barn cat, the wounded squirrel we were helping Grandfather rehabilitate, and—of course—the dogs. Probably wise of Rose Noire to take a short trip a few times a year, to remind us how much easier life was when we had a dedicated morning person around who enjoyed feeding both the two-legged and four-legged residents of our household.

According to the college radio station, the large and complicated weather system that had produced last night's snow was still moving through the area at a snail's pace, so more bands of snow could add to the precipitation total at intervals throughout the day.

Well, all the better for the tourists here for Christmas in Caerphilly. A light snow wouldn't slow them down—in fact, it would enhance the Dickensian ambiance we were aiming for, to say nothing of boosting business for all the shops selling hot food and warm beverages. And it would be interesting to see how much snow it took before the boys finally stopped asking if it would still be around on Christmas Day.

I'd thrown Janet's clothes into the dryer as soon as I

came downstairs, and a few minutes ago I'd ferried them upstairs and assured her that yes, she could take any and all of the baby gear with her.

The doorbell rang. Probably Robyn arriving to collect Janet and Lark.

Before opening the door I peered outside. I was a little surprised to see the van from the Caerphilly Cleaners parked in the street. But it was Robyn standing at the door.

I was even more surprised to find that Mother had accompanied Robyn. Normally it would be another few hours before Mother deigned to start the day with her customary hot jasmine tea and lightly buttered toast.

"We've come to collect those bits of furniture that need cleaning," Mother said as she stamped the snow off her boots before coming in. She said so rather loudly, so I assumed her words were for the benefit of any hostile lurking ears.

"I didn't realize we had furniture in need of cleaning," I said, once the door was closed, as I was helping her and Robyn shed their coats.

"Between the boys and the dogs, you almost always do," Mother said. "Of course everyone does," she added quickly.

In other words, we weren't the only utter slobs in the world. Just her pet utter slobs.

"We're going to take away a sofa, and a couple of smaller pieces," Robyn said. "We'll cover them with tarps. Janet can lie on the sofa, holding Lark, under the tarp, just until we get them into the truck. And we'll put the baby gear in a box and cover it with a tarp, and it will look like just another piece of furniture."

"And after we drop Janet and Lark off at the shelter, we really will take the furniture to be cleaned," Mother added. "You should have it back by Monday."

"Should?" I echoed.

Mother, I soon realized, was determined to remove not

just a sofa but every upholstered piece in the living room, plus the rug. I vetoed all of this.

"We have house guests arriving later today, remember," I said. "I'm not going to have them sitting around the fire singing carols on folding lawn chairs."

We finally reached an acceptable compromise. She took a sofa and two armchairs from the library, all pieces that had taken more than a few hits from after-school beverages and homework-fueling snacks. Mother wasn't happy, but I pointed out to her that the purpose of the expedition was to smuggle Janet and Robyn out unseen, not to clean up every item of furniture in the house—no matter how badly she felt we needed it.

"After our holiday guests leave you can empty the living room if you like," I told Mother. "The whole house, for that matter."

Possibly a mistake. I could see the look in her eye—the one suggesting that along with a thorough pre-spring cleaning she might do just a wee smidgen of redecorating.

Not a problem. I'd long since conceded the battle to keep her from redecorating the ground floor of our house whenever the mood struck her. I gave her free rein, as long as she followed two rules: She had to show us what she was planning before she ordered it, so we could veto anything we actually hated, and anything she did had to survive whatever the boys and dogs could do to it, because we weren't shooing them away from any part of their own house.

"Let's get this show on the road, then," Robyn said. "Any chance you and Michael could help us with the furniture?"

We could indeed, and so could Josh and Jamie. I swore them to secrecy, and wasn't too worried about their ability to keep their mouths shut. Unlike Dad—or, for that matter, Rob—they seemed to understand that if you managed to alert the immediate world that you were sitting on an important secret you'd already blown it.

Although I could see they really, really wanted to tell someone about this morning's adventure. First we covered one of the armchairs with a tarp, and Michael carried it out to the truck, allowing the tarp to slip off while he was waiting for me to open the truck doors, so the whole world could see that it was just an armchair.

Then we made Janet lie down on the couch, placed Lark in her arms, and hauled that out, with Michael and Josh on one end and Jamie and me on the other.

"Stay hidden until we take off," I murmured as we set the sofa down in the truck.

Josh and Jamie carried the second armchair out and managed, with my help to load it. Michael brought up the rear with an approximately armchair-sized object that was actually the portable crib, and the boys followed with a tarp-covered box in which we'd packed the diapers, onesies, bottles, and other useful baby gear.

While Michael and the boys were in the back of the truck securing the furniture so it wouldn't shift around and smash Janet or Lark, I pulled Mother aside.

"Any chance you could stay behind or come back and help with something?" I asked. "I have to hunt down Delaney and see if I can patch things together between her and Rob—and we have all those relatives arriving. If you could greet the relatives—"

"Of course," she said, almost purring. "At least I can greet the first one or two and get them settled. Then I can put them in charge of welcoming the later arrivals. I'll just go check out the guest rooms to make sure they're ready."

She sailed off toward the stairs. Another problem solved—provided we could all get out of the house before she decided that any of the guest rooms suffered from toxic feng shui and needed to have all their furniture rearranged.

"All systems go," Michael said as he came back inside. "Everything should survive the trip unscathed."

"Remember," I said as the boys waved good-bye to the departing Caerphilly Cleaners truck. "You can't tell *anyone* about this until the baby and her mother are safe. Not even Mason or Adam."

"But Adam's grandpa is the chief," Jamie protested. "Doesn't he know?"

"Yes, but he won't tell anyone, either, not even Adam, until it's safe. I'll let you know when that is. And then we can tell everyone how you helped rescue them."

They both beamed with pride. And then, luckily, Michael shifted their focus onto the upcoming sledding trip with Mason and Adam. We got them bundled up and on their way. I poured myself another cup of tea and called the Mutant Wizards security desk.

"Hey, Meg," Paton said. "Haven't seen him yet this morning."

"That's okay." I paused, trying to figure out a subtle way of finding out what I wanted to know, and gave up. "You seen Delaney again?"

"Not since yesterday. She wouldn't normally be here on a weekend."

Of course, neither would Rob.

"Can you let me know if you do?" I asked.

"Sure." A pause. "Um . . . is something wrong?"

"Nothing I can't fix if I can talk to Delaney," I said. With more confidence than I felt.

"Roger. I'll keep my eyes open."

I thought of texting Rob, but decided to wait. What could I say now, other than "I'm trying."

I drove over to Delaney's place. She lived in a neighborhood where Randall and I had succeeded in convincing the town council to ease up the draconian restrictions that had once made it almost impossible for a homeowner to set up a rental unit. So far the neighborhood hadn't gone to seed—in fact, it was thriving. Delaney lived in the top floor of what had once been a run-down three-story Victorian house. I liked to think the income from having rental apartments in the top floor, the basement, and over the garage had helped its owners bring the building back to something resembling its original glory. Then again, maybe the owners had simply paid attention when Randall and I warned that if the neighborhood started to look junky, the town council might reverse itself on the subdividing/subletting issue. The place looked particularly festive with its holiday decorations—wreaths and candles in every window, and several miles of evergreen garlands festooning the wraparound porch. The candles and any other lights were off, but I spotted fairy lights along with tinsel on all the garlands. The snow had nearly covered up the life-sized figures in the yard, but I could tell they were a trio of carolers—a nice change from the usual Santas and nativity scenes. Clearly Delaney's landlords had figured out that another way to reassure the town council that the new permissive rental policies weren't bringing property values down was to decorate lavishly for Christmas in Caerphilly, Halloween in Caerphilly, the Harvest Festival, and any other seasonal attractions Randall invented to enhance our growing success as a tourist destination.

The owners hadn't yet removed the latest installment of snow from their walks or their driveway. Well, it was early yet, and my car could easily handle a few inches of snow. I could see other tire tracks in the snow—tracks that drove in, circled around the wide end of the asphalt driveway, and then pulled out again. I followed them, which gave me a view of the parking area the owners created for their tenants, screened from the street by a privacy fence that in summer would be covered with a tangle of honeysuckle and morning glory vines. I found myself remembering one evening last summer when Delaney had invited me to a women-only chick-flick night. Walking past that fence, I'd had a moment of feeling almost dizzy from the sudden overwhelmingly sweet scent of the honeysuckle blossoms.

Nothing magical about the honeysuckle now. In fact, the dead, snow-covered vines gave the place a rather grim look.

Neither of the two cars in the parking area were Delaney's. No lights in the house. No tracks leading into the garage or the tenant parking area, so I suspected the tire tracks I was following were made by someone doing the same thing I was doing—turning in to see if Delaney was home, then leaving again when it was clear she wasn't. All the marks other than mine looked the same, and I rather thought they matched the tires on my brother's pricey little convertible.

Poor Rob.

Where to look? I knew the names of a couple of Delaney's friends. I had no idea where they lived, but I could probably look it up on my computer—my work computer, which had access to the town records. I headed toward the town hall.

Strange. There were Shiffleys perched on the roof of the town hall. Were they making some repairs to the multicolored Christmas lights decking the hall's roof and windows? No—they appeared to be scrutinizing the shingles. The shingles that had been replaced, at great expense, only two years ago. The great expense arose, of course, largely from the vast size of the roof—the Shiffley Construction Company had pared its labor costs to the bone. Obviously if there was anything wrong with the roof, the Shiffleys had the strongest possible incentive for fixing it right away—although 8:00 A.M. on a Saturday morning seemed a bit excessive.

But there shouldn't be anything wrong with a two-year-old roof unless the materials were defective or had been installed improperly. With Shiffleys doing the installing, I was pretty sure that wasn't the problem. And besides, if there was anything wrong, then given my role as Randall's special assistant, I should have already been told about it.

I went inside and took the elevator up to the top floor, then used my master key to unlock the door to the narrow corridor that led to the roof access. A few tools and bits of lumber lay along the sides of the corridor, and the pull-down access steps had been lowered. They were almost as steep as a ladder.

I climbed up and popped open the trap door. Small amounts of snow fell in. I took a deep breath and reminded myself that it was a very big roof with a very shallow slope, and the odds of my falling off were almost nil. Especially if I stayed near the trap door, which was smack dab in the middle of the roof. I climbed the rest of the way up, sat on the edge of the trap door opening, and looked around.

"Hey, Meg." It was Fred Shiffley, the cousin who was officially running the construction company now that Randall was mayor. The two other Shiffleys with him waved, and then went back to whatever they were doing. Peering at random shingles, from what I could see. And occasionally taking pictures of them with their phones.

"What are you doing up here?" Fred asked.

"I was about to ask you the same thing."

Chapter 18

"What are we doing? Inspecting the roof, of course," Fred said.

"In the middle of a snowstorm?" Okay, the snow had stopped for the time being, but the sky showed that was only temporary.

"Not a whole lot else we can do in the middle of a snowstorm," Fred said. "Too cold to pour concrete, too wet to paint. But Randall reminded me that we'd promised the manufacturer to send them regular data on the performance of the roof. Take pictures of the shingles every year or so, especially those in places where they're subject to more wear and tear. Give the manufacturer the data they want, and in return they give us a price break if anything does need repairing prematurely."

"Seriously?" I gave him what Rob would call my Mother look, a stare that always proved highly effective in extracting truthful information from Josh and Jamie.

"You don't think it sounds plausible?" Fred looked slightly guilty.

"Oh, it would sound plausible enough to an outsider," I said. "But remember, I was up to my ears in the administrative side of the roof deal. I don't remember any request from the manufacturer for ongoing data. What are you really doing up here?"

"You got me there." Fred grinned and shook his head. "We're on Dingle watch. We know y'all took Miz Caverly to the women's shelter this morning. We don't rightly know its exact location—not officially, anyway—but we do have a general idea of the part of town where we don't want to see interlopers from Clay County slinking around."

"That makes more sense," I said. "What if you do spot any Dingles? Or Plunkets or Whickers or Peebleses?"

"We call 911," Fred said. "And then we give a heads-up to a few cousins who are whiling away the afternoon playing poker in the backroom at Muriel's diner, so they can wander over and use their diplomatic skills to help defuse any tense situations."

I wondered if the chief knew about this. He probably did, although I'd make a point of mentioning it to him. I also wondered if I should tell Fred about the state-of-the-art security system Rob had donated to the shelter. Any Dingle—or, for that matter, any man—who attempted to enter the shelter would be spotted immediately in the security cameras, and the Caerphilly Police Department would probably hear about it before the Shiffleys had time to pull out their cell phones.

No, better not. For one thing, the less outsiders knew about the shelter's workings the better—no matter how well disposed they were toward it. And besides, why should I spoil the Shiffleys' fun?

"Carry on, then," I said. "And while you're at it—do you happen to know who Delaney McKenna is?"

"Not by name," he said. "Who is he?"

"She," I corrected. "My brother's girlfriend."

"The tall redhead." Fred nodded. "Yes, ma'am. I hope it won't rile any ladies too much if I say that most any red-blooded male in town has probably noticed her."

"If you happen to notice her around town today, could you call and let me know where?" I said. "I need to talk to her, and she's not answering her phone. Not to me, anyway."

"Can do. And I'd appreciate it if you could help convince

people we're just up here peering at shingles. And taking our own sweet time about it, on account of there being not much else to do today."

"You've got it. Later."

I climbed back down the access steps, closing the trap door behind me. I was relieved to have my feet back on solid ground.

Of course, now I had no reason not to return to my fruitless search for Delaney. For all I knew, she could have left town.

And it was ridiculous to keep trying alone. I needed to enlist some help.

First, I dropped by my office and used my computer to look up the addresses and phone numbers of the two friends of Delaney whose names I could remember. Even if they didn't know where she was, maybe they'd help me look.

Then again, maybe they wouldn't talk to me any more than she would yesterday. I needed to enlist someone I knew could help. I mentally put the friends on the back burner. Instead, I pulled out my phone and called Robyn.

"Can I drop by and talk to you?" I asked, after we'd exchanged greetings.

"Whenever you like," she said. "I'm over at the shelter for the next few hours, and then at noon I'm going over to the church for the Altar Guild's lunchtime meeting."

"I'll meet you at the shelter, then."

I retrieved my car from the lot behind the town hall and headed over toward the neighborhood of the shelter.

As I turned into the street where I was planning to park, I spotted Robyn's forest-green station wagon coming toward me.

Odd. I'd just said I'd meet her at the shelter.

When the car got closer, I was about to roll down my window to hail Robyn when I realized it wasn't her driving.

It was Janet Caverly.

I didn't think Janet recognized me, and she wouldn't have known my car as well as I knew Robyn's wagon. So with luck she had no idea she'd been spotted.

I pulled into the next open driveway I came to and turned around so I could follow her.

I trailed her through the side streets of Caerphilly for a few minutes, being careful to keep my distance. But from her slow pace I suspected she was more focused on driving safely on the snow-covered streets than on the possibility that anyone might be shadowing her. And dodging the tourists, who were already out in force in spite of the early hour. The snow, which had begun falling lightly while I was following Janet, didn't seem to be discouraging the tourists, who were swarming all the usual scenic spots with their digital cameras and smart phones, but at least it gave me some small degree of cover.

Eventually she headed out of town along the Clay County Road.

In the unlikely event that you were in Caerphilly and wanted to be in Clay County instead, you took either the Clayville Road or the Clay County Road. The Clayville Road led more or less straight to the center of the town, which was not only very small but quite unremarkable apart from being the site of the only traffic light in the county. The Clay County Road was a little more useful, since it led past the Caerphilly Inn and Grandfather's zoo before it crossed the county line. Once in Clay County, it meandered about seemingly at random until it finally entered Clayville and intersected with the Clayville Road at the aforementioned stoplight.

As I shadowed Janet, I tried to think of something along the Clay County Road that she might have some reason to visit. Nothing came to mind. And after we passed first the Inn and then the zoo, I began to wonder if she was actually heading for Clay County.

And apparently she was. She slowed down as if having second thoughts when she spotted the battered sign welcoming the unwary traveler to Clay County. Then she sped up again, until she was going more than a little faster than before. Not the safest thing to do in Clay County, whose snow removal policy seemed to be that plowed roads were for wusses and if you didn't own a vehicle that could handle a foot or so of snow you deserved to be snowbound.

I followed at a safe distance. In fact, I let her get out of sight. I knew this road reasonably well, and there were hardly any possible turns—just the mouths of lanes that led into the woods. Some, flanked by one or more mailboxes, clearly led to houses tucked back in the woods. Others were probably logging roads or maybe lanes leading to someone's hunting cabin. The storm had tapered off, thank goodness, but it had deposited about an inch of fresh snow before doing so, and I could see as I passed that no one had turned into any of the lanes recently—the snow lay deep and crisp and even, and most importantly, untouched by foot or tire.

I finally spotted a lane with fresh tire indentations in the snow, and a set of taillights slowly disappearing into the distance. I thought of turning in behind Janet, and then thought better of it immediately. Her destination couldn't be that far away, and I needed to find a way to continue my surveillance on foot. It was a lot harder to be stealthy in a car—cars were bigger, noisier, and especially in a wooded area like this, pretty much limited to the roads. On foot I could be swift and silent and had much more scope for taking a route that would let me sneak up on Janet. At least that's what I'd done the only other time I could remember trying to tail someone through the woods in a snowstorm, and it had worked out okay. Well, except for finding a dead body—but with luck I wouldn't be repeating that experience.

So I continued on until I came to a place where I could turn around. Then I drove back, again passing the lane with the fresh tracks. At the next mailbox-free lane I stopped and backed in. The snow might have paused for the time being, but from the way the sky looked I suspected that was temporary, and I wanted to maximize the odds that I could extricate the car when I returned. And while backing in was tricky, backing out with any more snow would be a lot worse.

Then it occurred to me that anyone who came along would spot my car. The lane was a curvy one, so I kept backing until my car was out of sight of the road. Then I grabbed a big branch and tried brushing my tire tracks away with it. That seemed to work pretty well. It wouldn't fool a Shiffley, or anyone else who was a seasoned tracker. Probably a few of those in Clay County. But at least it wouldn't jump out at the casual passerby that someone had driven a car down the lane. So I walked backward to the road, sweeping the branch behind me as I went. And once I reached the road I tried to walk only on one of the two packed-down ruts.

All this was probably overkill. But I couldn't shake the sense of being in hostile territory and wanting to keep a low profile.

When I reached the lane where Janet had turned, I brushed enough snow off the mailbox to read the name. R. PLUNKET.

Great. A Plunket. But then, what did I expect in Clay County? At least it wasn't a Dingle. Since both the mayor and the sheriff—and for that matter, the county judge—were currently Dingles, I tended to assume they were the most villainous of Clay County's denizens. If nothing else, they were the villains currently in charge.

I started trudging down the lane. Luckily it was a relatively short one—only a quarter of a mile from the main road I rounded a curve to find I was approaching a small, one-story bungalow. Robyn's station wagon was parked in front of it. A rather meager array of multicolored Christmas lights was strung around the door. A few puffs of smoke came from the chimney.

I could see lights in one of the windows. I slipped closer so I could peer in.

Janet was there, and she seemed to be talking a mile a minute to another young woman about her own age. They were clutching cans of diet soda and nibbling on potato chips. Both chips and sodas bore the logo of the Clay County Super Mart's singularly unappetizing house brand.

The other young woman looked pretty harmless. She had light brown hair tied back in a ponytail, and wore jeans and a navy blue sweater. I studied the room she and Janet were sitting in. I got the impression it belonged to someone just starting out in life. The furniture was a mixture of hand-me-downs and inexpensive assemble-it-yourself pieces. The colors were bright and airy, the whole effect feminine. Maybe the young woman Janet had come to see was the only one living here. I liked that idea.

But who was she? Apart from being a Plunket. I tried not to hold that against her.

Decision time. I could keep lurking out here in the cold until frostbite set in, or I could go in and confront Janet.

I strode up the steps and knocked on the door.

Chapter 19

I heard scurrying inside the house, and what sounded like a piece of furniture being shoved across the floor. Were they blockading the door against a possible home invasion?

"Who's there?" came a voice, finally.

"Meg Langslow," I said. "I'm a friend of Janet Caverly."

A pause.

"Who?"

"Oh, come off it," I said. "I know Janet's in there. I saw her through the window. I came to find out why she drove off in Reverend Smith's car. Let me in, or I'll call the police to report the vehicle stolen."

A pause. A fairly long pause. More furniture moving.

Then the door opened.

"Come in." The young woman opened the door and beckoned me in. She was looking down the lane a little wild-eyed, as if to make sure I was alone.

"It's just me," I said.

"It's okay." Janet had entered from what I assumed was the hallway to the bedrooms. Or maybe the only bedroom, given the small size of the house. "She's the one I told you about. Meg, what are you doing here?"

"I spotted you hightailing it out of town in Robyn's station wagon," I said. "I came to ask why?"

"It's a long story."

"I'm a patient person." I sat down on a lumpy couch covered with two brightly colored afghans. Possibly a tactical mistake—the afghans spruced up the look of the couch but they did nothing to make up for its broken springs, one of which poked uncomfortably into my rear. "Start with why you stole Robyn's vehicle."

"I didn't steal it." She perched on the edge of a lopsided easy chair draped, like the couch, in bright afghans. "I'm going to take it back."

"That's nice. But I notice you didn't say that she lent it to you."

"She didn't actually. But I didn't think she'd mind. She doesn't need it until she has to go back to the church, at eleven forty-five. I heard her say so."

"So why are you here?"

"I came to get my things."

"Your things!" I spotted a suitcase lying open on the floor. Clothes were spilling out of it—clothes and a few cosmetics. "You came here for a bunch of stupid clothes? Was that all a lie about being afraid of the Clay County sheriff?"

"It's not the clothes," Janet said. "I came for—"

Someone knocked on the door, heavily.

"Rachel! Open up!" A deep male voice.

"Oh, lord," Janet whispered.

"Back into the attic," Rachel hissed.

"Rachel! I know you're in there."

"Who is it?" Rachel called.

"Brad Peebles."

"*Deputy* Brad Peebles," she murmured to me. "Hang on a sec," she shouted to the closed door. "I just got up."

Rachel threw an afghan over the suitcase and scurried down the hallway, tearing her sweater and jeans off as she went. She ducked into a doorway. Janet tiptoed on past the doorway to where an access stair was pulled down—much like the one I'd recently climbed in the courthouse, but shorter and flimsier. A light curio cabinet was shoved aside—I gathered it would normally occupy the space right under the trap door. Janet hurried up the stairway. I followed. Rachel emerged from the doorway, tying a robe around her. She quickly lifted up the stairs and shut the trap door behind us. I heard the faint sounds of the cabinet being shoved into place. We were trapped here in the attic.

Not much of an attic, either. No floor—just bare joists with stretches of insulation between them and a few sheets of plywood thrown over them near the ladder. And it was only three feet tall at the peak of the roof. Janet and I crouched there on the plywood in the near dark on either side of the folded-up access stairs.

I hit my knee on something and the something made a faint hissing noise.

"Ssshh, Sammy," Janet whispered.

The something—presumably a cat in a carrier—uttered a faint yowl of feline protest and fell mercifully silent.

"I came back for Sammy," Janet whispered.

"Okay," I said. "I get it. Let's keep the noise down."

Downstairs, I could hear Rachel opening the door.

"You only just getting up?" Deputy Peebles's voice mixed disapproval with a hint of flirtation.

"Give me a break. I had to work late shift at the Burger Barn last night."

"Where is she?"

"Who?"

"Ms. Caverly."

"Janet? I haven't seen her since she and her husband went on the lam."

"Then why is her car parked in front of your house." The deputy's tone said "Gotcha!"

"Her car?" Rachel was a good actress. She sounded genuine puzzled. Then her tone changed. "Hey! What's going on? Lucius's truck was parked there when I went to bed."

"Then I'd say you got the worst of the bargain." Deputy Peebles seemed to be enjoying her reaction. "Someone takes a brand-new F-150 and leaves behind an old beater like that."

"Damn." Their voices were a little more distant now—I suspected they'd gone outside. "I should have checked to see if Lucius had left a spare key tucked up on the visor. As many times as I told him it was a stupid thing to do, and here I forget to look. But that's not Janet's car. It's from Caerphilly."

"She was driving it."

"What makes you think that?"

"Because Ben Dingle saw her doing it over in Caerphilly, and heading out of town in this direction. He's been hanging around Caerphilly, playing tourist and keeping his ear to the ground, on account of we figured one or both of the Caverlys would try to hide there."

"Well, what are you waiting for? Do I have to go down to the station to report Lucius's truck as stolen, or can I just tell you?"

"I'll call it in. And I'll get a tow truck out here to pick up this abandoned vehicle."

"No rush." Rachel's voice was closer now—they'd come back inside. "The abandoned vehicle's not going anywhere. But you might want to have your officers look out for Lucius's truck, because if Janet Caverly really did take it, I doubt if she's planning on staying around here much longer."

For the next forty-five minutes Janet and I crouched in the attic. We listened in as Deputy Peebles reported the stolen truck and called for the tow truck for Robyn's car. We overheard his heavy-handed attempts to flirt with Rachel. I could have assured Rachel that the insulation in her house did its job beautifully, but since that job was to keep the heat in the house—and out of the attic—I began to worry what would happen if we had to stay up here for a couple of hours. I must have checked half a dozen times to make sure the ringer on my phone was turned off. I'd have texted someone to tell them where I was and what was happening, but like much of Clay County, Rachel's house was in a cell phone dead zone. I fretted that Sammy would grow tired of sleeping in his crate and would begin yowling for food, a litterbox, or just a little attention. I had to suppress the urge to cheer when I finally heard the sounds of the tow truck hauling Robyn's car away. After all, getting it back was probably going to be a real headache. Deputy Peebles made a few final halfhearted attempts to get Rachel to agree to meet him that evening for drinks at the Clay Pigeon, the indescribably sleazy watering hole that was Clayville's only bar. Then he gave up and drove off.

Janet and I waited in tense silence.

A few minutes later, we heard the sound of the cabinet being moved. Rachel pulled down the steps.

"The coast is clear," she said. "I'll make you some hot coffee."

"I won't say no," I said. "But could you put it in cups we can take with us? Because I think the sooner we get out of here the better."

"Good idea." Rachel led the way into the tiny kitchen and poured water into a coffeemaker. "But just how are you getting out of here? For that matter, how did you get here?"

"I parked my car about half a mile away," I said. "On what I hope is a little-used lane. And I did what I could to hide it but I doubt if it would take local law enforcement long to find it if they started searching the area for Janet."

"Which they probably will when they find Janet didn't take Lucius's truck," Rachel said.

"If they tow my car, we'll have to hike back to Caerphilly." And wouldn't that be fun, I thought glumly. "Where is the truck, anyway?" I asked aloud.

"Grendel, my pig of a cousin came by last night and took it," Rachel said.

"Grendel?" I wasn't sure which seemed more unlikely—that anyone would knowingly name a defenseless child after an Anglo-Saxon monster, or that anyone in Clay County would have read *Beowulf.*

"Grendel Plunket," Rachel said, as if that explained anything. "He came around just after midnight. He had been threatening to do it if Lucius died—said it was too much truck for a little lady like me. I told him if he wanted the truck he should make me an offer. Well, let's hope this will teach him. I just hope I don't get the truck back full of bullet holes."

I shoved my curiosity over Grendel's name aside. Something had just dawned on me.

"Lucius Plunket?" I said. "Your brother was the one who was shot?"

"The one who was killed," she said. "You can say it. Your chief of police broke the news to me last night."

She turned away and began fiddling with something on the end of the kitchen counter—a bedraggled little Christmas tree. It only had room for about a dozen tiny ornaments, but she seemed intent on rearranging all of them.

"I'm so sorry," I said.

She nodded. Janet was patting her on the back. Rachel held up one grape-sized silver ball and frowned at it as if it were to blame for her brother's demise.

"That was how Rachel came to help me," Janet said. "Because Mark and her brother were working together."

"And Lucius wasn't shot by Mark Caverly—no matter what Sheriff Dingle says." Rachel turned back to me, still clutching the tiny ornament.

"Then what did happen to him?" I asked.

Rachel and Janet exchanged a look.

"She's okay," Janet said.

Rachel didn't look entirely convinced, but I could see the moment when she decided to take Janet's word for it.

"He was going to help Mark get the goods on the Dingles' crooked operation," she said. "Making moonshine, growing weed, and maybe even smuggling in other illegal stuff. Lucius worked for them for a while, mainly to earn money for college. He didn't realize exactly what they needed an electrician like him for until he took the job, and by that time he couldn't really get out. And he realized maybe they never would let him go. And that it was the small fry like him who'd end up taking the rap if they ever got caught. Mark knew the financial side, and Lucius knew a lot of the operational stuff, like how they managed to hide everything from the Feds."

"Mark had reached out to some federal agency," Janet said. "I don't know which—he never said. He told them that he and Lucius were willing to testify."

"A pity we don't know which agency." Rachel's voice shook with anger. "Because I think someone there's dirty, or at least damned careless. The next thing we knew Lucius had a bullet in his head and they were blaming Mark for it."

Janet frowned slightly, and I had the feeling she knew exactly what agency, and possibly how to contact it. Or maybe I was just being paranoid.

"By 'they' you mean the Dingles, right?" I said aloud. "So if something happens to Mark before he can testify, their problems are solved."

They both nodded. I didn't say it aloud, but it occurred to me that the two of them knew enough to make things awkward for the Dingles. Maybe Janet's fears for Mark and herself weren't entirely paranoid. Maybe Rachel should also be worried.

"You should get out of here, too," Janet said to Rachel.

Was she reading my mind? "Sooner or later they're going to start suspecting you know something."

"You're probably right." Rachel finally set down the little silver ball—miraculously still whole—and began pouring coffee into two plastic cups from the Burger Barn, Clay County's version of fine dining. "I don't know why I've stayed here this long. Our mother wasn't from around here," she added by way of explanation to me. "So I'm a lot more open to the idea that there might be someplace worth living outside Clay County. Let's get the two of you out of here first."

"The three of us," Janet corrected. "I'm not leaving Sammy behind."

She threw aside the afghan that had hidden her suitcase and began pulling out a few items. Then she went back to the attic and hauled the carrier down.

Sammy proved to be a smallish Siamese cat. He purred when Janet opened the door to his carrier, and when she picked him up he nestled against her and uttered one soft yowl that almost sounded like a baby. He wasn't as thrilled when she stuffed him back into the carrier and shoved half a dozen items of clothing in after him, but he quieted when she told him to.

"Ready," she said.

"If you're serious about leaving Clay County and worried about them coming after you, go see the Reverend Smith at Trinity Episcopal in Caerphilly," I said to Rachel. "She runs the local women's shelter, and she has helped quite a few women escape stalkers."

"Good to know."

She stood in her doorway and watched as Janet and I hiked away from her house. Hauling the cat carrier seemed to slow Janet down, so I took it over and set a brisk pace. If not for the snow, I'd have considered setting out through the woods, even if it took longer. But at least walking along the lane and then the Clay County Road we wouldn't be leaving quite such a glaringly obvious trail. Or taking quite so much of a chance of getting lost in the woods.

I was relieved to see the lane much as I'd left it, with my amateur camouflage efforts unsullied by any car tracks or footprints. While I'm fond of my old blue Honda, I don't usually feel an impulse to hug it when I'm reunited with it. I wanted to this time. I settled for patting its fender and mentally promising it an oil change if it got us safely out of Clay County.

While Janet loaded the cat carrier into the backseat, I retrieved the old blanket I kept in the trunk for impromptu picnics and handed it to her.

"If you see a car approaching, or if I say 'duck,' pull this over you and crouch down," I said.

"Why don't I just ride in the trunk?"

She sounded serious.

"If it makes you feel safer."

"If they stop you, you're just taking your cat to the vet," she said.

"They might know who I am," I said. "And they'd know my route to the vet wouldn't take me through Clay County. So if they stop me, I'm coming back from Tappahannock with a cat I bought there as a Christmas present for my mother."

"Whatever works. You're the local." She climbed into my trunk. I felt a brief pang of guilt. I had a habit of making good use of my time while waiting for the boys at school or at their various activities by tidying trash and clutter out of the body of the car and, if no trash can was readily available, stowing it in the trunk. The theory was that then it would be easy to complete the cleaning by emptying out the trunk. In practice, I didn't get around to that final phase nearly often enough.

But Janet seemed quite content to nestle down among

the power bar wrappers, empty juice boxes, and fast food detritus. Well, if cozying up to a few stale French fries was the worst thing that happened to her today, it I'd consider it a major victory. I tucked the blanket over her—more for warmth than concealment—and shut the trunk.

Then I took a deep breath and eased my car into motion.

Chapter 20

Hiding Janet in the trunk turned out to be a good thing. I didn't have to pull out my story of cat acquisition in Tappahannock, but half a mile from the county line I spotted a pickup truck approaching. As it drew nearer, I could see that the driver wore a deputy's hat. My heart began pounding, especially when he slowed down as we passed by. I kept my face neutral and nodded at him. He didn't nod back, and he made no bones about the fact that he was using his truck's superior height to look down into my car. He'd have spotted a blanket-covered lump in the passenger seat. Points to Janet.

When we passed the back of the WELCOME TO CLAY COUNTY sign and then the WELCOME TO CAERPHILLY sign, which was in much better repair than its counterpart, I breathed easier—but only a little easier. After all, we were still very much out in the country and spies from Clay County had definitely been lurking around Caerphilly.

And now I had to figure out what to do with Janet.

"All that effort to smuggle you into the women's shelter before dawn, and you go and pull a stunt like this," I muttered, with an irritated glance over my shoulder toward the trunk. And from the sound of it, Sheriff Dingle's spies hadn't spotted her until she'd taken off on her cat retrieval mission. Maybe taking her back there at this time of day wasn't such a good idea.

But where to take her instead?

We were approaching Grandfather's zoo. If it were after

hours, I'd use my key to smuggle her in the staff entrance. But the parking lot was swarming with tourists coming to see Grandfather's annual "Animals of the Bible" holiday exhibit. If the Dingles wanted to keep an eye on comings and goings from Clay County, a parking lot crowded with tourists would be an excellent surveillance point. I drove on past and kept my eye on the rearview mirror.

Soon we'd be passing the Caerphilly Inn. Of course! Normally, a snooty five-star hotel wouldn't be the first place I'd think of to hide a fugitive. But the Inn's assistant manager was a good friend of mine. I'd known Ekaterina Vorobyaninova since she'd been merely a junior member of the housekeeping staff.

And not only was she a friend but, as the daughter of a self-professed former Russian secret agent, she had a fondness for subterfuge and intrigue.

I turned into the Inn's mile-long lane, pulled out my cell phone, and broke my normally stern policy against phoning while driving. I rationalized that as long as I followed the Inn's five-mile-per-hour speed limit, it was almost indistinguishable from phoning in a parked car.

"Meg! Merry Christmas! What happens?"

"Merry Christmas to you, and can you hide a woman in peril for a little while?"

"Of course. Why are you in peril?" Odd, how matter-of-fact she sounded about the notion.

"I'm not in peril—at least I hope I'm not, now that I'm safely out of Clay County. But I just finished rescuing someone, and she needs a place to hide. She and her cat," I added. "Can I bring them in the back way?"

"I will meet you at the loading dock."

Janet was a little surprised to find herself being hustled past the Dumpsters and through the somewhat industrial back corridors of the hotel. But once we had her and Sammy installed in a room—small, by the Inn's standards, which meant it was still almost the size of Rachel Plunket's entire bungalow—she relaxed a little.

"This is rather nice," she said. Clearly she had a talent for understatement.

"You can stay here for the time being," I said.

"What about An—Lark?" Janet said. "I can't leave her at the shelter."

I decided not to point out that she already had, when she'd taken off to rescue Sammy.

"I'll make arrangements either to sneak you back into the shelter or to bring her out here, whichever will work better," I said. "But later. Let's give it a little time to make sure no one followed us here."

Janet didn't look as if she liked the idea, but she didn't argue with me.

Ekaterina and I left her and Sammy to settle in.

"Can we expect pursuit?" Ekaterina sounded as if she rather liked the idea.

"It's possible. Her husband's the one accused—probably falsely—of that murder in Clay County. She escaped with her baby, but she left her cat behind."

"And you helped her rescue him. Very good!"

I remembered that Ekaterina was herself a cat lover, and had recently engineered a repeal of the Inn's no-pets policy. Her two Russian blues, Alexei and Tatiana, could now usually be found in the Inn's lobby, basking by the fire and gazing superciliously at the guests. I decided not to mention that I would have vetoed the cat rescue mission if consulted.

"It would be nice if you could make sure she doesn't leave." Maybe I was too suspicious, but I still had questions about Janet's story.

"I anticipated that possibility." Ekaterina nodded with satisfaction. "I have placed her in one of the rooms that can be adapted to guests with special needs. Guests who should not, for one reason or another, be permitted unsupervised access to the rest of the property."

"Seriously? You have rooms like that?"

"From time to time, we have requests to accommodate, for example, a family party that includes a member who is less capable of independent action. Someone of advanced age and diminished mental capacity, for example. We can also provide a suitably discreet and safe environment for someone undergoing certain courses of medical treatment."

"Like sobering up?"

Ekaterina nodded.

Fascinating. The idea that the Inn also doubled, for its most elite clients, as a five-star residential treatment center for substance abuse or dementia was a new one.

"So she can't get out?"

"Of course she can get out," Ekaterina sounded shocked. "The fire code would not permit us simply to lock her in! She can get out by pushing the emergency exit bar on her door. But then of course the fire alarms would sound, our security office would see it immediately, and the appropriate staff member would be dispatched to deal with the situation. So it is preferable for her to use the house phone to request assistance. I will explain this to her in a few minutes when I take up her lunch."

"That sounds perfect," I said. "I'll try to get her out of your hair as soon as possible."

"No worry."

"Can you find me a quiet corner so I can make some phone calls?"

"You can use my office," she said. "And have you eaten?"

"No, but—"

"I will send up a tray," she said.

Ekaterina's office, like her, was elegant, serene, and

efficient. I sank into her butter-soft leather desk chair, pulled out my cell phone, and made a mental list of calls.

I'd start with 911.

"What's your emergency, Meg?" Debbie Ann said.

"I'd like to report a car theft," I said. "Not my car. Robyn's."

"She already reported it," Debbie Ann said. "Although she did add that it's possible she merely forgot who she lent it to. Which probably means that she suspects one of her stray lambs has taken it, and if we find it she'll suddenly remember having told the culprit they could borrow it any time they wanted."

"She probably will," I said. "As it happens I know who borrowed it—Janet Caverly."

"We were wondering about her."

"And I have at least a general idea where the car might be now."

"And that is?"

"Wherever Clay County deposits towed vehicles." I gave her as brief as possible an overview of my pursuit of Janet and our adventures in Clay County. About halfway through what was still a longish tale, a smiling uniformed maid delivered a tray laden with some of what Ekaterina knew were my favorite delicacies from the Inn's kitchens. As I finished my story I nibbled on the chocolate-covered strawberries, taking tiny bites that would not only make them last longer but also wouldn't interfere too badly with talking.

"Hang on a sec," Debbie Ann said when I'd finished. "I think the chief will want to talk to you."

I heaped clotted cream onto a scone as I waited.

"You've had quite a morning," the chief said when he got on the line. "Will it work to leave Mrs. Caverly at the Inn for the time being?"

"I think Ekaterina will enjoy taking care of her," I said.

"And given all the dignitaries who stay here, I imagine the Inn's security is pretty good."

"And Mrs. Caverly herself? Is she content?"

"I haven't asked her, and I don't much care," I said. "If you ask me, she lost her vote on the matter when she stole Robyn's car and very nearly got herself captured while trying to rescue her cat. I'm not criticizing her for wanting to rescue the creature, mind you. But if she'd told us about it, we could have arranged something. Sent a couple of Shiffleys to fetch it."

"Or one or two of my deputies. Water under the bridge now. Still, a good idea to have Ekaterina keeping an eye on her."

"I gather Debbie Ann gave you the headline version of our adventures," I said. "I left out a couple of bits that would have bogged down the story, but I should tell you." I rattled off the information Rachel had shared about why her brother had been killed, and her suspicions that someone in whatever agency Mark Caverly had consulted had been either crooked or careless.

"Great," he said. "So one of the agencies I've been nagging to come and deal with the situation in Clay County might have a Dingle mole inside. We just don't know which one."

"Sorry."

"Well, it's not as if any of them have been falling all over themselves to deal with Clay County."

He fell silent, and I wondered if he was thinking the same thing I was. What if Clay County did have a mole inside some federal agency? A mole who was not only warning the Dingles but even working to prevent or at least delay any federal involvement?"

"Well, it can't be helped," he said. "And I always operate on the assumption that anything you say to an agency is out there in public. Most of the Feds I deal with directly are career law enforcement and have their heads on straight, but sometimes the political appointees are a disaster."

"So I shouldn't hold my breath waiting for the Feds to swoop in and rescue Mark Caverly."

"I'm not optimistic that anything will come off until after Christmas," he said. "And yes, I know that's only three more days, but if Mrs. Caverly's fears are true . . . well, it's not as if the Dingles are going to observe any kind of Christmas truce on a guy who knows enough to put them in the slammer for a very long time."

Not much useful I could say about that, so I said nothing.

"At any rate, thank you for the update. You might tell Ekaterina I'll drop by later today to talk to Mrs. Caverly."

"Will do."

I thought about calling Michael, but I knew if I talked to him now, I'd probably give in to the temptation to vent about how idiotic Janet had been. And there was no need to interrupt the boys' sledding with anything stressful.

So I texted.

"Still looking for Delaney," I said. "How goes the sledding?"

He sent back a couple of photos of the boys on the slopes. I allowed myself a brief pang of envy. Then I dialed Robyn's number.

"Meg!" she said. "You'll never guess what happened."

"Someone stole your car."

"It was Janet Caverly, wasn't it?" She didn't sound angry—just sad and disappointed.

"Yes, but it's probably not what you think. She wanted to rescue her cat."

I gave her the highlights of my pursuit of Janet. When I finished, she was silent for a few moments.

"If she's going to stay at the Inn, we should probably

figure out a way to get Lark over to her," was all she said. I couldn't have resisted the temptation to mention what an idiot Janet had been.

"I'll see what I can manage," I said. "But I have a few other, more urgent things to do first. Like trying to find Delaney so I can convince her that Rob's not a two-timing creep."

"You've been trying to find Delaney?"

"In between bouts of rescuing Janet."

"She's at the shelter. At least she was an hour or so ago. Has been since last night. She said she didn't want to talk to Rob or even look at him, and the shelter was the one place she could be sure he couldn't come."

"Blast," I said. "If Janet had stayed put where she was supposed to be, I'd have found Delaney already. Any idea how long she's planning to stay?"

"She brought a big suitcase and her laptop. She was holed up in her room working on the computer all morning."

"You object if I go and try to talk to her?"

"As long as you leave her alone if she refuses to talk to you."

And Delaney probably would tell me to leave her alone. Well, at least she hadn't left town, I thought, as Robyn and I signed off. With luck, she'd be around when the news about the Caverlys came out.

I snagged a bit of beef satay from my lunch plate and dipped it in peanut sauce as I dialed Randall.

"Are your cousins still up on the roof keeping an eye out for infiltrators from Clay County?"

"Last time I looked."

"Wonder how they missed Janet Caverly sneaking out."

A pause.

"Are you serious?"

Chapter 21

Somehow I was no longer in the mood to give anyone chapter and verse of my morning's adventures. Randall was going to get the CliffsNotes version.

"Tracked her to Clay County and dragged her back," I said instead. "And stashed her at the Inn for the time being. FYI, there are definitely Dingles slinking about Caerphilly looking for the Caverlys."

A longer pause.

"Clearly I need to have a few words with Fred and the boys."

"Don't be too hard on them," I said, through a mouthful of pita bread and hummus. "They were watching for Dingles sneaking in, not damsels in distress sneaking out."

"Still. Maybe I'll pull them off the roof and send them out to look for Mr. Caverly."

"Rumor has it Clay County's already caught him."

"Rumor had it that way last night, but it turns out they'd just waylaid some poor random tourist who took a wrong turn when he left your grandfather's zoo."

"Yikes."

"Yeah. Your idea about that warning sign on our side of the county line is looking smarter every day."

"The one that would say 'Abandon hope, all ye who enter here'?"

"Truth in advertising. Maybe I'll get Fred and the boys to run one up, as a penance for letting their prisoner go."

"She wasn't exactly a prisoner."

"Maybe she should have been."

"Well, she is now." I set the phone on the desk so I could use both hands to remove the skewer from a steak kebab. "I've told Ekaterina to make sure she doesn't leave."

"Good. Meanwhile, I think we should leave Fred and the boys on the courthouse roof for the time being, if there are apt to be Dingles loose in town. I'll find someone else to make that sign."

We signed off. I surveyed my plate, trying to decide which delicacy to nibble next. One of the miniature quiches? The tempura veggies? The—

"Good news!" Dad bounced into the office. "Ekaterina was right," he called over his shoulder. "She's in here."

"What's the good news?" I asked.

"Rob's off the hook."

"So Grandfather's lab finished the DNA?"

"And Rob's not Lark's father." Dad beamed, and began rummaging through the bowl of Christmas candy on Ekaterina's desk. "It's definite."

"You can never be a hundred percent certain where paternity is concerned." Grandfather ambled into the office after Dad and slouched into one of the guest chairs.

"The odds are a million to one against." Dad's words were slightly garbled by the candy cane he was sucking. "Good odds."

"Stranger things have happened." Grandfather had also taken a candy cane, but he was just sitting and staring at it as if it were a dose of bitter medicine he was steeling himself to swallow.

"I think this good news calls for a little bit of celebration," Dad protested. "We can prove to Delaney that Rob's not the father."

"Yes, that is good news," I said. "The only problem is that while the DNA tests prove that Rob isn't the father—"

"They don't prove that." Grandfather sounded annoyed. Why was he sulking so? Did he want another great-grandchild that badly?

"I stand corrected," I said. "While the DNA tests indicate that, statistically speaking, Rob is highly unlikely to be Lark's father—"

Grandfather nodded with grudging approval.

"—they do nothing to eliminate the suspicion that he could have had the opportunity to become her father, so to speak."

"Oh, dear." Dad looked discouraged. "That's true. You think that's going to be a sticking point with Delaney?"

I shrugged.

"It's vital to recognize the limitations of science," Grandfather intoned. He had returned the unopened candy cane to the bowl and shifted his attention to my lunch tray. His hand was hovering over the plate as if undecided whether to sample a bite-sized quiche Lorraine or a prosciutto-wrapped melon ball.

"I think I'm going to need Janet to help me convince Rob." I grabbed one of the melon balls, before they all disappeared.

Clearly possessed by a contrarian mood, Grandfather frowned at the remaining melon balls and selected a mini-quiche.

"This would be much better with a nice white wine," he said, as he nibbled it.

"Ekaterina only brought me a light lunch." I tried not to emphasize the "me" too hard.

"You could ask her to bring up some chardonnay." He picked up a kibbe. "And a larger plate."

"The restaurant downstairs is open," I said. "I'm sure Ekaterina wants her office back before too long."

"Hmph." He dipped the kibbe into the tahini sauce and polished it off. "Very well. I can tell when I'm not wanted."

He strode off, wiping the excess tahini on his cargo pants as he went.

"It's not that you're not wanted," I called after him. "I just think Ekaterina's been more than helpful and—"

But he was long gone.

"I'll go join him," Dad said. "One of Chef Maurice's meals will calm him down."

"Sorry," I said. "I didn't mean to rile him up."

"Bear with him," Dad said. "He's a bit depressed today. He's been brooding about the cougars."

I tried to decipher that for a few moments, then gave up. "What cougars? The ones at his zoo?"

"No, they're fine. Thriving, in fact. It's the eastern cougars that have got him down."

"Because . . . ?" Sometimes conversing with my family felt like interrogating hostile witnesses.

"The U.S. Fish and Wildlife Service removed them from the endangered species list in January." Dad shook his head sadly.

"Isn't that usually a good thing? Or does Grandfather think they were removed prematurely?"

"Nothing premature about it." Dad sighed. "There hasn't been a confirmed sighting since 1938. Fish and Wildlife made an extensive review in 2011 and couldn't find any evidence of surviving individuals, much less a reproducing population. So this year they moved them from the endangered list to the extinct one."

"Took them long enough," I said. "But you said it happened in January. Grandfather only just heard about it, then?"

"He heard about it at the time. And he approves—declaring the eastern cougar extinct clears the way for introducing mountain lions from the western U.S. to take their place. We need a population of large carnivores in the ecosystem to keep the deer population down and curb the spread of tick-borne diseases."

Yes, Grandfather would be delighted at the prospect of turning mountain lions loose in the eastern woods. He was also strongly in favor of reintroducing wolves.

"So why is he brooding about the cougars today?" I asked. "What set that off?"

"He saw a headline that said 'Cougars on the Rise' and it got him all excited," Dad said. "Turns out it was about some college football team. He's been moping around and muttering 'damned farmers' all day."

"Why damned farmers?"

"They played a big part in doing in the cougar. In the interest of protecting their livestock, of course."

"But Grandfather infinitely prefers predators to livestock," I said. "I get it. Go feed him and cheer him up."

"Roger," he said. "See you later."

"The satay's particularly good today," I called after him. I knew it was one of his favorites.

I finished my food rather absentmindedly. Which was almost a sacrilege, given how good the food was.

As I ate, I pulled out my phone and called up the picture I'd taken of the paper in Janet Caverly's pocket. On a hunch, I borrowed Ekaterina's computer and looked up the two numbers, using a reverse phone number lookup site.

The phone number with *R* beside it was registered to an R. Plunket in Clayville. Probably Rachel.

The other phone number didn't produce any results. Which seemed weird. Then again, I didn't have all that much experience with the reverse lookup site. Maybe a lot of numbers weren't there.

Ah, well.

I finished off the last bite of mini-quiche and stuck the

tray outside the door, where the staff would eventually collect it. I made sure I hadn't left any grease spots or little bits of food on the sleek surface of Ekaterina's desk. And after allowing myself a brief pang of envy over how elegant and uncluttered her office was, I let myself out and headed back to the loading dock.

Time to tackle Delaney. Maybe even bring her out to the Inn to talk to Janet. Surely hearing Janet's story would convince Delaney.

I had a sense of déjà vu as I turned into the street where I was planning to park for my walk to the shelter. Of course, the first time I'd been here, I'd had no idea where Delaney was, and had been merely planning to ask Robyn for help finding her. Now at least I knew Delaney was—or had been—here. And I'd rescued Janet—and Sammy—in the meantime. So I was making some progress, wasn't I?

Before leaving my car I popped the trunk and fished out the small tool kit I always kept there. The house where the shelter was located was old, and had been in terrible repair when Robyn had first found it. In my notebook I kept a running list of things that needed fixing when I could find the time. If I walked in with my tools, maybe it wouldn't look quite so much as if I was there just to tackle Delaney. And if she absolutely refused to talk to me, I could fix a few of the more urgent things on my list, and at least my time wouldn't be completely wasted.

I went through a small alley and emerged onto the street where the shelter's entrance was. And then I saw something that made me pop back into the mouth of the alleyway and peer carefully out.

Two men were standing a little farther down the block, a short ways from the shelter's gate. This wasn't a section of town where the tourists came, except by mistake, and these two certainly weren't tourists. If they'd been dressed in Victorian costume, I'd have assumed they were two of

Michael's drama students rehearsing a new bit for the ongoing street theater: two inept burglars trying to be inconspicuous while scouting a potential target. Trying and failing miserably. But I didn't recognize them, and they looked a little old for students.

I hunkered down a little so there was a bit of shrubbery between me and the men. Probably a good thing. When I'd emerged from the alley, they'd both been looking away from me, craning their necks to stare down the street. Now they both turned and did the same thing in my direction.

"There are two of you," I muttered. "You could cover both directions at once."

But evidently subtleties like that were above their pay grade. If this day in my life had a cast of characters, they'd show up as First Dim Thug and Second Dim Thug.

Given the cold weather, perhaps it wasn't surprising that they wore knit caps drawn low over their eyes. But it was a little odd that their bulky coats were open at the front. Then one of them moved slightly, and I saw that he was holding a pistol, half-concealed beneath his coat. The other one had a sawed-off shotgun.

Okay, so they were not here to provide a charming comic interlude between two dramatic scenes. The odds were they were Dingles, or Dingle minions, and up to no good.

One of them—I mentally dubbed him Shotgun Dude—pulled out a cell phone and began talking on it. The other—Pistol Guy—was trying to look nonchalant, as if standing around doing nothing on a snowy back street in sub-freezing weather was something he did all the time.

I pulled out my own phone and dialed 911.

Chapter 22

"What's up, Meg?" Debbie Ann said.

"Two armed men are eyeing the women's shelter," I said. "I think they're about to barge in there. Dingles, probably, or some of their Clay County allies. No one I know, anyway, and certainly not tourists."

"Roger," she said. "Sit tight; help is on the way."

But as I watched, the men seemed to come to a decision. Pistol Guy picked up something that had been lying on the ground beside his right foot. A sledgehammer. They both started walking toward the shelter. No, they were actually tiptoeing, which would have struck me as hilarious if I hadn't seen the guns. Shotgun Dude had stuck his weapon under his coat, which didn't do a whole lot to hide it. Pistol Guy's attempts to conceal the sledgehammer beneath his coat were even less successful.

I ended my call with Debbie Ann and silenced the ringer. Then I threw open my tool kit and rummaged in it for weapons. About the only weapon-like objects I had were the hammers. Nothing as big as Pistol Guy's sledgehammer, alas. I stuck a ball peen hammer in my coat pocket and took a good grip on my largest claw hammer.

The men reached the gate to the shelter. They were on camera now, although there was no way they could know it. In whatever remote location the security system monitors were located, I hoped alarms were now going off. Wouldn't the security staff be surprised to find the Caerphilly PD already knew about the intrusion?

The men seemed surprised to encounter a locked gate. They rattled it a couple of times, and seemed to confer for an unnecessarily long time over what to do about it. Then Pistol Guy seemed to remember he was also Sledgehammer Guy. He tucked his gun in his pocket, hefted the sledgehammer, and used it to break the latch.

As the men strode through the gate, I thought of calling Debbie Ann to say that the men had escalated from lurking to trespassing. Or did this count as breaking and entering? Either way, by now the security company would have seen it, too. I decided to let them share the news.

As soon as the men tiptoed through the gate I took off toward the gate in a half walk, half run, hoping they wouldn't hear my footsteps.

In my pocket, my phone vibrated. Debbie Ann calling back, no doubt. I looked around, hoping to see a police car racing up the street.

Nothing. Not even a tourist. And no sirens in the distance.

This was stupid. What was I thinking of? Running in after a couple of armed men waving my little claw hammer? I wasn't the Lone Ranger. I should find a good observation post and wait for the people who were trained and equipped to deal with this.

I heard a crashing noise—the shelter door being broken in? Screaming erupted from inside the shelter—though no shots, thank goodness. Suddenly waiting for help didn't seem that feasible.

I peered through the gate. The house's front door was hanging from one hinge. The men had gone inside.

"Where is she?" one of them was shouting, over the screaming. "Janet Caverly—we know she's here. Bring her out or you'll be sorry."

Definitely Dingle foot soldiers. When I had crept a little closer, I could see that the one with the pistol was standing just inside in the open doorway. Evidently it was Shotgun Dude doing the shouting. Pistol Guy was just holding his gun pointed into the room.

"Stop all the yapping!" Shotgun Dude sounded exasperated, as if the women's screams were a total overreaction. "We're not going to hurt anyone. Just bring out Janet Caverly."

I figured the screaming would cover the sounds of my approach, so I snuck up behind Pistol Guy and raised my hammer. But what target? The head? What if he had a hard skull and the blow had no effect? Or worse, what if I killed him? There was probably some pressure point on his neck that would drop him like an ox if I hit it, but I didn't have Dad's expertise in anatomy.

The hand holding the gun. He wasn't all that big—absent the gun, I figured I could probably take him. Of course, there was also his friend with the shotgun. One problem at a time.

So I brought the hammer down on his gun hand with all my strength. It hit with a satisfying crunch, and he shrieked bloody murder and dropped the pistol. He also half-turned toward me, so I grabbed him, brought my knee up hard between his legs, and then dragged him outside and tried to keep his now-limp body between me and the door, in case Shotgun Dude came out to retaliate. Which I could tell almost immediately wasn't going to work—Pistol Guy wasn't tall but he was beefy. I let him fall, looked around for the pistol, and kicked it out of his reach.

"What the hell!" Shotgun Dude shouted inside. And then I heard a loud clang! Followed by the sound of something falling.

The screaming continued, but I heard nothing from Shotgun Dude, so I stepped into the doorway, hammer at the ready.

Josefina, who would have been maybe five feet tall in

heels—if she ever wore them—was standing over Shotgun Dude, holding a cast-iron frying pan. Delaney was standing behind her with what I thought at first was a baseball bat, given the way she was holding it. Then I recognized it as the leg that had been nearly falling off the dining room table. Maybe a good thing I hadn't put fixing the table high on my chore list. Our eyes met. She nodded, smiled slightly, and lowered the table leg.

I shifted the hammer to my left hand, pulled out my phone, and called 911.

"Meg! What's going on there?"

"Send an ambulance along with the deputies." I strolled outside as I spoke. "We've neutralized the threat to the shelter."

"Neutralized? What do you mean neutralized? And who's 'we'?"

Just then help arrived, in the form of Horace and Aida, who ran into the yard, service weapons at the ready.

"They're all yours," I said. "One's over there by the door, and Josefina's got the other one inside."

Chapter 23

What I really wanted to do was go home. No, first I wanted to go wherever Michael and the boys were and collect them, and then go home. Instead, I was standing in the living room of the women's shelter, waiting my turn to be interviewed by the chief.

A lot had been happening here. Aida had handcuffed the conscious intruder while Horace checked the vitals of the one Josefina had felled. Vern Shiffley arrived and recognized the two thugs as both denizens of Clay County and frequent occupants of the Caerphilly jail's drunk tank.

"Tyler Whicker and Urisha Peebles, as I live and breathe," he said. "Fancy seeing you again."

Aida read the conscious prisoner his rights and then, about the time she'd finished, the other one came to and she had to do it all over again. Horace fetched his forensic bag. Robyn showed up, with Noah adding his shrieks to the sirens that had suddenly erupted in the area. I deduced from the sirens that word had gone out that the bad guys were in custody—Horace and Aida had arrived in silence. Dad showed up, medical bag in hand, and checked out both prisoners. Shotgun Dude didn't seem to have taken any damage from Josefina's frying pan, but Dad sent him off to the hospital anyway, so he could be observed for signs of concussion. To be followed when the ambulance returned by Pistol Guy, who'd need an X-ray to see how many bones my hammer had broken.

"Do you have any idea how many bones there are in the human hand?" Dad exclaimed.

"Twenty-seven." Not that I had any practical use for this information, but I'd heard him quote it often enough. And twenty-six bones in the human foot, which seemed rather odd—what did the hand have that the foot didn't?

"Very good," he said. "And you may have broken quite a few of them."

Robyn was already making plans to move the shelter's occupants to another location.

"We'll have to decide later if this location is completely ruined," she said. "But for the short term, I think the ladies will all feel safer elsewhere. There could be press coverage."

Or more intruders, I thought, but I decided I didn't need to remind her of that.

"Of course, I still have to think of a place to take them," she went on. "Or places—it's not easy to find someplace that can take in twenty people on such short notice—"

"And this close to the holidays, and in the middle of a snowstorm," I finished for her. Then a thought hit me. "Ask Cordelia." I knew my grandmother Cordelia's house sometimes served as a stop on the modern day Underground Railway that had sprung up to help get abused women and children to safety. "She's very big on supporting the shelter—maybe she could take some of them."

"Do you think she would?"

Instead of answering, I pulled out my phone and called my grandmother.

"Merry Christmas, Meg," she said when she answered. "I should be at your house in an hour or two."

"I might not be there till later," I said. "We've had a major security breach here at the women's shelter. Robyn needs to move everyone someplace else until we're sure the danger is past."

"Have her take them up to my place," she said. "There's room enough. You still have your key, don't you?"

"Yes. You're sure you don't mind us using your house?"

Robyn breathed a visible sigh of relief.

"Happy to have them," she said. "You can tell me all about it when we get there."

"See you soon."

"Your grandmother is an angel," Robyn said. "One of these days I'll find a way to repay her. By the way, is—" She stopped and looked around to see if anyone was near enough to overhear. "Is you-know-who safe?" she went on, in a softer tone.

"Our car thief? Yes, she's fine. I may wring her neck if she ever tries anything like that again, but for the time being, she's safe and sound."

"And where?"

"Ekaterina has hidden her. Which reminds me—where is Lark?"

"Josefina is looking after her. But Janet must be worried sick about her—or she will be when she hears what happened here."

"Any chance you could find a subtle way to deliver her to Ekaterina?" I asked.

"Can do." Robyn smiled. "And maybe I can enlist Delaney to help me. Might do a world of good to put those two in a room together and get them talking."

"I like the way you think," I said. "I suspect I'll be tied up for a while, making statements to the chief, so I'll leave it in your hands."

"Right. So much to do. I've got a couple of people coming over to ferry the residents to the police station, and then when the chief's finished with them, over to Trinity—

they can stay there till I round up a bus to take them to your grandmother's. Must go make a few calls." Robyn took the copy of Cordelia's key that I'd teased off my key ring, and dashed off.

"I want to talk to you at much greater length," the chief said. "But I think I should deal with the shelter residents first. Get them ready to move as soon as possible to wherever Robyn is taking them."

"No problem." I could use some time to process what had happened. Regain my composure before I rejoined Michael and the boys.

"Meg?" I turned to see Delaney standing behind me. "Can we talk?"

"Sure." Processing could wait.

I followed Delaney to the other end of the living room, where it was quiet. Most of the shelter residents were upstairs packing. A few were walking out, suitcases in hand, presumably to be transported over to Trinity.

"I'm an idiot sometimes," she began.

If she expected me to contradict her, she was doomed to disappointment.

"Of course, Rob can be, too," she went on.

Also a good point.

"Why the hell is he dodging me?"

"Dodging you?" I said. "He spent most of yesterday wandering around looking for you, when he wasn't begging me to talk to you. You weren't answering his phone calls—or mine either, for that matter."

"I wasn't answering anyone's calls yesterday," she said. "I turned my phone off for the rest of the day. But then this morning—well, I'd had time to think it over and realize maybe I was overreacting."

"Maybe?"

"It's just that I thought things were going really well and we were getting pretty serious, and I actually thought he was kind of creeping up on saying the *M* word, and then he started acting weird and furtive."

"Yes, he probably has." I sighed. "He's been trying to come up with some really brilliant, original, impressive way of surprising you with a proposal. And I've been shooting down his ideas because I thought they were all pretty hideous. Maybe I'm wrong; maybe you'd like to be proposed to by a troop of clowns, or with an animated cartoon involving Bart Simpson and SpongeBob SquarePants, or by Rob leading a mariachi band or—"

"Oh, God," she said. "Thank you. I was hoping maybe he'd just pop the question over dinner at Luigi's—it's where we had our first date. I was even wondering if maybe I should reverse the roles and propose to him. But then he started acting weird, and when that Desiree person jumped out of the box—"

"Is that who was in the box?" I exclaimed. "Relentless Stalker Desiree, as we call her in the family?"

"Yeah." She giggled slightly. "I guess he really didn't look so happy to see her."

"So Rob was acting weird, or weirder than usual, and when you were blindsided by the idea he might have cheated on you, you overreacted," I said. "But now you've cooled off—why not call him?"

"I've tried—he's not answering his phone. I figured maybe he'd gotten mad at me for doubting him."

"More likely he ran down the battery trying to call you and forgot to plug it in." I took out my phone and punched my shortcut to call Rob.

"Goes to voice mail immediately," I said. "Either it's off or out of power. In either case, last time I talked to him, he hadn't gotten any of your calls and may not even know you've been trying to reach him."

"We have to find him!" She jumped to her feet as if ready to run out.

"I'll help you look," I said. "But first, can you do me a favor and take Lark back to her mother?" I brought her up to speed on why Janet had left Lark at the church, and why she was now hiding out at the Caerphilly Inn. I figured if Delaney had any lingering doubts, Janet's story would dispel them. "And in the meantime I'll get everyone I know looking for Rob."

She brightened slightly, and looked much more cheerful when she took off with Lark in tow.

I made a few phone calls. At Mutant Wizards, Paton answered the phone again.

"What are you doing still on duty?"

"Some of the guards went home for the holidays," he said. "So I'm pulling a double shift. Voluntarily—the holiday overtime pay's awesome. Do you know where Rob is?"

"Damn," I said. "I was going to ask you that. Why are you looking for him?"

"I'm kind of worried," Paton said. "He left around nine, and then when I made my rounds, I saw that he left his phone in his office. That's not like him. I mean, usually it's like he's surgically attached to it."

"True," I said. "And it explains a lot. Can you bring his phone down to the front desk? If I figure out where he is I may pick it up and take it to him. Or if I reach him before you do, I'll tell him you have it."

"Roger."

Of course, without his phone, finding Rob wouldn't be easy. I strolled over to where Aida was helping the last few shelter residents carry their suitcases.

"Any chance you could talk the chief into putting out a BOLO on Rob?" I said. "He's wandered off without his phone, and that's not like him."

"Will see what I can do," she said. "And I'll definitely keep my eyes peeled, and tell everyone I run into to do the same."

"And if the chief balks at doing the BOLO, remind him how Delaney heard about the paternity accusation against Rob."

She chuckled and nodded.

The chief would probably do it, I thought. But the shelter would keep most of his officers busy for a while. Was there anyone else I could enlist to find Rob?

I called Fred Shiffley.

"You guys still on the roof?" I asked.

"For the time being." Fred sounded glum. "Maybe through New Year's, the way things are going. Randall's pretty ticked off. Is it our fault we didn't spot those clowns going into the shelter?"

"I'll talk to him," I said. "Meanwhile, if you want to redeem yourselves, keep an eye open for Rob. He's wandered off without his phone and I need to talk to him."

"Yes, ma'am."

At the other end of the room, the EMTs had returned and were lifting Pistol Guy onto the stretcher. I leaned against the wall and closed my eyes. Once he was out of the way, I'd head over to the police station. I thought of pulling out my notebook. Perusing its contents usually cheered me up, especially if it involved checking off items I'd already accomplished. But for once I wasn't in the mood.

"You broke his hand." I probably started slightly when the small voice came from my right side. It was the girl, the slightly older one who had had her doubts about Santa. She was leaning against the wall beside me and staring at the front hall.

"I was afraid he was going to hurt someone," I explained.

"Yeah." She nodded. "Is the guy Josefina hit going to die?"

"Probably not." I'd have said, "Absolutely not," but I decided anyone who was old enough to grapple with doubts about Santa wouldn't take kindly to grownups trying to sugarcoat the truth.

"Mom says now that those bad guys found it, we all have to leave the shelter."

"Not really," I said. "The shelter's just going to move someplace else for a little while, and you'll move with it. Someplace nearby. And then once Reverend Robyn's sure this place is safe again, the shelter will come back here."

"Will Josefina still be at the new place?" she asked.

"Why wouldn't she?"

"And will the doctor come?"

"Of course," I said.

"And the lady who came last night to give us computer lessons?"

"Absolutely." Delaney was passionate about getting girls to love math, science, and especially computing.

"What about those guys?" She nodded in the direction of Pistol Guy. "What if they find the new shelter, too?"

"Odds are they're going to prison for a long, long time," I said. "Chief Burke is determined to make that happen."

She nodded as if that reassured her.

"And if the shelter is going where I think it's going, it's a nice place. Out in the country. Very quiet." I'd have added "very safe," but up until an hour ago I'd have thought the shelter here in Caerphilly was pretty darn safe.

On impulse, I put an arm around her shoulder. She stiffened slightly, then relaxed and leaned against me. We stood there, side by side, leaning comfortingly against each other, until her mother came to collect her for the ride to the new shelter. Or possibly some temporary refuge, if Robyn needed more time to organize a stealth transport to Riverton, where my grandmother lived.

Pistol Guy was gone now. No one here but Horace, who

was slowly and meticulously doing his crime scene routine, and Aida, who seemed to have been assigned to guard the shelter for the time being. Or maybe she was there to watch Horace's back in case more Dingles showed up. I strolled over to her.

"Chief's gone to the station," Aida said. "He said to ask you to stop by if you can."

I nodded and headed outside. I found Randall Shiffley standing in the front yard, surveying the damage Pistol Guy and Shotgun Dude had done to the fence and the front door.

"Helluva thing," he said. "I heard you did good."

"They were stupid and I got lucky," I said.

Behind Randall, Fred and several of the other Shiffleys who'd been perched on the roof were marching in with tools.

"We'll be fixing everything up so the place is in tip-top condition," Fred said. "As a donation, on account of us not being able to stop those creeps before they got here. I want those ladies to come back to perfection. But don't worry—we left Austin on the roof to keep an eye out for your brother."

"And if Robyn figures out it's not safe for the shelter residents to come back?" I didn't want to dampen their enthusiasm, but I was feeling pessimistic about the prospect.

"Then we'll have this fixed up so nice that Robyn can sell it for enough money to afford an even nicer replacement," Randall said. "Or if whatever replacement she finds is in bad shape, we'll do a renovation there. Is the chief here?"

"He went down to the station. Which is where I'm heading myself. Just trying to decide if I should walk or drive. My car's almost as far away as the station, and in the wrong direction."

"Drive," he said. "Then if you need to go anywhere in a hurry, you'll have your car."

"Excellent point."

"Also, you can give me a lift."

On the way over, Randall was busy craning right and left, checking to see that the carolers and musicians had started their performances, that the shops and refreshment stands were open, that no stray patches of ice or snow were lingering to trip the unwary, and most important, that the tourists were starting to show up in suitably large numbers, looking happy—and thus, presumably, unaware of the exciting events that had been happening a few blocks away.

We arrived at the police station to find it bustling. Most of the shelter residents were there, digging into a stack of pizzas from Luigi's, everyone's favorite local Italian restaurant. Some of the women still looked a little shell-shocked, but the kids were having a blast. And since the station—like nearly every other building in town—was decorated to the hilt, I was hoping the grownups would recover some of the holiday spirit they'd had the last time we'd seen them. We could even bring Santa back for an encore if need be. He never minded a chance to hang out at the police station—especially in the holiday season, when he could play with all the miniature handcuffs and revolvers and other themed decorations on the small blue-and-silver tree that graced the front desk.

"Chief can see you." Kayla, my friend Aida's daughter, was home from music school and filling in here at the station.

"What's the plan for getting them to their temporary quarters?" I asked, nodding at the shelter refugees.

"Soon as we round up Deputy Shiffley to take over from Mom, she and Deputy Crowder can drive them to the new place." Kayla didn't have to explain that Deputy Crowder was one of the department's other female deputies.

"Good. In the meantime, did Luigi donate the pizzas? Because if he didn't—"

"He did, and Muriel's going to bring over some food from the diner for them to take with them, and if you want to contribute to paying for any of it, you're about number twelve or thirteen in line, so I don't think they'll be here long enough for us to need you, but if we do, I'll let you know. And Merry Christmas!"

I should have expected as much. Randall and I went down the hallway to the chief's office. His door was open, and as we drew near we could see he was on his phone. Then as we walked in—

"Damnation!" The chief slammed down his phone.

Randall and I both stood and stared. I couldn't remember the last time I'd heard the chief say anything stronger than "blast it!" or "tarnation."

The chief looked up and winced.

Chapter 24

"Sorry," he said. "Dealing with the federal bureaucracy has me at the end of my rope. That officious son of a biscuit eater just had the nerve to tell me that I'm overreacting to a mere case of domestic violence. Mere! Domestic violence being second only to auto accidents as a cause of death for women under fifty, I take exception to the word 'mere'—but that's beside the point anyway. Where does the idiot get off, calling what happened here domestic violence?"

"Seriously?" Randall exclaimed. "Thugs from Clay County invade our women's shelter looking to kidnap an inconvenient witness, and those clowns think it's domestic violence?"

"Just the one clown so far," the chief said. "A Fed by the name of Inman, in the ATF's Office of Interagency Coordination. Whatever that is—apparently a recent addition to their org chart, and not at all the useful find I first thought it was. But unfortunately he also seems to be the clown who has the clout to get us the federal help we need."

"Are your prisoners claiming it was a domestic incident?" This sounded suspicious to me.

"Apparently." The chief scowled. "At the moment, they've clammed up and asked for a lawyer. But before they did, one of them claimed that he thought his girlfriend was there. And the other chimed in that yes, they were looking for the girlfriend. Someone named Ellie Peebles."

"That's nonsense," I said. "I heard them asking where Janet Caverly was."

"As did Ms. McKenna and Mrs. Diaz." The chief shook his head. "Of course, when the matter comes to trial, it won't matter if they were looking for Mrs. Caverly or this Ellie Peebles, if she even exists. I'm sure our town attorney will have no difficulty proving breaking and entering. But that doesn't help us now."

"What's the penalty for breaking and entering?" I asked.

"Since they were carrying firearms when they did it, twenty to life." The chief smiled grimly. "There's also the fact that both Mr. Peebles and Mr. Dingle have done time on a string of larceny charges, which means an additional one to five years, unless they've successfully petitioned to have their firearm privileges restored, which strikes me as improbable. And then there's that sawed-off shotgun Mr. Dingle was carrying—another twenty to life, since he was carrying it during the commission of a violent felony. All of which I expect will come as a nasty surprise to those two clowns. I might be able to use that to pry some information out of them—assuming that their lawyer, when he finally gets here, isn't bought and paid for by the Dingles. But again—doesn't help us right now."

"Maybe it's just me," I said. "But something strikes me as weird. You got this bureaucrat sitting in Washington or wherever—"

"Richmond, actually."

"And only a couple of hours after what went down here he already knows it's a 'mere' domestic violence incident."

The chief nodded almost imperceptibly.

"Which just happens to tally precisely with the story our two thugs are telling." I paused, then forged ahead. "I know you probably don't want to think badly of a fellow law enforcement officer—"

"Inman's not law enforcement." The chief waved his hand dismissively. "Just a jumped-up bureaucrat with an inflated sense of his own importance. Probably a political appointee, or owes his job to one. You're not saying anything I haven't started thinking myself."

"He's the guy with the clout to get you the federal help you need," I said. "And also the guy with the clout to sabotage it?"

The chief nodded.

"Holy cow," Randall said. "You mean the Feds are bent?"

"Only one Fed," the chief said. "One damned clever son of a gun. I thought I'd struck pay dirt when I first talked to him. Someone who took seriously what I was telling him about Clay County, instead of making Dogpatch jokes. And now it's looking as if he was playing me all the time."

"Weird question," I said. "Remember those phone numbers I sent you? The ones on the slip of paper I found in Janet's pocket? One of them was marked with an *R* and belonged to Rachel Plunket, and I thought other wasn't marked, but there was this kind of random line beside it—"

"Apparently not a random line but a carelessly written letter *I*," the chief said. "Yes, Janet had Inman's number. If he was her contact—and Mark's—maybe it's not surprising that nothing's been done to rescue him. Not yet, anyway."

"Can you think of anyone you do trust absolutely?" I asked. "In that agency or elsewhere?"

"Yes. Several people. That's my next step. But it's going to be a little difficult, getting hold of any of them on short notice this close to Christmas. And what if Inman's managed to poison the well—convince his colleagues that I'm overreacting. Or worse, that I'm dirty."

Hard to believe that anyone would suspect that of the chief. But then maybe to someone sitting in Richmond or Washington it was hard to see the difference between Clay County and Caerphilly.

"We need to get the goods on Inman," I said.

"Takes time." The chief sounded despairing.

"Building an airtight case you can present in court takes time," I said. "Finding just enough dirt to convince a savvy federal law enforcement agent that a petty bureaucrat might not be entirely trustworthy? That might not take so much time."

"Please tell me you're not planning to go down to Richmond and burgle the ATF office."

"Of course not." Although if it had been closer than Richmond, I might have given the idea some consideration.

"Then what are you suggesting?"

I pulled out my phone and dialed Delaney.

"Any news?" she said in lieu of "hello."

"I've got people looking for Rob." I glanced at the chief, who nodded. "Including the police. Meanwhile, can you do me a favor? The chief needs some help."

"Will it help us find Rob?"

"Not directly," I said. "But it could go a long way toward getting things around here back to normal, which I think will help both Rob and you in the long run."

"Okay." She sounded resigned. "What do you need?"

"I want to borrow some hackers."

"What for?"

She sounded cautious.

"Aren't you supposed to say, 'I am *shocked—shocked*—to find that *hacking* is going on around here!' or something?"

"Shocked—shocked, I tell you," she said flatly. "Yeah, I could probably find you some white hat hackers if I tried. What do you want to do with them?"

"I want to help the chief get the goods on a crooked Federal agent," I said.

The chief raised an eyebrow and leaned a little closer.

"Sounds worthwhile." Delaney was also starting to show some enthusiasm.

"Would it make a difference if I told you that this guy

was connected with the armed invasion of the women's shelter earlier today?"

"That son of a— Okay, how many hackers do you need?" she said. "And do you need them down at the police station or can they work remotely?"

"Let me turn you over to the chief."

"I have my reservations about encouraging these young people to do something that could be illegal," the chief said, as I held out my phone.

"Then tell them to stick to legally available information until we can get them some warrants," I said. "I can call the town attorney."

"I'll call Aunt Jane," Randall added. Yes, Judge Jane Shiffley would be a help.

Within half an hour, the town attorney was on her way to Judge Jane's farm to get the first set of warrants approved.

"Have her plan to stay here awhile," Judge Jane said. "I don't want her to have to drive out here in the snow if something else comes up. I can feed her a good dinner—even give her a bed if this goes on into the night."

And Delaney's cadre of white hat hackers were already starting the search for information about the chief's nemesis. Starting, I hoped, as instructed—with publicly available information.

"I think our work here is done," I said to Randall, as I watched the chief talking on the phone to Delaney. Probably just as well it was Delaney doing this. While Rob had an uncanny knack for coming up with the ideas for computer games that would turn out to be enormous hits, he would be the first to admit that he had no technical skills whatsoever. Fortunately, he also had a knack for hiring really good staff, and the self-awareness not to micromanage them. But still—Delaney was not only motivated, she was also highly skilled in whatever needed doing and could deploy her hackers strategically.

"We'll leave you to it," Randall said to the chief. The chief mouthed "thanks" and turned back to his phone.

"Any chance you can give me a ride over to Osgood's?" Randall asked as we strolled out of the police station.

"Sure. Car trouble?" Randall's cousin Osgood Shiffley ran the local service station and car repair shop.

"Engine cooling system's shot. Needs some five-cent part that will cost a bazillion dollars in labor to install, even at the family discount." Randall rolled his eyes. "And Osgood didn't have it in stock, so he had to have it sent from Richmond. Odds are it hasn't come in yet, but if that's the case, I can guilt trip Osgood into giving me a lift home. I was just dropping the car off when the call came in about the doings at the shelter."

"I wondered how you got there so fast, and on foot," I said. "I can take you all the way home if you like."

"Thanks, but it's completely out of your way, and right on Osgood's, and he owes me."

We had turned right, and were heading toward the service station, chatting about nothing in particular, when Randall's phone rang.

"I should take this," he said. "Hey, Vern. What's up."

"I can't stop them." Vern's voice carried, even though Randall didn't have the phone's speaker on. "So I'm going in with them."

"Going in with them? Are you crazy? Vern? Vern?"

Evidently Vern had hung up.

"Great," Randall muttered.

"What's Vern going into?" I asked. "And who's he going with?"

"When a bunch of my crazy cousins heard last night's rumor that the Dingles had captured Mark the whistleblower, they decided to go all Rambo and rescue him."

"But the Dingles hadn't captured him, last I heard."

"Only a matter of time, they figure. They were going to

wait till tonight, but after they heard about the daring daylight raid on the women's shelter, I guess they moved up their timetable. Vern was supposed to be talking the fools out of it, not joining forces with them."

"Damn," I said. "Have you told them the chief's doing as much as he can to bring in the Feds?"

"And pointed out that, quite apart from being completely illegal, what they're trying could warn the Dingles that the outside world is onto what they're up to. Make it harder for the Feds when they go in. Couldn't get through to them. Look—forget Osgood's. Can you take me a little farther away?"

"Sure," I said. "But where?"

"Start out as if you were going to your grandfather's zoo," he said. "I think I know where my idiot cousins would go to start their bone-headed rescue mission. Place in Cousin Dwayne's woods that we sometimes use as a rendezvous when we're forming a hunting party. I'll tell you where to turn off. If you can drop me off there, I can try to track them and talk them out of it."

"Roger. By the way, should we warn the chief?"

"Probably." Randall sounded grim. He took a deep breath before dialing the chief.

While listening to Randall's side of the conversation—and deducing that the chief was not pleased—I pushed the speed limit as much as I dared, and we flew out of town on the Clay County Road. Grandfather's zoo was way out of town and right on the border with Clay County, so it made sense that the Shiffleys would choose someplace out that way to launch their mission.

About a mile short of the zoo gate Randall pointed ahead and to the left.

"See that dirt road? Turn in there. And take it slow, if you're fond of your transmission."

I took it slow, and we lurched into the woods on what

was definitely an unimproved road. If it was a road at all. More likely it was the faint track the Shiffley trucks had carved out on their way to that family hunting rendezvous. In some places I had to be careful not to scrape against the trees on one side or the other. I reminded myself that the Shiffleys would be coming this way in trucks that were a good bit wider than my car, so I probably wasn't going to get stuck. The road was so narrow that the trees, many of them evergreens, met overhead, making it so dark I turned on my headlights. On the plus side, not much snow had made it through the leaf canopy.

A mile and a half down the road we spotted vehicles ahead. They were parked in—well, it wasn't exactly a clearing, just a place where the woods didn't come right up to the edge of the road. I could probably even turn my car around if I worked at it for a while.

"I guessed right," Randall said. "The blue pickup's Vern's. The red one belongs to our cousin Taylor."

"I'd have thought either of them would have more common sense." I pulled my car in behind Vern's truck.

"I think Taylor misses his army days." Randall was scanning the woods. "Maybe this won't be a total disaster—all of them are expert woodsmen, and a couple of them ex-military to boot."

"But that doesn't change how stupid it is."

"Exactly." He hopped out of my car and strode over to feel the hood of Vern's truck. "Still warm. Look, I'm going to see if I can catch up with them and talk them out of this. You skedaddle back to town and let the chief know we've found their cars."

"Why don't I just call him?" I suggested. "And wait here in case you end up wanting a ride out of the woods in a hurry?"

"If you can get a signal, call away," he said. "But don't wait here. I have a spare key to Vern's truck, so if I need a ride in a hurry, I can take that. You get to someplace with cell phone service and work on sending in the cavalry."

With that he disappeared into the trees. I turned on my cell phone and looked at the screen. Randall was right—no signal. I got out of the car and waved my phone around—sometimes that helped in the more remote and cell-signal-forsaken parts of the county.

Not this time. I contemplated, just for a moment, climbing one of the enormous evergreens whose thick, drooping branches were probably part of the reason for the lack of signal. Maybe if I got higher up?

But it would be faster to drive to the zoo. Cell phone service wasn't great there, either, and the zoo would be closed by now, but I probably had a key to the staff entrance in my purse—and even if I'd left that at home there would be night shift staff on duty, so I could get them to let me in to use a land line.

I was about to slide back into my driver's seat and turn around when I heard a noise. A vehicle. It seemed to be approaching along the same route Randall and I had used to get here.

Maybe it was the cavalry already coming to the rescue. Just in case it wasn't, I grabbed my purse and tote and slipped into the woods. I took shelter under one of those drooping evergreen branches and resolved to stay hidden until I'd figured out who the new arrival was.

Chapter 25

A truck lumbered into sight. A tow truck. As it passed by, I saw the words CLAY COUNTY TOWING on the cab door.

I resisted the urge to retreat farther into the woods. Staying still and quiet was my best option.

The truck slowed to a stop behind my car and idled. Then a man jumped out of the passenger door of the truck's cab. He was stout and bearded, with a red plaid jacket and a red knit hat.

"Dammit, there's three of the bastards." His words were slightly slurred—with drink? He was holding a beer can. "This is going to take forever."

"No, it's not." Another man, similarly dressed, but not as stout, hopped out, also from the passenger's side. "Anse tows one and you and I hotwire the other two and drive them out."

"First I gotta find someplace to turn this rig around," said the man still in the truck—presumably Anse.

"You go on that way and see what you can find. Bo, get started on one of them vehicles."

Great. I was about to watch my car being stolen.

Bo grunted. He polished off his beer, crushed the can, and tossed it into the woods. Then he lumbered over and began fiddling with Vern's truck. The other man went to work on my car. Well, at least he seemed sober. Unlike Bo, who was visibly impaired. Maybe if I ever saw my car again the wiring wouldn't be completely messed up.

I pulled out my phone, made triple sure the sound was

turned off, and took a little video of the two men hotwiring my car and Vern's truck. Evidently Anse eventually found a place to turn around—the tow truck lumbered back into the clearing, now heading in the other direction. Anse hopped out, and he and Bo began to hook up Taylor's red pickup.

"Cy, I still think it would be safer if we just dumped them in the quarry," Anse said. "What if someone shows up at the shop before we get them stripped?"

"Stuff that goes into the quarry can get hauled out of the quarry again," Cy said, from where he was watching their labors. Clearly Cy was both the leader and the brains of this operation. "They're not coming back to claim them for while. And if someone else shows up before you get them stripped, you can claim you bought them from someone and it never occurred to you that they were stolen. But that's pretty unlikely. And any danger's long gone once they're broken down into a couple thousand used parts. So we have a busy night ahead of us."

I hoped my camera captured their words along with the video. I kept it running until Anse had driven the tow truck off, with Bo following in my car and Cy bringing up the rear in Taylor's truck.

I waited until the sound of the engines had faded into the distance. Then I scrambled out from my place of refuge and tried to brush all the twigs and spruce needles out of my hair and off my clothes.

I felt a moment of panic. I was stranded out in the middle of nowhere, with no way to call for help. And what if one of the Clay County car thieves suddenly realized he'd left something behind and came back to find it?

Then I reminded myself that I wasn't in the middle of nowhere. I was a mile and a half from Clay County Road. Once I reached that, I was only a mile or so from the zoo. And if the car thieves returned, I'd hear them coming.

But they weren't just car thieves. They'd almost certainly come here with their tow truck because they'd found out about the Shiffleys' expedition. "They're not coming back to claim them for a while," Cy had said. What if Vern and Taylor and whoever else had gone in with them were already on their way to join Mark Caverly in the Clay County Jail? Or worse—no. I wasn't going to let my imagination run away with me.

Perhaps it was a good thing I wasn't a savvy tracker and woodswoman. Because if I was, I'd probably be dashing off right now to catch up with Randall and warn him, and maybe falling into the same trap I was afraid was waiting for him.

Okay, no cell coverage right here and right now, but I might hit a pocket sometime soon, and so might he. So I composed a text.

"Look out!" it said. "Three Clay County people just came and took your cousins' trucks and my car away. Something may have happened to Vern and Taylor's party. Or they may know you're coming. Be careful!"

I followed that with an email, saying the same thing. He probably wouldn't get either one until it was too late for the message to be useful, but at least I'd tried.

I couldn't think of anything else to do, at least not until I got back to civilization.

"You've got this," I muttered to myself as I started down the uneven track. I set as brisk a pace as I dared, given the dim light and the uneven surface of the road. At least the snow had eased off for the time being. Every so often flakes would start drifting down

Two and a half miles to the zoo. How long was that going to take me? I almost reached for my phone to look up "average human walking speed." Just in time, I reminded myself that if I had the signal I'd need to do an internet search I could just call the police.

I worried for a while about whether Randall was going to find his cousins and convince them to abort their mission before Clay County captured them. Or whether that had already happened. Whether Delaney's hackers were having any luck at finding something the chief could use to prove his suspicions about Inman the bureaucrat, or at least make some other Fed suspicious enough to want to go in and find out what was really happening in Clay County. Then, just for a change of pace, I worried for a while about the fact that Michael would have expected me to be home already, and would be worried sick. Well, at least I'd had my purse and my tote bag with me when my car was stolen. I wasn't sure which would stress me the most—having to replace my driver's license and credit cards, or trying to reconstruct the contents of my notebook-that-tells-me-when-to-breathe.

When I reached the Clay County Road, I wasn't sure whether to feel optimism or dread. I was probably halfway to the zoo. Over halfway. But I still had a long slog ahead of me. I was more visible to any rogue Dingles still sneaking around in Caerphilly. But also more visible to any friendly souls who might come along and give me a ride. Should I feel relieved or anxious? I settled for feeling a sense of progress, and tried to be alert for any sights or sounds that might herald either danger or rescue.

A wave of relief swept over me when, at long last, I turned into the zoo's parking lot. Followed by a wave of cranky that I struggled to keep in check, or at least save up until I ran into someone who deserved to be the target of it.

The enormous front gates would be locked, of course. But clearly the place wasn't deserted. I could see three—no, four vehicles in the parking lot, all of them at the far side, the staff were encouraged to park. At that end of the lot there was both a side gate for deliveries and a door for staff use, with a doorbell marked FOR DELIVERIES on the wall between them. This was the door my key would unlock if I had it, and also where they usually let me in when I arrived after hours—to pick up Grandfather, for example. I trudged toward it.

As I drew nearer, I recognized several of the vehicles. A white van with the logo of the Willner Wildlife Sanctuary painted on it. Not surprising—we were expecting our friend Caroline Willner up for a Christmas visit, and while here she'd probably spend a lot of time at the zoo, checking on the welfare of animals she'd once fostered and arguing with Grandfather about the finer points of zoology. I was a little surprised to see her here so late, though. And why was Dad's blue sedan here?

I'd find out soon enough. I rang the doorbell, and smiled up at the hidden security camera.

"Meg? What's up?" Caroline's voice crackled through the overhead speaker.

"Can I come inside and tell you? It's damned cold out here."

"Of course."

Something buzzed. I grabbed the door while I could, and ducked inside, making sure to close the it securely behind me. I was in a small courtyard with the Small Mammal House on my left and Admin—the Education and Administration Building—on my right. A rectangle of light appeared in the side of Admin, and I hurried toward it.

"Merry Christmas, Meg." It was Cordelia, my paternal grandmother, also expected for a Christmas visit. Although I was surprised to see her since, unlike Caroline, she tended not to spend much time at Grandfather's zoo. Or anyplace else where she'd have to share space with Grandfather. They got on each other's nerves very quickly. I sometimes wondered how the two had managed to stay together long enough to produce Dad during their youthful romance. Not a question I'd ever managed to ask.

Since Cordelia was a highly sensible woman, she waited until I was in out of the cold to give me a warm hug and a kiss on the cheek. "We could use your help."

"Hang on a sec," I said. "Let me see if my cell phone works."

It did, so I called the chief.

"We've got a problem." I broke the news that both the Shiffleys' vigilante mission, and Randall's effort to thwart it, might already have failed. And being an expert in multitasking, while I was talking to the chief, I texted Michael, saying "Car trouble. Catching ride home soon." It wasn't untrue—just a woefully incomplete description of my last few hours.

"Blast," the chief said when I'd finished my story. Either he was in a slightly better humor or he'd gotten his vocabulary back under control. "So any time now I could get a call from Clay County telling me they've locked up one of my off-duty deputies for trying to break a prisoner out of their jail."

"Your off-duty deputy and our mayor," I said. "Remember what you said about them trying to railroad Mark Caverly on some kind of fake charges? I bet they'd love doing the same thing to a posse of Shiffleys."

The chief didn't rush to say anything reassuring, so I gathered he shared my worry.

"I'll do what I can," he said. "If I can think of anything to do."

"Can I at least report my car as stolen?" I said. "Because if Cy and his minions take it apart and I never see it again, I think my insurance company will want to know that I've reported it."

"Consider it reported," he said. "And you can drop by the station tomorrow and finish the paperwork. I might even make a courtesy phone call to Sheriff Dingle. Warn him that we seem to have a rash of car thefts here, and he might want to keep his eyes open in case the perpetrators hit Clay County as well. Although it's going to be a little hard to explain how you managed to have your car stolen in the middle of the woods during a snowstorm."

"Nature walk," I said.

"He might buy that. Then again, I'm not sure I care if he buys it or not. It'll put him on notice that I know what those jackasses of his did. If they called him Cy, the clown in charge of the tow truck operation is almost certainly Cyrus Whicker. Owns the repair shop over in Clayville, and as far as I know his is the only tow truck in the county. Anse Dingle works for him. Maybe if they know I have my eye on them they'll be a little less ready swipe any more cars."

"Here's hoping," I said. "Talk to you later." I hung up and turned back to Cordelia. "What's up?"

"I'll let *them* explain it. This way."

Clearly she was highly displeased with *them,* whoever they were.

We took the elevator to the third floor, where Grandfather had what I called his penthouse—his office, his conference room, and the reception area that served as an anteroom to both. It could actually have been a fairly luxurious and impressive executive suite if Grandfather cared even a tiny bit about décor. Or tidying up. But even when he was expecting important visitors and his long-suffering administrative assistant had done a whirlwind cleaning triage, all three rooms invariably looked like a movie-set designer's idea of a mad scientist's lair. Books and scientific papers filled every available shelf and overflowed into piles in front of the shelves and in every corner. The small kitchenette along one wall held more test tubes than coffee cups. The trash cans invariably overflowed with pizza boxes and Chinese carry-out containers. Any flat surface not covered by books or papers generally held a cage or aquarium containing one or more small creatures that

Grandfather currently had under special observation for some reason or other. Though not usually because of illness—the well-equipped veterinary clinic on the first floor provided round-the-clock care for any zoo residents that were under the weather. And if you happened to know a large party in need of any kind of what Grandfather called "expedition gear"—binoculars, telescopes, compasses, freeze-dried food, hiking boots, thermal underwear, space blankets, fisherman's vests, backpacks, fanny packs, tents, camp stoves, etc.—you could have equipped them easily from the items that littered the rooms, ranging from well-worn favorites to brand-new equipment he was testing.

I followed Cordelia into the reception area to find it contained half a dozen black-clad people, some wearing ski masks. Was Grandfather hosting a delegation of ninjas? No, he was one of the ninjas. So were Dad, Rob, and Clarence Rutledge, the town veterinarian. I recognized the remaining two as longtime members of Blake's Brigade, the loose organization of volunteers Grandfather called on whenever he needed help with any kind of animal welfare project.

"Here's Meg!" Caroline exclaimed, coming over to give me a hug. "Monty, why don't you tell Meg what you're planning?"

Chapter 26

Caroline didn't actually add "so she can help us talk you out of it, you old goat," but she didn't have to. Her tone got her point across.

"Well?" I turned to Grandfather. The rest of the party looked cowed and ready to slink away, as if they'd already been the target of enough withering scorn to last a lifetime. Only Grandfather looked unperturbed. In fact, he looked pleased to see me, no doubt thinking that at last a sensible person had arrived—someone capable of appreciating the beauty of his plans.

"We think it's time to do something about the little cuckoo's father."

"Lark," I corrected. "And just what are you planning to do?"

"The chief's hands are tied, you know," Grandfather said. "He can't just go barging into some other lawman's jurisdiction with guns blazing."

I had a hard time imagining the chief barging in anywhere with guns blazing. Had Grandfather been watching too many Westerns?

"I understand the chief has to wait until he can bring in the Feds. But we can't just stand by and let those wretched Clay County crooks do away with the kid's father. So"—he drew himself up to his full height and stuck out his chest belligerently—"we're going commando!"

Rob and one of the Brigade members burst into

laughter. The rest of us managed to stifle ours. Rob sidled over and said something softly in Grandfather's ear.

Grandfather harrumphed.

"Picky, picky," he said. "Some people can see a double entendre in the weather report. Going to behave like commandos, then—although that doesn't quite have the same ring to it. Anyway, we're going to infiltrate Clay County and rescue the chap."

"That's an interesting idea," I began.

"Meg!" Cordelia and Caroline exclaimed in unison.

I held up my hand to suggest that they let me finish.

"But I happen to know that a posse of Shiffleys came up with the same idea and is already sneaking through the woods around Clayville." At least I hoped they were still sneaking, not sitting in the Clay County lockup. And optimally sneaking back toward Caerphilly under Randall's guidance, not still onward. But Grandfather and his usual suspects didn't need to know that. "Experienced woodsmen all, and most of them ex-military," I continued aloud. "So, not to disparage the abilities of your crew, but the Shiffleys are pretty darned qualified for this, and more importantly, they're already there."

"We could join forces with them!" Grandfather suggested.

"You really think you could find a handful of Shiffleys in the middle of the woods?" I asked. "I know I wouldn't want to try it. I'm not even sure Randall's going to succeed, and he has a head start on you. Let's focus on giving them a clear shot at achieving the mission." Or being persuaded to drop it and get home safely.

"Damnation." Grandfather looked almost bereft. Perhaps it was my imagination, but I thought a few of the others looked relieved rather than disappointed. Rob for sure. "A pity they didn't consult me first. We could have joined forces. Well, I suppose there's no help for it. We don't want to compromise the mission. Stand down, men!"

As if to emphasize his words, he whipped off his black knit cap and tossed it aside. It landed on top of a cage containing some kind of scruffy rodent.

I turned to Rob.

"Delaney's been trying to get in touch with you, you know."

"You could have fooled me." He sounded glum.

"She calmed down overnight, and tried calling you to talk things through. Of course, by now she's probably ticked off because you haven't answered any of her calls."

"What calls?" Rob dug into his pocket and pulled out a phone. "I think if she'd called I'd have— Hey! This isn't my phone."

"No, you left yours plugged in the charger in your office," I said.

"Wonder who this belongs to," Rob said.

"Call Paton at your security desk," I said. "He's holding your phone for you—maybe whoever lost this one has called in to ask about it. Let's get back to the important stuff. Delaney's been trying to call you."

"Right." He rushed over to Grandfather's desk and picked up the desk phone. Then he paused and looked at me.

"Um . . . do you have her number?"

"You don't know Delaney's number?"

"I don't know anyone's number anymore. They're all in my phone."

Good point. I pulled out my own phone and read off Delaney's number. He punched it in. I looked around at the family and friends who were watching him.

"Anyone think maybe we should give him a little privacy?" I asked.

Clarence was already heading for the door, and Caroline

and Cordelia were hovering near it. But Grandfather, who had taken a seat on the cluttered sofa and begun reading another scientific paper, didn't appear to have heard me. Nor had Dad, who was peering into the cage containing the rodent, evidently fascinated by the way it had pulled the edge of Grandfather's discarded ski cap through the bars and was rapidly shredding it—no doubt for nest material.

"Dad! Grandfather!" They both looked up, startled. "You can go home now."

"Don't bother on my account," Rob said. "The number's busy."

"Then try again." Rob looked sheepish. I went over to the desk, wrote Delaney's number down on a piece of paper, and held it out.

"Thanks."

We all watched as he dialed again. And then hung up almost immediately.

"She's probably on the phone with Chief Burke," I said. "Helping him find some data. Keep trying."

"Probably a good idea for the rest of us to go home," Dad said.

"You know what sounds like a good idea?" Clarence said. "Pizza."

"Luigi's?" Rob brightened at the thought of a visit to the family's favorite pizzeria. "I'll go with you. Dad, can I use your phone to keep calling Delaney on the way?"

"Of course!" Dad handed it over and they headed for the door.

"May as well, if we can't be useful." Grandfather cast his scientific paper aside.

The ninjas departed, with Rob programming Delaney's number into Dad's phone for ease of redialing while the others cheerfully debated the competing merits of pepperoni and Italian sausage on pizza, and whether it was too late in the day to safely eat something as spicy as Luigi's *penne alla arrabiata.* I wondered what Luigi would make of them in their inky black outfits. Dropouts from mime school, maybe. And whether Rob would desert them when he got through to Delaney or invite her to join them.

"Good job," Caroline said when the door had closed behind them.

"I didn't want to ask in case I gave them ideas, but they weren't planning to go in armed, were they?"

"With stun guns and tranquilizer dart pistols," Caroline said. "The same ones we used last month when we went to film that documentary on the Alaskan moose herds."

"I don't suppose it occurred to them that what would stun a moose might kill a human being," I said.

"I was just arguing that point with them when you arrived to save the day." Caroline beamed at me.

"Can one of you give me a ride back to town?" I sank down onto the sofa, feeling suddenly tired. "I drove Randall out this way so he could take off after his crazy cousins, and to make a long story short, my car has now gone to join Clay County's growing collection of illegally impounded Caerphilly vehicles."

"Happy to give you a ride," Caroline said. "And your grandmother is riding with me. But would you mind if we stayed here just a little longer? We were going to offer to share our tea with the menfolk, but that fell by the wayside when we found out what they were up to. And frankly, right now I'm more in the mood for a ladies-only meal anyway."

"Not that Monty would have appreciated anything as civilized as tea," Cordelia added, with a sniff.

"All the more for us," Caroline said.

She led the way into the conference room, where she'd spread a red-and-green Christmas tablecloth over the conference table, and began laying out delicacies. Cordelia found a small saucepan in the kitchenette, washed it carefully—after all, we had no idea what kind of scientific experiments Grandfather had been using it for—and boiled some water for the tea. Then we sat down to a feast—scones and clotted cream, ham biscuits, cupcakes, cucumber sandwiches, and half a dozen kinds of Christmas cookies. Accompanied, of course, by catching up on all the town and family gossip.

"You're lucky to have your grandfather around this Christmas," Caroline remarked at one point, when we'd reached that portion of our tea that hobbits would have called "filling up the corners."

"That's a matter of opinion," Cordelia said.

"He was all fired up to do a few more of those live wildlife webcasts of his," Caroline said.

"The ones where he goes out and bothers some poor creature that's just trying to hibernate or catch its dinner in peace?" Cordelia asked.

"You've seen them, then." Caroline nodded. "Only this time he wanted to do them from the northern part of Norway or Finland. Someplace really cold, at any rate. I told him if he wants to spend Christmas somewhere north of the Arctic Circle and freeze his rear end off, he was welcome to do it, but he could count me out."

"Good for you!" Cordelia exclaimed.

"So we compromised," Caroline went on. "He came here as planned, and between Christmas and New Year's we're going to do a bunch of webcasts from the woods around here. I hope the snow stays around. I think he'll grumble a lot less if he can still stride across some kind of frozen landscape."

"You're in luck," I said. "It's supposed to remain subfreezing until after New Year's."

"Well, I can't hold another bite," Caroline said. "Any of you want to finish those scones?"

Cordelia and I both shook our heads.

"Do let's scatter a few leftovers around, so those idiots know what they've been missing," Cordelia suggested.

"See if there's room in the minifridge," Caroline suggested.

"Just barely," I said as I peered into the fridge. "What is *Lasiorhinus latifrons*?"

"The Southern hairy-nosed wombat." Caroline frowned. "He doesn't have one of those in there, does he? They're a threatened species."

"Just its urine," I said. "Unless labeling chicken broth as wombat urine is Grandfather's idea of a joke."

"It probably is." Cordelia rolled her eyes.

"No, it probably is wombat urine," Caroline said. "For a pregnancy test—he's been having a great deal of success breeding them."

I succeeded in wedging the little bits of leftover food in between the wombat urine and something that was either a long-forgotten container of lo mein or the start of a new exhibit on molds, spores, and fungus. Then we made our way down to the parking lot. I was relieved to see that Caroline's van was the only remaining vehicle in the parking lot.

We when we got close to the town limits, we took a small detour to show Cordelia the Christmas decorations. In spite of the snow, the streets were still thronged with tourists, come to enjoy the holiday ambience that we piled on with such enthusiasm.

And I quickly realized one reason my holiday spirit had been lower than usual: in my job as Randall's assistant, I'd been spending far too much time organizing Christmas and not enough time simply enjoying it. Maybe it was time for me to stop worrying about whether we had enough carol singers on enough corners throughout town and just enjoy the sound of voices raised in joyous song. Maybe I should stop looking at the minor infractions in the Victorian dress code—like the bright pink snow boots on one of the carolers—and focus on the singers' smiling faces.

The town Christmas tree looked splendid. When we'd lost the previous tree after one of last winter's terrible ice storms, Randall had agonized for weeks over how big the replacement should be. For years, he'd proudly boasted that our tree was almost—but not quite—as tall as the National Christmas Tree. Would it be arrogant and prideful to plant a larger one, he wondered?

"For heaven's sake," I said at last. "Stop worrying about the size. Get the most beautiful one you can find. Who cares whether it's half or twice the size of the National Christmas Tree? If anyone in Washington is bent out of shape, I'm sure they can manage to find an even bigger one."

I had no idea how the new tree compared with the National Christmas Tree, but at sixty feet high it was considerably taller than our previous tree. We'd had to invest in twice as many lights and ornaments, but it was worth it.

In fact, it was all worth it—all the work I'd done to make this year's Christmas in Caerphilly even better than last year's. So I sat back and basked in Caroline and Cordelia's enjoyment. As we drove down the residential streets, I shared their delight in how many of the houses were so beautifully decorated, instead of fretting about the houses that hadn't bothered.

Eventually we tired of oohing and aahing and took the road that led out of town and toward home.

Since Caroline was driving, I used the ride to call Michael.

"I heard about what happened at the shelter," he said, after we'd exchanged greetings. "I'm not sure whether to say 'well done!' or 'what the hell were you thinking of'?"

"I'll consider them both said. It probably wasn't as

dangerous as it sounds—they were pretty incompetent thugs. And I snuck up behind them. Josefina tackled them head-on with her frying pan."

"I am in awe of you both. And I will look forward to celebrating your being safe and sound when you get here. When will that be?"

"Ten minutes," I said. "I'm riding with Caroline."

"Oh, by the way," Michael said. "Rose Noire appears to have had a wonderful time at her retreat—in fact all the ladies there did. So much so that they want to keep it going for another day or two."

"That's great," I said. "She deserves a bit of R and R." Although the idea of managing without Rose Noire for another day or two, now that the family hordes had descended, was a bit daunting. I was already trying to calculate which visiting relatives I might be able to guilt trip into doing some of the extra work that came along with having the house full of family for the holidays.

"So it's okay that I told them they could move into our barn for a day or two?" he went on. "Rose Noire swears they won't be any trouble or cause any extra work—they'll be too busy meditating, doing yoga, and mixing up herbal concoctions."

"They probably will cause extra work," I said. "But at least Rose Noire will be around to figure out how to get it done. And to help with all the family guests."

"Exactly what I thought. See you soon."

I was looking forward to a quiet evening at home. Of course, it would never be all that quiet with several dozen relatives underfoot. But still—at home. Though I didn't say so aloud, because I didn't want to jinx us.

Chapter 27

As we drew near the house, I could see light shining from almost every window. Christmas carols were playing. No, the Christmas carols sounded live—someone was playing our piano, and the assembled relatives were singing.

"They sound rather nice," Cordelia said.

"They also sound rather numerous," I said. "I put Mother in charge of sorting out which relatives stayed where—how many do you suppose she assigned to us?"

"You've only got so many guest rooms," Caroline said. "So it can only be so bad."

"You underestimate how annoying my relatives can be when they reach critical mass," I said. "And what if she carried through with her threat to turn the library into a bunkhouse for the teenage boys?"

"Then you think up chores for them," Cordelia suggested. "And I guarantee they will make themselves delightfully scarce."

"And then there's feeding them."

"The menfolk should be down at Luigi's," Caroline said. "Have them bring home a dozen pizzas. Any that don't get eaten tonight will give you a head start on lunch tomorrow."

"Or even breakfast," I said. "Knowing kids and pizza. Good idea."

Caroline parked her van in the space where my car would normally have been, if it wasn't over in Clay County, possibly being disassembled into spare parts. But with my regained Christmas spirit, even that didn't bother me as much. The Honda wasn't exactly new. In fact, Michael and I had recently agreed that it was time to replace it with a newer model.

So I was in a downright festive mood when we walked into the house to find dozens of friends and family members singing Christmas carols, accompanied not only by a cousin playing our piano but also half a dozen who'd brought along their own musical instruments—two guitars, a trumpet, a flute, an oboe, and a harmonica.

I'd have been a little alarmed at the sheer number of cousins in the house—even over the caroling I could hear voices and laughter from other areas of the house, which meant the fifty or so people in the living room were only part of the crowd. But shortly after I walked in I spotted Rose Noire circulating with a pitcher of hot cider and I relaxed a little. In fact, a lot.

And Mother reigned supreme in the kitchen and dining room, supervising both the arrival of all the food people had brought with them and its disposition, either onto the dining table to feed tonight's crowd, or into the refrigerator or the pantry to fuel upcoming meals. At least I assumed she was saving some of it for the future, though you couldn't have guessed from the spread in the dining room—ham, turkey, roast beef, mushroom casserole, macaroni and cheese, potato salad, tossed salad, green bean casserole, stewed tomatoes, pickled okra, succotash, mashed potatoes, sweet potatoes, tomato aspic, ham biscuits, croissants, and of course every kind of pie, cake, and cookie imaginable.

"Hello, dear." Mother gave me a quick kiss on the cheek. "Isn't it looking wonderful? Everyone has been so kind."

Yes, they were kind, although the sheer extravagance of the spread owed at least as much to the usual genteel competition among the family's many cooks. Thank goodness agreeing to host the whole thing gave me a graceful out.

“I can’t imagine what’s keeping your father,” she said.

“I think he was helping Grandfather with something,” I said. “I’ll give him a call and see how much longer he’s going to be.”

I went out into the backyard to make the call. Michael and the boys and a few other cousins their age were there, dragging some of the littler cousins around the yard in sleds, producing squeals of delight from the children and interested humming from the observant llamas.

Dad’s phone went to voice mail immediately. I hoped that meant Rob was using it for a long productive talk with Delaney. “It’s Meg,” I said. “You’re missing the feast. Call me when you get this.” Grandfather’s phone just rang on and on, because he couldn’t be bothered listening to voice mail and had never set it up.

“Annoying,” I muttered. What if I’d been calling about something really urgent? Even more urgent than getting back before the food disappeared? But I had one more option. I called Luigi’s.

Unlike the men in my family, Luigi answered promptly.

“Merry Christmas, Meg,” he said. “You want pickup or delivery?”

“Actually, I just wanted to know if you could give a message to my family, if they’re still there.”

“Still here?” He sounded puzzled. “Were they supposed to be?”

“I thought they were heading your way when they left the zoo over an hour ago,” I said. “Grandfather, Dad, Rob, and Clarence Rutledge.”

“Let me check.”

He put the phone down. I tamped down my impatience by taking a few deep breaths of the cold, crisp air, and listened to the background noise. People talking and laughing, and the soaring voice of Luciano Pavarotti singing “Gesù Bambino.”

"No, they are not here, and Angelica says she has not seen them at all tonight."

"Weird," I said. "Well, maybe they got delayed and will be coming in later. If you see them, tell me to call me."

"Of course! *Buon Natale!*"

I pondered for a moment. Maybe Grandfather had enjoyed his lunch at the Inn so much that he'd asked to go back there again.

But when I called, the Inn hadn't seen them, either.

At Mutant Wizards, Paton was still on duty.

"They're not here," he said in answer to my question. "But Rob picked up his phone an hour or so ago, so you could try reaching him on that."

An hour ago? He must have gone by the office as soon as he'd left the zoo. And his phone went straight to voice mail, just like Dad's.

Had they all arrived back at the house while I was out here? I couldn't spot any of their cars, but there were rather a lot of cars by now, and they might have had to park quite far down the road.

In the living room, the carolers were just finishing up "Good King Wenceslas." Their numbers had grown, but Dad, Grandfather, and Rob weren't among them.

They weren't in the kitchen, sipping hot toddies or mugs of eggnog.

Or in the dining room digging into the feast.

Or in the library, reading in companionable silence with the few family introverts who'd showed up.

Or out in the yard inspecting the llamas and cheering on the sledders.

They weren't in the barn, where a dozen women had rolled out sleeping bags and were sitting cross-legged in a circle with their eyes closed, humming "ommmm." Presumably Rose Noire's retreat companions, although, apparently, she was still inside wrangling our guests.

I was getting really worried now. So I went up to the third floor and checked out Rob's room. He wasn't there. His laptop still sat on the desk. I started it up and logged in once more to the site that would let me find his iPhone.

I watched the little compass icon spin. It seemed to take forever. And it finally gave up searching, and showed me the last location it had for Rob's phone.

I was still staring at the screen when Cordelia came up behind me.

"What's wrong?" she asked.

"What makes you think something's wrong." I wasn't sure I should tell her.

"Because even allowing for the fact that it's midwinter, you wouldn't normally look that pale."

"See that little green dot?" I pointed at it.

She took out her reading glasses, donned them, and peered through them at the screen.

"Yes," she said. "What is it?"

"The location of Rob's phone."

She peered more closely.

"It appears to be near your grandfather's zoo."

"Near it," I said. "I'd say about two miles away. But two miles in the wrong direction."

"Meaning?" She looked up at me.

"That dot is slightly over the Clay County line. And that was an hour ago."

Cordelia uttered a word one doesn't usually expect to hear from one's grandmother.

"My sentiments exactly," I said.

"That old fool!" she exclaimed. "I could have sworn you talked him out of it. But he's gone and done it anyway, and taken James and Rob with him. And poor Clarence. What are we going to do?"

"First, we tell the chief." I was already pulling out my phone. I'd called 911 so often in the last two days I was surprised there weren't dents in my phone screen over the 9 and 1 keys.

But then a thought hit me. Instead of dialing 911, I searched through the pictures I'd taken until I found the one I'd taken of the piece of paper I'd found in the pocket of Janet's jeans. Then I dialed Rachel Plunket's number.

It rang once. Twice. Three times. Was no one answering the phone tonight? Then the fourth ring was interrupted.

"Hello?" A very tentative sounding hello.

"Hello, Rachel. This is Meg Langslow. Remember me?"

No answer.

"Hiding in your attic? If you can't talk freely, just pretend I'm an aunt."

"That's nice, Aunt Tilly," she said. "I'm kind of busy right now. Is this important?"

"The Burger Barn's pretty close to the sheriff's office and the jail, isn't it? Like across the street?"

"Uh-huh."

I'd thought it was, from my occasional visit to Clayville. And of course, Clayville was only a few blocks long, so nothing was all that far from anything else.

"Have the deputies arrested any groups of people tonight?"

"Yes, ma'am."

"Two groups?"

"Yes, that's it."

"One group of Shiffleys, and one group led by a really tall old guy in a pith helmet?"

"Yes, that's exactly it, Aunt Tilly."

"How much longer will you be there?"

"Yes, ma'am. Look I should go— I've got a bunch of deputies who just got off duty and I have to take them their orders. And my shift doesn't end till midnight, so maybe I should call you back tomorrow."

"Thanks," I said. "If there's any way you can send me any more information, please try."

"I will. Tell the family I said Merry Christmas, and I hope I can get down there soon."

She hung up.

"Clay County has them," I said.

"Monty's silly expedition?" Cordelia asked.

"And also the Shiffleys."

"You're sure?"

"As sure as I can be."

"Well, at least there's safety in numbers." Cordelia shook her head in exasperation. "They can't very well knock off Mr. Caverly with half a dozen witnesses in jail with him. And maybe a night in jail will teach your grandfather a lesson."

"We won't have a very merry Christmas if Sheriff Dingle keeps them all in jail until the new year," I pointed out.

"I hadn't thought of that."

I was already dialing 911.

"Nine-one-one. What's the emergency, Meg?" Debbie Ann sounded a little terse.

"So Randall already reported to the chief that he was going in after Vern and his cousins, right?" I began.

"He did," she said. "And we're already aware of the possibility that the Shiffleys may have been captured, so as you can imagine, we're a little busy right now."

"It's more than a possibility, according to my sources in Clayville."

"You have sources in Clayville? Let me put you through to the chief."

I waited, tapping my fingers impatiently on Rob's desk. Cordelia sat down on the end of Rob's bed and folded her arms as if rehearsing what she wanted to stay to Grandfather.

I really hoped she got the chance sometime soon.

"Meg, Debbie Ann says you have confirmation that

those blasted Shiffleys managed to get themselves arrested in Clay County."

"Not only the Shiffleys but another vigilante party, probably composed of Grandfather, Dad, Rob, Clarence Rutledge, and a couple of really unlucky members of Blake's Brigade."

"Blast! Are you sure?"

"Pretty sure. I called Rachel Plunket—Janet's friend. She works at the Burger Barn."

"Which happens to be right across the street from the Sheriff Dingle's station," the chief said. "So she confirmed it?"

I repeated my conversation with Rachel, as close to word for word as I could manage.

The chief was silent for a few moments after I finished.

"Okay," he said. "This should help."

"Help?" I exclaimed. "Are you saying you're glad the Shiffleys and Grandfather's motley crew are in the Clay County jail?"

"Of course not. I meant the information you got from your source. Judge Jane and I are raising Cain down here, trying to get some kind of state or federal intervention organized. Your brother's hackers are uncovering some very suspicious links between Inman and the Dingles and we're making headway. Your information will also help—please pass along anything else you hear."

"I will."

We hung up.

"We have to do something," Cordelia said.

"Trying to do something has already gotten a whole bunch of people into trouble," I said. "Are you suggesting we go join them?"

"Or course, not," she said. "But—"

"Meg, dear." Mother and Caroline appeared in the door of Rob's room. "What's going on?"

Chapter 28

Cordelia and I looked at each other.

"Bad news," Cordelia said. "You heard that Clay County captured the man they were looking for."

"Yes," Mother said. "Poor soul."

"Apparently Monty decided to go in and rescue him," Cordelia continued.

"The old fool," Caroline said. "Did he finally manage to get himself killed?"

"Not yet," Cordelia said. "But only because I haven't yet gotten my hands on him. He took James and Rob and Clarence Rutledge with him. And a couple of Brigade members."

"Oh, my God," Mother murmured.

"They've also got Randall and Vern Shiffley and one or two of their cousins," I added. "Who had already failed in their own separate rescue mission. The chief's afraid Sheriff Dingle will try to keep them in jail over Christmas—and after that, he might even try to get them all convicted on some kind of phony charges that would keep them locked up for—well, who knows how long."

"What is the chief doing?" Mother asked.

"As much as he can," I said. "He can't just interfere in another county. He's working to bring in the ATF or the FBI or the DEA or—"

"We must do something," Mother said.

"Absolutely," Caroline said. "Just because Monty's an idiot sometimes doesn't give those Clay County creeps the right to lock him up. And it could be dangerous—he's a tough old bird, but he's no spring chicken. And Rob and James and Clarence were just led astray."

The door opened.

"Rob, how are— What's going on?" Rose Noire stood in the doorway, looking puzzled. "Where's Rob."

"Welcome home," I said.

"Shut the door and come have a seat," Mother said. "We're going to need your help."

"Her help for what?" If Mother had a plan, I wanted to hear it.

"I was rather hoping you'd figure that out, dear." Mother took a seat on the edge of Rob's bed and smiled up at me, as if to say she had complete confidence that of course I'd figure out a way to rescue her husband, her son, and her annoying father-in-law from durance vile. And before their absence ruined Christmas.

"Yes, help for what?" Rose Noire echoed, taking a seat beside Mother. "What in the world has been going on here?"

"Someone fill her in," I said. "I'll be back in a few minutes."

The ghost of an idea was starting to form in my mind, but I needed some peace and quiet to think, if I was going to tease it out.

"In fact, meet me in the library in half an hour," I called over my shoulder. "No, wait—the library's full of teenage boys. Make it the dining room. Kick out any men who are there—tell them it's a women's shelter business meeting. Any woman who wants to can stay provided she's willing to be sworn to secrecy."

"We'll take care of it, dear," Mother assured me.

Yes, Mother would definitely take care of anything I asked her to do if she thought it would bring Dad and Rob back in time for Christmas. And heaven help the person who got in her way. In the way of any of the formidable women who would soon be making their way to the dining room with stern faces and worried minds. If I gave them a plan, they'd make it happen.

But I still had to think of the plan.

Normally, if I had to do a lot of thinking, I'd make my way to the barn. I'd fire up my forge and do some blacksmithing. Nothing delicate or complicated, just the rough shaping needed to start a project. Heating iron to just the right temperature requires concentration, and then there's no way to think when you're hammering it out. But if you put a problem into your brain and let it alone to marinate while you do something else that takes your full attention, it's amazing how often the brain will come up with a solution.

I didn't think Rose Noire's retreat ladies would appreciate my hammering iron at this time of night, even if they were still awake and meditating.

I couldn't even go to my office to think, since it was also in the barn, in what had started out as the tack room, and I'd probably wake them up getting there. Still, I drifted into the kitchen and glanced out over the backyard.

The sledders had gone inside. Michael was leaning on the fence around the llama's pen. The llamas were standing nearby. Not touching him, of course, since like all llamas they hated to be touched. And they were probably humming at him. That seemed to be one of the ways they tried to offer comfort when they sensed that one of their chosen humans was upset.

I grabbed the old coat I kept by the back door and trudged out to join him.

"How are you doing?" I asked when I'd joined him in leaning on the fence.

"A little melancholy. I heard they'd captured Mr. Caverly."

"That's not all." I brought him up to speed on the failed attempts to rescue Mark Caverly, and our fears that the would-be rescuers would be locked up long after Christmas. When I'd finished we stood for a few moments listening to the humming of the llamas, which was strangely soothing.

Maybe there was something to this hanging around with the llamas. A plan was starting to take shape in my mind. It was still ill-formed and downright peculiar. It might not succeed. But if I could put together the pieces . . .

"Non sequitur of the day," I said. "But have most of your students gone home?"

"You're thinking about tomorrow night's pizza party, right?" Actually I'd completely forgotten about it, but he didn't need to know that.

"Most of the undergrads have gone," he was saying. "But we have quite a few grad students still around, since so many of them are doing the street theater. We should have about three dozen for pizza."

More than I'd expected.

"Do any of them happen to be women with tech experience?" I asked. "As in knowing something about running a video camera? I need someone ASAP for a shelter-related project."

"I can think of several who might fit the bill," he said. "You want me to call them?"

"I'd rather call myself," I said. "I can explain better. Can you get me their contact info? I'd like to send an email tonight, and then be ready to call them as soon as possible."

Actually, I was planning to call them as soon as I got their numbers, but probably better not to tell him I was planning to wake up his students.

"Sure. I've got the guest list in my office. I should be heading that way anyway—I agreed to take the first night of riding herd on the teenage boys in the library. Time I showed up to make sure they don't burn the house down."

Excellent. That would make it easier for me to sneak out to execute my plan.

"I'll go back in with you, then," I said aloud. "We're having an emergency women's shelter steering committee meeting in the dining room."

When we got to his office, Michael printed out a list of the students who'd accepted our Sunday night pizza party invitation. I was delighted to see that he'd already put the emails and phone numbers on it. Delighted, but not surprised. Given the possibility of snow in the weather forecast, we'd wanted to make sure we had no delay in notifying them in case of a change in plans. He ticked off a couple of women's names.

"Any of those should be able to do your video project, whatever it is."

"Thanks." I wanted to tell Michael what we were up to. But I was afraid he'd say it was crazy. Or dangerous. Or that he'd insist on coming with us. And I had a gut feeling that for my plan to succeed, we needed to keep it all female. Not that I thought the Dingles were models of chivalry, but I suspected they'd take a bunch of women a little less seriously. Give us a little bit of the good old boy "now, now, little lady" nonsense before taking any drastic action. At least I hoped so.

"Well, wish me luck." He braced himself and opened the library door. A chorus of voices arose.

"No grownups allowed!"

"Hey! I'm getting dressed in here!"

"Did you bring the pizza?"

The door closed behind him.

I studied the list. I knew two of the women. I'd call them in a little bit. First I had to see if my own family and close friends thought my idea was worth trying.

I strolled back to the front of the house. I was hovering

between entering the dining room and sitting in front of the fire in the living room for a few more minutes, to let my idea take a little more shape.

Someone knocked on the door. I peered out the window to see Minerva Burke, the chief's wife.

"What are you doing here at this time of night?" I opened the door and beckoned for her to come in. "Which doesn't mean your visit is unwelcome—just unexpected."

"Henry seemed to be worrying that you might be planning to do something stupid and foolhardy and dangerous." She shed her coat and handed it to me. "Like invading Clay County to rescue your menfolk."

"What makes him think that?" She'd realize, of course, that I was avoiding the question.

"Who knows how men get these ideas? Anyway, I told him you hadn't done a stupid thing in your life, and I didn't think you were going to start now. And then I told him I was going to go lead a prayer vigil for the safe return of our friends and neighbors."

"Great idea," I said. But if she was planning to lead a prayer vigil over at the New Life Baptist Church, why was she taking off her snow boots?

"He probably thought I was headed over to the church," she said, as if reading my thoughts. "I figure I can pray on my feet as well as anywhere else. When are we leaving for Clay County?"

"First I have to see if anyone else thinks I've come up with a plan that will work," I said. "You can join us. In the dining room, in a few minutes."

She nodded and marched down the hall. When she opened the dining room door, I heard glad cries of welcome from some of the others. Then the door shut again.

Time for me to join them.

I was about to walk over to turn out the porch light when I heard a car pull up outside. Then footsteps coming up the front walk. By the time the doorbell rang, I was peeking through the window to see who else was arriving.

Robyn. And Josefina.

"You're out late," I said as I opened the door. "And without Noah. What's up?"

"Matt's watching Noah," Robyn said. "And in case you're worried, the shelter residents have arrived at their new temporary quarters, and Mo Heedles is holding down the fort there. She sends her regards."

"Good." Mo was both a friend of Cordelia's and the very savvy police chief of Riverton, where the shelter occupants had gone to take refuge in Cordelia's house. The shelter residents were in good hands. "So what brings you here so late?"

"Your mother said you have a plan to rescue Mark Caverly," Robyn said. "And the other jailbirds. No matter how silly they are, we can't let them spend Christmas in jail."

Evidently Mother had already been busy rounding up recruits.

"I'm not exactly sure I have an actual plan yet," I said. "I'm still working on it."

"Whatever it is, count us in," Robyn said. "We want to help."

"For my ladies," Josefina said. "And their babies."

Okay. I could fit them into my still-vague plan.

"Go on into the dining room," I said. "And—"

Another car was parking in front of the house.

Chapter 29

Robyn, Josefina, and I all tensed as we turned to study the new arrival. Then we simultaneously relaxed when we saw Ekaterina emerge from the driver's seat, wearing a quilted jacket that managed to look both effortlessly chic and toasty warm.

I threw open the door.

"We have come to join you," Ekaterina called out, throwing back the hood of her jacket. "My sister Oksana and I."

Oksana, wearing a very similar elegant coat, but with the hood pulled low over her face, strode up the walk behind Ekaterina.

"Welcome," I said to them both. "I didn't even know you had a sister."

"I do now." Ekaterina shut the door and beamed at Oksana. Oksana threw her hood back, revealing that she wasn't Ekaterina's sister after all.

"Hello, Janet," I said.

"I made Ekaterina bring me," she said. "If you're going to rescue Mark, I want to help."

"Join us, then." I still had those residual doubts, but maybe it was better to have her where we could keep an eye on her. I'd drop a quiet word to Ekaterina on that.

"A moment." Ekaterina was looking out of the window. My stomach knotted again. First with anxiety and then with anger that those thugs from Clay County had made me feel unsafe in my own house.

My tension must have shown on my face.

"Is nothing," Ekaterina said. "Only that there should be one more car arriving. Ahh—there she is."

A bright red convertible skidded to a stop right behind Ekaterina's car, sending up a small wave of snow, and Delaney hopped out.

I opened the door again.

"Sorry!" Delaney called as she loped up the front walk, heedless of the patches of ice yet somehow managing to miss them all. "I know I'm the last one here. Did I miss anything?"

"You're just in time." When she arrived at the door I gave her a quick hug, on impulse. She tightened the hug and held on to me as if she might need the support.

"Did Rob reach you?" I asked.

"I'm an idiot. I was ignoring every call that wasn't from his number, I was even getting mad at your father for calling over and over when I wanted to keep the line free for him to get through. By the time I realized it was him calling on your father's phone, I guess he'd despaired and gone off on that stupid rescue mission. If anything happens to him it will be all my fault."

"Then we won't let anything happen to him," I said.

"We are all back in harmony." Ekaterina nodded with approval. "Good. Now let us begin."

"Follow me." I led the way to the dining room, still thinking furiously. Granted, the plan evolving in my mind would take a bunch of people. But I hoped we didn't get any more arrivals for the time being. We were going to run out of chairs.

It took a few minutes for everyone to get settled, with friends who hadn't seen each other in the last few days—or hours—exchanging warm greetings. I introduced Janet to those who hadn't already met her. Delaney fetched a couple of chairs from the kitchen. And then they all sat down around the table and looked expectantly at me.

Mother. Cordelia. Caroline. Robyn. Josefina. Delaney. Rose Noire. Minerva. Ekaterina. Janet.

I suddenly felt a lot more optimistic. With this group on my side, maybe my vague plan had a chance.

"Okay, I think I have a plan," I said. "Or at least the glimmerings of one. I'm going to need all of you to start making a whole lot of phone calls. And I apologize in advance, because I bet most of the people you'll be calling will be pretty mad about being awakened in the middle of the night. But it can't be helped. We need to have our troops ready to head into Clay County at dawn."

"Troops?" Robyn said. "I don't want to sound oppositional, but should we really be thinking in terms of sending in armed people? Hasn't Clay County already captured some of our most skilled hunters and woodsmen? Along with . . . um . . . some of our most adventurous souls?"

A tactful description of Grandfather's band.

"And do we really want to stoop to their level?" she went on.

"You're right," I said. "We don't want to stoop to their level, we don't need to add armed people to an already tense situation, and most importantly, we absolutely don't want to repeat the mistake that both the Shiffleys and Grandfather's crew made."

"I'd say their mistake was going to Clay County in the first place," Janet said.

"No," I said. "Their mistake was to think they could sneak into Clay County, stealthily break your husband out of jail, and then whisk him back to Caerphilly before the Dingles figured out what was going on."

"I admit, it's a long shot," Caroline said. "But isn't that what we have to do? Or at least try to do? What else can we do that would help?"

"We're not going to sneak into Clay County," I said. "Not most of us, anyway."

"And we're not going to be armed, right?" Rose Noire asked.

"Of course we'll be armed," I said. "Just not with firearms. We'll be armed with brains. And common sense, which both of the previous expeditions were probably a little short on."

"Amen to that," Cordelia muttered.

"And the Christmas spirit—that's it. We're going to bring the Christmas spirit to Clay County."

"Dibs on playing the Ghost of Christmas Yet to Come," Delaney said. "I dig the costume."

"And our goal won't be to break Mark Caverly and the other prisoners out of the jail," I went on. "Although I'm hoping we can convince Sheriff Dingle of the wisdom of turning everyone loose. But even if we can't do that, our mission will be to distract and delay them. And if possible to shine enough light on what they're doing that they'll realize they can't get away with hurting Mark or locking up everyone over Christmas."

"You think light will scare them?" Rose Noire asked. "It's not as if they're beetles."

"I was speaking figuratively," I said. "By light, I actually meant . . . well, eyes. The light of publicity. Caroline, how fast do you think you could get hold of the equipment you and Grandfather use to do those live webcasts when you're in the field doing some kind of animal rescue? And the shortwave radios that you use when you're someplace where there's no cell service?"

"All that stuff's already at the zoo," she said. "Want me to fetch it?"

"No, just round it up when you get back to the zoo. That's where we're going to rendezvous before heading into Clay County," I said. "Everyone will rendezvous there at the zoo—everyone here, and everyone we recruit. And if possible, get your recruits to show up there half an hour before dawn. Six A.M. With their official town Christmas carol books," I added.

"You're serious about the Christmas spirit thing, then?" Robyn asked.

"Absolutely. Think what total jerks they'd look like if they were rude to us while we were singing 'peace on earth, goodwill to men.' But the more of us there are, the better this will work—so I want most of you to start rounding up volunteers. Mother—you work on the ladies of St. Clotilda. Minerva—can you bring the sopranos, mezzo-sopranos, and altos from the New Life Baptist choir? Robyn, see if you can get any recruits from the rest of the Ladies' Interfaith Council. The rest of you—if you can think of women's groups or single individual women who would be good additions to the project, see if you can recruit them, and if you can't, help the others with their phone calls. Although I do have special jobs for some of you."

Mother, Minerva, and Robyn took out their phones. The rest looked at me expectantly.

"Delaney—you're in charge of the webcasting. Whatever happens when we get to Clay County, we want the world to be watching."

"Got my laptop in the car," she said. "I'll get on it."

"Go out and set up at the zoo," I said. "I'll call and tell them we're having an emergency women's shelter meeting in Grandfather's conference room. Caroline, you can go out with her and work on the video equipment. Although I seem to recall that all of Grandfather's cameramen are male, right?"

"That's usually who's willing to put up with him," Caroline said.

"I have a line on some camerawomen," I said. "Janet, can you convince Rachel Plunket to help us?"

"I can try," she said. "What do you need her to do?"

"She works at the Burger Barn," I said. "Do they open for breakfast?"

"No." Janet shook her head. "The Clayville Market has a monopoly on serving breakfast—if you call bad coffee and stale doughnuts breakfast. The Barn doesn't open till eleven."

"Then the Barn could be a good place to set up our equipment," I said. "If there's any way Rachel could meet us there and let us in, that would be great. She doesn't have to stick around. And we can make it look as if we broke in, if she'd prefer."

"I'll see what she can do."

"Most of us will be going in openly at dawn," I said, turning back to the rest of the crowd. "I'm going to sneak in beforehand to arrange setting up the camera equipment. Ekaterina, do you think you could get hold of a van or a panel truck? And would you like to be part of the vanguard?"

"Yes, to both questions," she said. "I am good at covert and clandestine activity. And the Inn has a small panel truck we could use."

"Are you sure you want us to use something with the Inn's name on it?"

"This is the truck we use when discretion is required," Ekaterina said. "It is unmarked."

Was I the only one here wondering what discreet missions the Inn needed an unmarked panel truck for?

Evidently not.

"'When discretion is required'?" Caroline repeated. "For what?"

"When, for example, our landscaping department needs to acquire a bulk supply of fertilizer," Ekaterina explained, "from one of the local organic farms."

"Oh, like manure," Caroline said.

"Yes." Ekaterina wrinkled her nose. "We would not want the Inn's logo associated with that. And, of course, I always ensure that it is thoroughly cleaned after such expeditions," she added to me.

"Awesome," I said, "Anyone have any ideas they'd like to propose?"

Everyone looked back and forth at each other. I was a little disappointed that no one was speaking up. Because at the moment, sneaking into Clay County and singing Christmas carols sounded a little thin as plans went. Maybe they were just eager to start phoning.

"If you think of anything, speak up," I said. "I'm going to go off and make a few calls of my own."

"Before you go." Robyn's voice had a tone that even the non-churchgoers in our band could recognize, and we all fell quiet and listened as she asked a blessing on our endeavors. I wondered if it had occurred to her that our endeavors were likely to include a wide variety of deceptions and misdemeanors, and maybe even a felony or two. And then I decided from her expression that yes, she probably did.

Chapter 30

I retreated to Michael's office for some privacy. Occasionally a burst of shouts or laughter or fake screams would erupt from the library next door, from which I deduced that the teenage boys were watching a horror movie.

I settled comfortably into Michael's desk chair and dialed up the first of the grad students he'd flagged.

To my relief, she answered, and didn't sound all that sleepy.

"Hi," I said. "This is Meg Langslow—Professor Waterston's wife."

"Hi," she said. "I bet you're calling to cancel the pizza party on account of the snow."

"No—what's a few inches of snow?"

"I've lived in Florida all my life," she said. "This is more snow than I've ever seen at one time."

"So does that mean you wouldn't be interested in going out in the snow to help with a video project that might be dangerous but could be fun and might even go viral on the internet?"

"Sure—when?"

"Can you meet me at the Caerphilly Zoo at six A.M.? We'll have the equipment if you can come prepared to run it. And if you can find one or two other women who can help with the behind-the-camera stuff, that would be great—but only women. And don't tell anybody else. Not even my husband. I'll fill you in at the zoo."

"Okay, now I'm curious. I'll see you at six at the zoo. And I'll bring my roommate."

Okay. I had someone to run the cameras. And with any luck Janet would talk Rachel into letting us set them up in the Burger Barn. Now I needed a way to smuggle them in there. And someone to handle the sort of tech issues that might be beyond a film studies major who'd never tried to film outside of a studio.

I looked in my phone's contact list. Yes, I had phone numbers for both Amber and Brianna, the two young Shiffley women who helped out at the shelter. I knew Amber better, but I decided to call Brianna. Amber was a very skilled Jill-of-all-trades, but Brianna was a licensed electrician. From a family of electricians. That could be useful.

Her phone only rang twice before she answered. Maybe I was in luck, and she was a total night owl.

"Hello—Meg? What's up?" Her tone said, Why the hell are you calling me in the middle of the night? but she was polite.

"I hope I didn't wake you." She sounded pretty awake—if a bit annoyed—but some people went from zero to sixty in the time it took me to figure out which end of the phone was up.

"No, I was up. Whole family's in a tizzy—you heard what happened to Uncle Randall and Uncle Vern, right? I doubt if anyone will get much sleep tonight."

"Please tell me they're not planning to send in more cousins to rescue the ones who've already been captured," I said. "They're probably already running out of room in the Clay County jail."

"Naw—some of the young hotheads wanted to dash right over there, but Aunt Jane raised holy hell and ordered everyone to stand down. It's not setting too well with some of the young hotheads, but nobody disobeys Aunt Jane."

"I want to grow up to be just like your aunt Jane." Thank goodness Judge Jane was laying down the law for her clan. And it occurred to me that Judge Jane was maybe another person I should enlist to help with my scheme. "By the way," I went on, "did you hear that apparently my grandfather led another expedition into Clay County? No idea whether he was planning to rescue Vern and Randall or join forces with them, but he didn't succeed, either, and he got my brother and my father captured with him."

"This is crazy," she said. "You know those creeps are going to keep them locked up as long as they can—and it's only two days till Christmas. We can't let them get away with this."

"I agree." I took a deep breath. "So I was wondering if I could enlist your help for something. Something that I hope will help bring your relatives and mine safely home tomorrow. Something that I hope is a little smarter than what any of the men did. Although if you want to run it by Judge Jane, that's fine with me."

"Aunt Jane generally seems to think you have a pretty level head on your shoulders," Brianna said. "What do you need?"

"Off-the-wall question, but do you think there's any way you could get hold of a Dominion Energy truck? Or even something that could be mistaken for one?"

A slight pause.

"Yeah, pretty sure I can," she said. "My brother Brady works for them, and he's pretty careless with his keys. I could bring along Brady, too, if you like."

"No, we're making this a testosterone-free project."

Brianna giggled at that.

"If you have to give a reason why, say it's women's shelter business," I went on. "So borrow if you can, steal if you must, but show up at the Caerphilly Zoo as soon as possible in some kind of Dominion Energy vehicle."

"You mean like right now?"

"Like five minutes ago if possible."

"Okay, cool," she said.

"One more thing," I said. "If I showed you some equipment that needed a portable generator to power it, could you get it running?"

"You need a generator?"

"No, I have one of those, but I could use someone who knows which end of it is up."

"No problem. I rebuilt a generator when I was eleven or twelve. Running one's a piece of cake. Anything else?"

"Not that I can think of. Thanks."

"No problem. Sounds like this is going to be fun!"

Nice that someone was so enthusiastic about our project. I took a deep breath, marshaled my mental resources, and called Judge Jane.

"Tell me you have good news," was how she answered the phone.

"I wish," I said.

"Half my family wants to run over to Clay County and get themselves thrown in jail."

"The half with Y chromosomes?"

"Pretty much. I used to think Randall was the one man in the family smart enough to think with his brain most of the time, and then he goes and joins the craziness."

"In Randall's defense, he chased after the others to try and talk them out of invading Clay County," I said.

"I'm sure that will be a comfort to us while he's away serving time for whatever phony charges the Dingles manage to pin on him. Sorry, Meg; you find me in a rotten mood. The county attorney has taken up residence in my study, so if she and the chief can come up with any valid warrants that will do them any good I can run in and sign them. I'm calling anyone I know who might have any clout with any government agency that might possibly step in and do something, and the chief is tearing what's left of his hair out. What can I do for you?"

"Can you keep a secret?"

"I'd be a pretty piss-poor judge if I couldn't."

"I know you're doing what you can to help Chief Burke get the Feds involved in what's going on in Clay County. But I also know that the crooked Fed he's been dealing with has made that an uphill battle, and that in the meantime your relatives and mine are stuck over there in the Clay County jail."

"Please don't tell me you're planning on dashing over there all by yourself to rescue them," she said. "Because I know you're smarter than that."

"That was my first thought," I said. "But yeah, I'm smart enough that it didn't take me too long to realize it was a stupid idea."

"Good."

"So I'm not dashing over there all by myself," I said. "I'm taking as many other women as I can—and only women. I figure we're less likely to rile the Dingles up to the point that they get stupid and vindictive. And we won't necessarily be trying to rescue anybody. We're just going to create a distraction, maybe shine a little light on what's going on in Clay County. Pretty much doing everything we can to buy as much time as possible until the chief can get the Feds to take action. Of course if our presence causes the Dingles to repent and let their prisoners free, I won't complain."

A pause.

"If anyone can pull it off, you can," she said. "What do you need me for?"

"Do what you can to keep the chief in the dark until we're underway," I said. "And in case he gets wind that something's up, anything you can do to make him think it's just more women's shelter business would help."

"No problem."

"And can you help round up the Presbyterian women?" Shiffleys who were churchgoers tended to belong to First Presbyterian, and Judge Jane was an elder there.

"I can try," she said. "You mean all of them? Just what are you planning to do to those wretches in Clay County—or do I want to know?"

"Send anyone who can carry a tune, or thinks she can," I said. "Don't tell the chief, but Minerva and the Baptist ladies are already on board. We're going to Christmas carol Clay County into submission."

When she stopped laughing, she promised to round up as many Presbyterian ladies as she could find.

I let out the breath I'd been holding. Maybe this was going to work.

Time for me to head out to the zoo.

I went up and changed into clean, warm clothes. Not all black, though, like Grandfather's party. I wondered, for a few moments, what he and Dad and Rob and the rest were doing.

And then I shoved the thought out of my mind, changed into jeans and a comfortable old sweatshirt, and hurried downstairs.

I was feeling a little blue as I started up the Twinmobile—technically the Twinmobile II, since we'd recently replaced the sturdy minivan we'd bought just before the twins' arrival with a newer edition of the same model. Would the Twinmobile join the growing collection of Caerphilly vehicles languishing in some Clay County junkyard? Worse, would its innards soon find their way to the gray market for automotive parts, joining the scattered pieces of my ancient Honda and the Shiffleys' trucks? Was I worrying about cars to keep myself from dwelling on how the prisoners might be suffering? I suspected the Clay County jail was neither modern nor comfortable.

I hoped not to find out for myself.

After starting the engine, I paused long enough to take a few deep, calming breaths. They didn't seem to help much, but what did help was the sight of the house in all its holiday finery. This year Mother had gone in for thousands of white fairy lights, outlining all the architectural features of the house and the shape of the hedge and all the shrubbery. And it wasn't just the house—the barn, the llama shelter, and all the assorted sheds that filled the yard were also outlined in light. Even the fences that surround our several acres carried a strand of lights. All very modern LED lights, Mother had assured us, so the cost of operating them was almost nonexistent. Suddenly it all felt very peaceful and welcoming.

For a moment, I found myself wanting to go back inside. To take refuge in the gaily decorated living room, make a big fire with aromatic fir and cedar logs, turn on the system that played soft carols through hidden speakers, and forget about Clay County and the Dingles.

And then I put the Twinmobile in reverse, backed out of the driveway, and drove away, trying not to look back. I'd have to earn my Christmas festivities this year.

I wasn't going to let Clay County ruin anyone's Christmas. Not mine, not Mother's, not Delaney's, not Janet and Lark's. The odds were probably against the Dingles seeing the light like Scrooge and the Grinch—and didn't even miserable old Mr. Potter reform at the end of *It's a Wonderful Life*? I wasn't sure of that last one. But even if the Dingles remained unreconstructed, we'd show them a thing or two.

Chapter 31

I was the first one to arrive at the zoo. I briefed the security guards on duty with our cover story about an emergency meeting of the women's shelter board. If the women's shelter hadn't existed, we'd have had to invent something like it for tonight's project.

When I got to Grandfather's office, I realized it was only 3:00 A.M. Time enough for me to take at least a brief nap before my troops began arriving. Or at least lie down and rest—I'd probably be too wired to sleep. So I cleared several piles of papers and the skull of some animal with very sharp teeth off Grandfather's sofa, grabbed a rather ratty overcoat from the coat rack, and settled down.

I was fast asleep when someone rang the doorbell downstairs.

I leaped off the sofa and scrambled over to Grandfather's desk, where a small monitor let me see who was at the gate, I saw Brianna Shiffley's face as she pressed the intercom button.

"Reporting as ordered with the semi-hot Dominion truck."

"I'll be right down," I called back. There was a button somewhere I could have used to buzz her in, but I'd still have to show her the way to the Admin building. And besides, I wanted to see the truck.

When I opened the "staff only" door, I realized what she'd brought wasn't just a truck—it was a full-sized repair vehicle, complete with a bucket lift. The familiar blue

Dominion Energy logo gleamed on the white paint of its door and body.

"Awesome!" I exclaimed. For once, the boys' favorite adjective seemed like an understatement.

"I figured maybe the bucket lift might come in handy."

"It very well might," I said. "I don't know how yet, but our plans are still evolving."

We stood admiring her prize for a few moments.

"I also lifted a couple of Dominion uniforms," she added. "As long as I was there. I figured they also might come in handy. They're in the passenger seat."

"You are a coconspirator with class," I said.

"So I assume we're going to sneak into Clay County posing as a power line repair crew."

"That's the plan," I said. "I figure right now they're going to be a little hyper about strangers coming into town. But given all the snow, there could be outages. Even if someone who spots the truck still has power, they'll probably assume we're on our way to someone less fortunate."

"It'd be even better if they had a real power outage," she said. "Add veri-whatsit to our scenario."

"Verisimilitude," I said. "Yeah. But we can't expect miracles."

"Wouldn't take a miracle," she said. "Just a little old pine tree dropping on the lines. The supply line for all of Clay County runs through the woods no more than half a mile from here—why don't I just run out and take care of it?"

"Why not?" I said. After all, if real Dominion repairmen showed up in Clay County, it would only help our plans.

Brianna sprinted back to the truck and opened up the passenger-side door. After a little rummaging, she emerged holding safety goggles, work gloves, and a gasoline-powered chainsaw.

"Don't leave without me," she said. "Unless you absolutely have to, in which case, hang on to this."

She tossed me a set of keys, and sprinted off toward the woods.

I pocketed the keys and went inside. But just inside the gate—not inside the building. Other arrivals should be following on Brianna's heels.

Sure enough, a few minutes later a nondescript white panel truck drove up with Ekaterina at the wheel and Janet in the passenger seat. Both of them were in what I recognized as the kind of uniforms that the Caerphilly Inn maintenance workers wore. They weren't identical to the uniforms I'd seen on Dominion repair crews, but close enough that they'd probably serve our purposes.

"This will work?" Ekaterina asked. No doubt she'd noticed the scrutiny I'd given her and the truck.

"Perfectly," I said. "If you tag along behind the Dominion truck, they probably won't notice yours doesn't have the markings."

"Ah, but it will." Ekaterina held up a spray-paint can. "Is a shade of blue we use behind the scenes at the Inn. Very close to the official Dominion Energy blue. And if I can use a computer, Delaney will send me a template to use. Is there someplace where we can do the painting out of sight of any unfriendly eyes?"

I opened the large gate so she could pull the truck into the little courtyard, escorted them to Grandfather's office, and set Ekaterina up with a computer.

"Have you reached Rachel?" I asked Janet.

"Yes. If we come to the back door of the Burger Barn, she'll let us in. She doesn't promise she'll stay if things get crazy—she's packing her car, and one way or another she's leaving Clay County tonight. But she'll let us in."

"That's all we need."

By the time I returned to the gate, Caroline and Cordelia had arrived.

"I figured you'd need me here a bit early to organize the video equipment," Caroline said.

"What else needs doing?" Cordelia asked.

"Can you let in the arriving troops and have them gather in the lecture hall?"

"Can do," she said. "I hear someone coming right now.

I also heard the sound of engines. We all peered out. Two vehicles were crossing the parking lot. One looked as if it had been driven out of a time warp—it was a vintage Volkswagen bus painted in a predominantly pink-and-purple paisley pattern. I suspected that it probably belonged to one of Rose Noire's fellow retreat members. The other vehicle could also have emerged from a time warp, although it would have to be one pointed at an even earlier era. It was an old-fashioned slat-sided livestock truck that looked ancient enough for the Joad family to have ridden in it on their way out of Oklahoma in the Dust Bowl days. When I first spotted the truck, I thought it was, for some reason, filled with snow. When it parked near the staff entrance, I realized that the fluffy whiteness I could see between the slats wasn't snow. It was sheep. At least two dozen of them.

"Meg!" Rose Noire leaped out of the passenger side of the Volkswagen. "Everyone in the retreat group wants to come along!"

"Do they realize it could be dangerous?" I asked.

"I've been marching in demonstrations since Birmingham and Selma." A tall, rangy woman in jeans and a purple quilted jacket, with a wild mane of iron-gray hair, was getting out of the driver's seat of the Volkswagen. "I survived Bull Connor's bully boys—I'm not afraid to face your local thugs."

"This is more of a rescue mission," I explained.

"But a nonviolent one, from what Rose Noire told us," she said. "And for a good cause."

"Mona has a lot of experience with conflict de-escalation and resolution," Rose Noire said. "And the rest of us brought along some herbs that we think will help manage the situation."

Of course. Because herbs were the answer to just about any problem, to hear Rose Noire tell it. Still, a group of militantly nonviolent New Age herbalists should add to the effect I was hoping we'd create.

I was less sure what the contents of the other vehicle would add.

"What's with the sheep?" I asked. "They're not members of your retreat group, are they? Or do you plan to give shearing and spinning demonstrations between choruses of 'We Shall Overcome'?"

"I borrowed them from Seth Early," Rose Noire said. "I think they'll help with the ambience. I mean, look at those calm, peaceful faces. Who could see those faces and still have an angry, violent thought?"

I could, quite easily. That was probably because Seth Early's sheep regularly invaded our house to graze on our curtains, deposit sheep droppings on our rugs, and drink from our toilets like oversized cats.

"Does Seth know you're taking them to Clay County?" I asked. "And what if they wander off over there? It could take them a while to get home."

"Oh, didn't I tell you? This summer I talked Seth into attaching those cute little tracking devices to all his sheep. That means it will be much easier to keep track of them."

It occurred to me that it also meant that Seth was now able to figure out when his sheep strayed across the road and onto our property, so if they lingered overly long it meant he was relying on us to deliver them back, rather than fetching them himself. I'd keep that in mind.

"As long as he's okay with it," I said aloud.

I was starting to have some ideas on how we could make use of the sheep.

"You know, that's not a bad idea," Caroline said. "Animals will make a nice addition to the chaos."

"Don't you mean festivities?" I asked.

"That too. I think I'll round up a few from the zoo. And arrange for a truck to haul them over."

She hurried off.

"Not the wolves," I called after her.

"Surely she wouldn't even think of bringing the wolves," Cordelia said. "Not with so many sheep about."

"She might have a sentimental moment and remember how fond Grandfather is of wolves," I said. "Sometimes he's a bad influence."

"Sometimes? I'll go along and make sure she chooses relatively harmless animals." Cordelia strode off in the direction Caroline had taken.

"And can you get her to bring down the video equipment first?"

"Of course," she called over her shoulder.

"While Cordelia's doing that, could you mind the gate?" I asked Rose Noire. "Send any new arrivals to the lecture hall?"

"Of course."

More people arrived. Caroline returned and unearthed the video equipment. Devon and Annika, Michael's two grad students, arrived and fell upon the equipment with enthusiasm. I gathered what Grandfather had bought for himself was a lot nicer than what the college had provided for the students to use. I vowed that when we got him back safe and sound with their help I'd make him donate some state-of-the-art equipment to the department. He'd probably protest that he'd already given the drama department a very nice new building, and I'd point out that he'd probably still be in the slammer without Devon and Annika.

Brianna returned from her sabotage mission. Ekaterina and Janet finished stenciling the Dominion logo onto the white van. It probably wouldn't fool a real Dominion employee, but with luck no one in now powerless Clay County would look too critically at an arriving repair truck. They'd even stenciled logos on a half-dozen white hardhats for those of us who would be masquerading as repairmen.

I checked my watch: 6:00 A.M. Time for my advance party to take off. I gathered them in the courtyard: Brianna driving the real Dominion repair truck with me riding shotgun, both of us in Dominion uniforms; Ekaterina driving the fake Dominion panel truck with Janet riding shotgun, both in generic maintenance uniforms; Devon and Annika in the back of the panel truck with the video equipment. Janet and I were both armed with shortwave radios, as were Delaney, now ensconced in Grandfather's office with several extra computers, and Caroline and Cordelia, whom I was leaving in charge of supervising the gathering crowd here at the zoo.

"Wish us luck," I told them as I stepped into the repair truck cab.

"We'll be coming to join you before you know it," Cordelia said.

We were only a mile down the road when my shortwave radio erupted into life.

Chapter 32

"Blue team leader," the radio sputtered. "This is blue home base—do you copy?"

I recognized Delaney's voice.

"Blue team leader here," I replied.

"Can someone drop off a few cases of paintballs? Because Jack forgot to bring any, and there's no way we can defend the fort with no ammo."

Since there was always the possibility that our adversaries could intercept our shortwave transmissions, we'd agreed to pretend that we were participants in a giant paintball game. Still, I wasn't sure why she'd chosen now to start creating this illusion.

"Roger," I said.

"And we've figured out what radio frequency the Yellows are using. Will let you know if we pick up anything useful."

"Good." Presumably that meant she'd figured out how to listen in on the Clay County Sheriff's Department's radio transmissions. That could indeed be useful.

A text arrived in my phone. I glanced down at it. A series of numbers—the radio frequency, I assumed. Good to have, though I had no idea when or how I'd use it. But reassuring to know Delaney and her cyber corps were monitoring it.

We were approaching the county line. If I were driving, I'd have been tempted to pause or at least slow down a little as we neared the WELCOME TO CLAY COUNTY sign, and try to think of something suitably momentous to say to mark the occasion. "The die is cast." "This was their finest hour." Whatever. Brianna just kept the big rig lumbering steadily along.

Though she did point out the Clay County Sheriff's Department cruiser parked in a side road just inside the county line.

"Looks like they're guarding the borders," she said.

For the next few minutes, I kept my eyes glued to the side mirror, and I suspect Brianna spent as much time glancing in the rearview mirror as at the road ahead. But nothing happened. No sirens splitting the night. No flashing lights looming up behind us.

"Guess we fooled them so far," she said.

Never had the road to Clayville seemed so endless. Brianna drove the hulking repair truck with practiced ease. I kept my hardhat pulled low over my eyes and tried to maintain the calm, resolute demeanor of a leader who had no doubts about the success of her mission. I also kept a map of Clay County propped on the dash in front of me—an honest-to-God old-fashioned paper map, which had taken some finding, but I assumed any Dominion worker who'd ever ventured into Clay County would be well aware of how useless a GPS device would be in its more remote corners.

"Outskirts of town," Brianna said finally. "Still looks pretty dark."

In fact, as we drove slowly toward the center of town, we only passed one or two houses with any lights, and those were clearly lanterns or flashlights.

"You'd think more people would have generators," she said.

"Probably not a lot of people awake to start them up when you knocked the power out," I said.

"Yeah." There was enough light in the cab for me to see her grin.

Even the combined sheriff's office and jail only had a few dim lights.

We had arrived at the stoplight in the center of town. It was dark, of course. The only other moving vehicle in sight was Ekaterina's van, directly behind us, but Brianna came to a full stop, the way you're supposed to at a dead stoplight. Always a good idea not to commit minor traffic offenses in Clay County. Stopping also gave us a few extra seconds to reconnoiter. To our left was the Burger Barn. I'd forgotten that it was housed in a run-down two-story building—atypical of Clayville. Not the run-down part—just about everything in Clay County was run down, if not actually falling apart. But land was so cheap that most people found it more economical to expand horizontally rather than vertically. There were very few two-story buildings. Even the jail was only one story. The Burger Barn also had a six-foot false front at the top, along the street side of the building, with the restaurant's name rather sloppily painted on it. This could be useful.

"Hang a left," I said. "And then another left into the parking lot behind the Burger Barn."

Once in the parking lot, we pulled the vehicles close to the restaurant's back door in a formation we'd hoped would be possible, with the real Dominion truck on the outside, screening the panel truck as much as possible from view. Brianna popped the repair truck's hood and went to peer into it. Ekaterina grabbed a small automotive toolkit and joined her, thus completing—I hoped—the illusion of two power company drivers conferring over an engine problem.

The back door of the restaurant opened a crack and Rachel peered out. She opened it wider when she saw that Janet was with us.

Devon and Annika and I began quickly hauling the equipment from the panel truck into the restaurant. After a brief and slightly tearful reunion, Janet and Rachel pitched in as well.

When we'd finished unloading, I glanced over to see that Ekaterina and Brianna appeared to have completely disassembled the real Dominion truck's engine, scattering parts in a wide delta around the cab of the truck.

"Um . . . do you think you could put the engine back together pretty soon?" I asked them in an undertone. "Because while our plans don't necessarily call for making a quick escape in the trucks, it would be nice if we could do it if we had to."

"Do not distress yourself," Ekaterina said. "These parts are not essential to the operation of the vehicle."

"Seriously? Because it looks to me as if you've taken out the spark plugs and the battery and the radiator hose, and that's just the parts I recognize."

"Ah, but we did not remove those parts from this truck." Ekaterina looked triumphant. "These are decoy truck parts I brought along just in case. If anyone is observing us, these will create the false impression that we are immobile."

Sometimes I actually believed Ekaterina when she claimed that her father had been a Russian spy for the CIA.

"Great idea," I said. "Can you stay here and keep a lookout while maintaining the illusion that you're trying to solve the engine problem?"

"Of course."

"Brianna, they could use your help getting the video stuff set up."

She nodded and strode inside.

I pretended to be watching Ekaterina's engine tinkering, while actually scanning our surroundings. No one seemed to be stirring. Of course, it was only just beginning to get light.

I strolled inside and found myself in the Burger Barn's

kitchen. Most of the video equipment had vanished, except for two metal cases that Annika and Devon were hoisting. Brianna and Janet were nowhere to be seen. Rachel seemed to be directing traffic.

"Where's the rest of the stuff?" I asked.

"Upstairs," Rachel said. "It's just storage up there, and not very full, so we thought that would be a good place to set up the cameras."

"Better camera angle," Devon said.

"And we're going to put the antenna on the roof," Annika added.

"We can hide it behind the Burger Barn sign," Devon said.

Exactly what I would have suggested. I left them to it, and they trudged upstairs, leaving Rachel and me in the kitchen. Not a pleasant place to be—it was so cramped I wondered how even a single cook could manage to work in it and so filthy that I was glad I'd never had any reason to consume food at the Burger Barn. I tried not to show my reaction—for all I knew, cleaning the kitchen was one of Rachel's job responsibilities—but my face gave me away.

"I know—it's a pig sty, isn't it?" she said. "I offered to clean it once, and Rocky wouldn't let me—said he didn't want anyone else messing with his work space. Just serving the slop he churns out in here makes me worry that I could get arrested as an accessory to murder. And it's not as if any of it tastes good enough to risk dying for. I'll be glad to get out of this dump. And by dump I don't just mean the barn; I mean the whole county."

"Where are you going?"

"Dunno. Maybe Richmond. Or maybe D.C. I was saving up money to go to college—I'll probably end up spending it all to make a new start somewhere else, but it'll be worth it."

"Come to Caerphilly," I said. "Everyone there will be grateful to you for helping us out—we can work on finding you a job and a place to stay."

"I'll think about it."

I opened the door from the kitchen to the public part of the restaurant and peered out. At the far end of the room, two large, old-fashioned bay windows flanked the double doors to the street. Although the windows ran nearly to the twelve-foot ceiling, they didn't let in much light—window shades were pulled down over the top two-thirds of each window, and the café curtains that screened the bottom third were drawn. Still, there was a gap between the bottom of the blinds and the top of the curtains, so some light crept in—mostly moonlight reflecting off the snow. And someone could peer in, so I slipped along one side of the dim space, brushing against the outside edges of the booths. I remembered one time when I'd stopped in here for a cool drink on a sweltering August day. I'd thought that the vintage vinyl banquettes, liberally mended with duct tape, and the chipped Formica tables had a certain seedy charm. But even without seeing the kitchen I'd been wary of trying the food.

I reached the front window and ducked down below the level of the café curtains. They'd have added a homey touch to the place if anyone had washed them within living memory, or even given them a good shake to remove some of the dust. If I owned the place, I'd also have cleaned out the impressive collection of dead insects that littered the window ledge and replaced the mummified potted plants with living ones.

But most of all I'd have put up a few Christmas decorations. Was I just overlooking them in the dark? No. With the exception of a small half-dead poinsettia near the cash register, the Burger Barn showed no signs that anyone was celebrating the holiday season. No lights in the window. No wreaths or candles. No nativity scene. Not even a cutesy plastic Rudolph with a light-up nose.

In fact, as I peered around the town square, I realized the same could be said of every building here in the center of town. Granted, taking out their power would have darkened any Christmas lights people had strung up—but I should still be able to see the glass of the bulbs glittering in the moonlight. I didn't spot any. I counted exactly one door wreath within sight.

"They really do need a transfusion of Christmas spirit," I muttered to myself.

And then I reminded myself to focus. I hadn't crept to this observation point to pass judgment on the Clayville citizens' lack of Christmas spirit. I needed to scout out what was happening across the street at the jail.

And at the moment, not much was happening. Reassuring. I nodded with satisfaction as I scanned the building's old-fashioned red brick exterior. I estimated that it had been built in the 1930s, and it would have looked rather charming if they'd done any repairs or painting in the last fifty or sixty years. Or maybe I only found it charming because the dim light inside reassured me that the power was still out in Clayville. Along the street in front of the jail was a row of angled parking spaces, all but two empty. A pair of Clay County Sheriff's Department cruisers sat side by side near the right end. They probably belonged to the deputies on duty inside. Most of the spaces had signs. Two VISITOR signs at the far right, beyond the deputies' cars. A handicapped space at the far left. The rest were marked DEPUTY, except for the middle one, directly in front of the door, whose oversized sign said SHERIFF.

Well, that should make it easy to notice when Sheriff Dingle arrived.

Next door to the jail was the county office building, a squat, utilitarian one-story cinder-block structure. It probably didn't have to be very big if, as rumor had it, most of the real business of governing happened down the street at the Clay Pigeon, the sleazy bar whose owner also operated the Clayville Shooting Range next door. And what did it say about a town when their jail was almost as large and a great deal prettier than the building that housed their mayor's office?

Where was everyone? Surely somewhere Mayor Dingle and Sheriff Dingle and their minions must be making plans to deal with the sudden epidemic of prisoners in their jail?

Maybe they were—in some back room at the Clay Pigeon, perhaps. Out here on the street, not a creature was stirring.

I heard the kitchen door open.

Chapter 33

I congratulated myself on not starting at the sound of the door. Rachel slipped through it and made her careful way to my side.

"Brianna says they've got proof of concept on the video transmission, whatever that is," she whispered. "What's this all about—are you planning to broadcast whatever you're doing?"

"That's the plan. Where's the courtroom, anyway?"

"Back of the county office building."

"Next door to the jail. Convenient. Can you keep watch here and let me know if you see any signs of activity? At either building?"

"Sure." She pulled over a vintage metal diner chair and sat down in the shadows, eyes scanning the street outside.

I crept back into the kitchen.

"Check this out." Brianna handed me a laptop. "Careful—it's tethered to the wall with an Ethernet cable." Her tone seemed to suggest that this was an annoying if quaint eccentricity, rather like writing with a quill pen. "The Barn's owner doesn't hold with newfangled gadgets like wireless. I guess we should be glad he's got internet at all."

I moved to where I could hold the laptop without disconnecting it and looked at the screen. It showed the front of the jail. From the angle, I deduced that they'd put the camera upstairs, as planned.

Then the view shifted. This new view was from slightly to the left, and a little higher up.

"The roof?" I guessed.

"No—the Dominion truck's bucket lift. We taped a camera to it and hoisted it up. Also, Ekaterina's picked out a couple of likely spots where she can fly up the drones later, but we don't want to do that until there's enough ambient noise to cover the sound, or at least distract from it."

"Drones?"

"Yeah, she figures if they seize our cameras upstairs and in the bucket lift, we can still get some shots from the drones."

Clearly I had made the right decision when I recruited Ekaterina for the mission. Maybe I should have put her in charge.

"But we're not webcasting this, right?" I asked. "I mean not yet. We don't really want to tip our hand until the crowd gets here."

"It's on a password-protected site for now. We can make it public as soon as the buses are in sight. And Delaney's rounding up a massive network of people to push it out on Twitter and Facebook and whatever other social media seem useful."

"Excellent," I said. "Then we're as ready as we'll ever be. Any word from the zoo?"

"Caroline texted," Brianna said. "Maybe five minutes ago? She said Operation Overlord is in motion. With three exclamation marks, so I assume that's good news. Does it mean something to you?"

"Operation Overlord was the code name for the Battle of Normandy," I said. "As in D-Day. So yeah, I assume it means the rest of our troops are on their way."

"Good."

What was not so good is that now we'd have to wait—how long? Twenty minutes, maybe, if Caroline had texted when they were already on their way. More like half an hour if she was merely announcing that they'd started loading. And I could already tell that thirty minutes here would feel like thirty hours.

Rachel slipped back into the kitchen.

"You might want to see this," she said, pointing behind her.

Brianna and I followed her back to the bay windows.

Two more vehicles had arrived at the jail. Another police car—a much newer-looking one—had arrived and parked in the sheriff's space.

Sitting beside it in one of the deputy spaces was a pickup truck whose bed was filled with red plastic gasoline cans.

"What do you suppose they're doing with that?" Brianna asked.

"No idea," Rachel said. "But it can't be good."

"Find out how much longer till the first bus gets here," I said.

Brianna dashed back to the kitchen.

"I don't like this," Rachel muttered.

I didn't either. I wasn't sure what the Dingles could possibly be planning with several dozen gallons of gasoline, but I couldn't like the look of it.

Another sedan pulled up and parked in one of the deputy slots. Mayor Dingle got out and walked quickly into the building.

The door to the kitchen opened.

"Fifteen minutes at the earliest," Brianna said.

A deputy came out of the building, grabbed a pair of red gas containers, and carried them into the building.

"They could be up to something," I said. "No idea what. I hope our diversion doesn't arrive too late. Delaney's recording all this, right?"

"Yup, every frame," Brianna said.

"Tell her to go live as soon as the first bus appears."

"Why can't you tell her?" Brianna sounded suspicious.

"Because I'm going over there to figure out what they're up to," I said. "And if necessary, create a mini diversion until the big one arrives."

I went through the kitchen, out the back door, and over to where Ekaterina and Janet appeared to be discussing the Dominion truck's engine.

"This does not look good," Ekaterina said. She nodded at a tiny monitor on which I could see what I gathered was the picture from the camera over our heads in the bucket.

"I'm going in to distract them." I took off my fake Dominion hard hat and tossed it into the cab of the truck. They'd figure out how we'd sneaked in soon enough—no need to give them a clue.

"Would you like me to accompany you?" Ekaterina asked. "Strength in numbers."

"I'd rather have you out here, keeping an eye on things," I said. "If anything happens to me, you're hereby in charge. If anything . . . bad seems to be happening, improvise something."

"You may rely on me."

Yes, I could.

I decided to approach the police station from the other side, so I ran along the back of the building beside the Burger Barn, and then the one beside that, until I reached an alley. I half ran to the mouth of the alley. Then I stopped, took a deep breath, and peered out into the street.

I could see the deputy disappearing into the building with another pair of gas cans.

Show time.

I stepped out of the alley and headed straight for the door of the station, setting a pace that I hoped looked reasonably nonchalant while covering ground efficiently.

The deputy reemerged from the door just as I started

up the steps. He stopped dead in his tracks and stood staring at me.

"Good morning," I said. "And Merry Christmas."

Any of Chief Burke's officers, man or woman, would have put down the box they were carrying to open the door for an arriving member of the public. This deputy—Deputy B. Peebles, by his name tag—just stared.

The deputy at the front desk—D. Plunket—looked equally surprised. Sheriff Dingle and Mayor Dingle, who were standing near the desk, looked not just surprised but downright unwelcoming. I pretended not to notice them. It was fairly easy to pull that off since the room had no lights other than a few camping lanterns scattered here and there.

Deputy Plunket didn't react to my greeting any more warmly than his colleague.

"What are you doing here?" he blurted out.

Luckily while crossing the street I'd thought of an answer to that question.

"I came to report a stolen vehicle," I said. "At least I originally thought it was stolen, but from what Chief Burke tells me it's possible that it was merely towed by mistake. So maybe I should have said I need to reclaim a towed vehicle. I was hoping you'd be able to help me figure out which."

I smiled what I thought was the harmless smile of someone confidently expecting help from the forces of law and order. Deputy Plunket just stared at me. Clearly the entire Clay County force could benefit from some remedial training in customer service.

"Let me handle this, Darnell," Sheriff Dingle said. "So what can we do for you, Ms. Langslow?"

So he knew who I was. Probably to be expected, but still—creepy.

"My car's missing." I rattled off the make, model, year,

and license plate number. It would have been nice if he'd even pretended to be taking notes, but Dingles weren't noted for niceness.

"How come you came all the way over here to report it?" he asked. "Your car wouldn't be here—unless you've been visiting my county without my knowing it?"

"I didn't know it required a visa." I bit back several even sharper things that occurred to me and told myself to chill. Getting them mad wouldn't help. "Actually, I may have been visiting your county without knowing it myself. I drove out into the woods yesterday to find Randall Shiffley, and I found the place where his truck was parked. At least I assumed it was his truck—I have to admit, one pickup looks pretty much the same as another to me. Or one car, for that matter."

All three of them were looking as if they thought I'd lost my mind. Maybe I had. But I didn't need to make sense—I just had to keep talking until the big diversion arrived. I leaned against the counter and tried to adopt the body language of someone who had absolutely nothing better to do with her morning than tell a long, convoluted tale.

"Anyway," I went on, "I waited there awhile, and then I thought I'd poke around and see if I could find him—which turned out to be a pretty stupid idea, because I'm not much of a tracker. My sons have been learning about it in Scouts, and they've been trying to teach me about it, but I think I need a lot more practice. Or maybe there's a knack, and I don't have it. When I finally found my way back out of the woods to the road where I'd parked, my car was gone. I had to walk to the zoo, and someone there told me they'd seen a tow truck go by hauling my car away."

"What makes you think it's here in Clay County?" the sheriff asked.

"Well, neither Osgood Shiffley nor his cousin Wilmot has it," I said. "And they own the only tow trucks in Caerphilly. So Chief Burke asked if I was sure I hadn't crossed over into Clay County while looking for Randall. I didn't think so, but who knows? Maybe I did and whoever tows for your county thought it was an abandoned vehicle and hauled it off by mistake. I came over so I could report it and get your help figuring out if it's over here."

I assumed the expression of someone who was confident that she has explained everything perfectly and could now expect to have all her problems resolved.

The two Dingles, sheriff and mayor, exchanged a look. Deputy B. Peebles peered in the front door, with a questioning look on his face. I wasn't sure, but I thought I could see two more red gas cans in his hands. Mayor Dingle waved him away.

"How come you were looking for Randall Shiffley in Clay County?" the sheriff asked.

"Well, was I? I thought I was looking for him in Caerphilly County," I said. "But it was out by the zoo—that's near the county line. Maybe I wandered over the line by mistake and the truck I thought was Randall's was someone else's."

"I mean what was Randall doing wandering in the woods near the county line?"

Obviously he already knew what Randall had been doing. But it was probably a bad idea for me to bring it up. Inspiration struck.

"Looking for my grandfather," I said. "He—Grandfather, that is, not Randall—was leading some people on a nature walk in the woods near the zoo and hasn't come home yet, so Randall and some of his cousins went out to rescue them. Say, you haven't seen any of them, have you? The reason I'm so much in a hurry to find my car is that I want to drive around and help look for them. It'd be great if some of your deputies could have a look around for Grandfather. I can give you a description: he's—"

"You think your grandfather and his nature walk might have wandered across the county line by mistake?" I could tell by the slight look on the sheriff's face that he thought it was pretty funny, asking me that when he knew all the time where Grandfather was.

And what was that noise I was hearing outside. Could it be—?

"He once came close to walking off a cliff because he was staring up in the sky at some rare bird," I said aloud. "I don't think he'd even notice a mere county line. I mean, it's not as if there's anything to mark the county line if you're not on one of the main roads."

Sheriff Dingle glanced at the mayor as if asking a question.

"Well, little lady," the mayor began.

Deputy B. Peebles burst into the room.

"There's something kind of weird going on out here," he said. "I think you should come and see this."

Mayor Dingle and Sheriff Dingle looked at each other, then turned to follow the deputy back out. But just as he opened the door for them—

"JOY TO THE WORLD! THE LORD IS COME!"

Christmas had arrived in Clay County.

Chapter 34

Both Dingles rushed outside to stand staring at the spectacle taking place in front of their jail. Deputy Plunket walked to the double front doors and peered out. I joined him.

Six buses had arrived and were discharging their passengers on one side of the street or the other. Only a few of the passengers had emerged from the buses, but they were all singing at the top of their lungs. As they disembarked, they were arranging themselves in a semicircle in front of the jail and the county office building, singing all the while. The far greater number still sitting in the buses had opened the windows so we could hear their singing better. Even the women climbing down the buses' stairways sang all the way.

"LET EVERY HEART PREPARE HIM ROOM!"

Two of the buses were the special purple-and-gold ones used to transport the New Life Baptist Choir. Another was the one from First Presbyterian—thank you, Judge Jane. The remaining three were Caerphilly County school buses, which seemed to be what Mother and Robyn had rounded up to transport the ladies of St. Clotilda's Guild.

Beyond the buses I could see a flock of smaller vehicles. The pink-and-purple paisley Volkswagen bus was there, and Seth Early's sheep truck. Also two trucks from the zoo. I hoped Cordelia had been successful in convincing Caroline to leave the wolves at home.

"AND HEAVEN AND NATURE SING!

"AND HEAVEN AND NATURE SING!"

I decided to make sure my presence in the police station was known to the rest of the world, so if I disappeared they'd know where to start looking. With that in mind, I followed the Dingles out onto the wide concrete landing at the top of the jail steps. They glanced at me and hurriedly moved to the far right side of the landing, as if fearful that I'd overhear what they were saying.

Some of the singers waved to me. I waved back cheerfully.

I spotted Mother floating through the crowd. She appeared to have just arrived, which would have meant she didn't come on any of the buses. Not surprising—the idea of Mother on a bus was rather hard to imagine. Two of my younger women cousins were trailing along after her carrying what looked like a stretcher. What was that for? Surely she wasn't anticipating casualties, was she?

The cousins reached a spot near the center of the gathering choir and, under Mother's direction, they unfurled a large banner that read MERRY CHRISTMAS, CLAY COUNTY!

Two more cousins hurried up carrying stands in which the poles holding the banner could be planted, and then all four cousins breathed a sigh of relief—obviously both pole and stands were heavy—and joined the singing multitudes.

I looked past the singers to see how the locals were reacting. A few people were standing on the sidewalk or peering out the doors or windows of nearby buildings. They didn't look hostile. A little bewildered, some of them, but mostly curious or even friendly.

I thought of walking down the steps and joining the crowd. It would certainly feel more comfortable, being among friends and family. But I also suspected there might be an advantage to going back inside. Maybe I could find a way to communicate with the prisoners, or at least confirm that they were here and okay.

So I took a place just outside the doorway and remained a spectator to the Christmas caroling. "Joy to the World" was followed by "Bring a Torch, Jeanette, Isabella." During "Silent Night," Rose Noire and the rest of the herbalists lit bundles of sage and circumnavigated the choir, smudging all the way. The Presbyterians brought out a set of hand bells and performed "The Holly and the Ivy" on them. Kayla Butler performed a solo on "O Holy Night," which was beautiful, but I wondered what her mother would think. Then again, since the chief's wife was here leading the choir, why not a deputy's daughter doing a solo?

I decided to see what else I could learn inside. I opened the front door. Deputy Plunket frowned as if he wasn't sure he should let me back in.

I walked in anyway.

"Mind if I use your ladies' room?" I asked.

"We don't have a ladies' room." His voice had the petty, triumphant air of someone who enjoys catching the small and meaningless mistakes of others. "We have a plain old one-stall bathroom over there."

He pointed to a door in the far corner of the room. Over the door was a sign that seemed to have been sliced out of a piece of well-weathered driftwood, with the word HEAD burned into it in old English style letters. Charming.

"Thanks." I was tempted to comment on the irony of finding a unisex bathroom in a place as backward as Clay County, but I decided it was better not to annoy them. Not yet, anyway.

I went in, locked the door, and took a deep breath. And then immediately regretted it—clearly no one in the Clay County Sheriff's Department cared much about cleanliness. I gave in to the temptation to wet a paper towel and wipe off any surface I might be about to touch.

The caroling was a little less overwhelming in here, but still easy to hear. They'd started "Good King Wenceslas." Good—that had a lot of verses. I found myself thinking "maybe we've pulled it off," but then I backpedaled. "Don't jinx it," I muttered. The prisoners were still prisoners. We hadn't pulled off anything yet. We just hadn't yet crashed and burned.

Now that it was clean—or at least noticeably less dirty—I used the toilet. Not because I had to all that badly, but in many ways I'd turned into Mother once I had kids of my own. I frequently found myself uttering sentences like "Go while you can, because if you wait until you really need to, there might not be a bathroom nearby." And I usually took my own advice.

As I was washing my hands, my radio crackled into life.

"Meg? You there?" Delaney.

"Yes."

"The other officer went outside. Looks as if you're alone in the station."

Clearly she'd been keeping up with the video of events outside the jail. I left the bathroom and looked around. Deputy Plunket had vanished. The Dingles had not returned.

"Yes, they're all outside watching the performance," I said. "The coast appears to be clear."

"These guys are idiots!" she exclaimed.

"I've probably just done a good job of convincing them that I'm harmless," I said. "I'm sure if they knew me better they'd be in here watching me like hawks."

"No, they really are idiots. Just how stupid *are* these people?"

"Shall I assume that's a rhetorical question, or do you really want me to attempt an answer?"

"I always thought Rob was exaggerating when he told stories about how backward Clay County was," she went on.

"I assumed it was just some long-standing intercounty rivalry turned toxic. In fact, sometimes I thought you guys were all just a little mean, what with some of the things you'd say about Clay County. But oh, my God! You weren't exaggerating!"

"What has brought about this revelation?"

"Apparently at some point they decided it would be kind of cool to have surveillance cameras in the jail cells, so whoever was on duty at the front desk of their police station could watch the prisoners."

"Makes sense." I took a seat in one of the decrepit folding metal chairs that seemed to be Clay County's idea of hospitality for citizens who had to visit the sheriff or the jail. "They have a small department—even smaller than Caerphilly's. The cameras probably let them get by with one deputy on duty here at the jail."

"Oh, I get *why* they did it—no argument there. But they should have gotten someone who knew something about computer security to set it up for them."

"Wait—does this mean you can see into the cells?"

"Yes, and before you ask, they're all fine. Rob, your dad, your grandfather, Dr. Rutledge, Randall Shiffley, two old guys dressed a lot like your grandfather, three guys who look so much like Randall that I assume they're his cousins, and a guy who under the bruises and contusions matches the picture the DMV has for Mark Caverly. None of them look very happy, but they're alive and well."

I breathed a sigh of relief.

"So how did you happen to find these cameras?" I asked aloud.

"Wasn't hard. I take it you don't want the technical explanation, so I won't bore you with stuff like IP addresses."

"Yeah, just give me the version you'd give Rob."

She chuckled at that.

"They set up the cameras so that you can see the pictures

over the Web," she explained. "Maybe the sheriff likes to sit in his den and watch his captives wither away or something. Clearly it never occurred to them that they should maybe install some kind of security. It's just out there for anyone to see."

"And just out of curiosity, what made you look for camera feeds?"

"Ever since you told me what happened to Rob, I've been looking—and had people looking—for any data going into or out of Clay County. There's not a lot of it, actually, so this was pretty easy to find. We also figured out that Deputy Darnell Plunket, the one who's usually on the overnight shift, likes to do video chats with his girlfriend to while away the long, boring hours on desk duty. Pretty lively video chats."

"Oh, good heavens," I said. "Do I really want to hear about this?"

"Probably not," she said. "I wouldn't even be mentioning it except that one of my guys was watching the videos. Supposedly just in case he could glean any useful information from it. Not because he has the emotional maturity of a thirteen-year-old or anything like that. But weirdly, he actually did find something useful. He spotted where Plunket hides his keys. Top left desk drawer. You could actually just go in and open all the cell doors."

I pulled open the drawer. Yes, sure enough, there was a set of keys.

"Tempting," I said. "But getting them out of the cells is only a start. We also have to get them out of Clay County, and even that won't do much good if Clay County claims they're escaped fugitives and makes us give them back. I'm not sure letting them out of the cells is going to help with that."

"Might make them happy, though," she said. "We'll keep snooping around for anything useful. Oh, by the way, I'm recording some video of them moping around in their cells. Pretty boring but it could come in handy. If you do decide to let them out, I can substitute that for the live feed."

"Excellent idea," I said. "I'll let you know."

I stared at the keys for a few seconds, then pushed the drawer closed again.

I went over and peeked out the front door.

More buses had arrived, from the Methodists, the Lutherans, St. Byblig's Catholic Church, and even Temple Beth-El, although I wondered how useful Rabbi Grossman's flock would be at the carol singing. And quite a few people that I assumed were Clay County residents were gathering on the sidewalks and gaping at the spectacle.

No, not just gaping—joining in. Singing.

The combined church choirs were doing a slow, poignant version of "We Three Kings"—well, as poignant as three hundred or more voices raised in joyous harmony could manage—and at the foot of the jail steps Rose Noire and her retreat buddies were doing a sort of interpretive dance, now pretending to be camels traversing afar, now gazing heavenward at the star of royal beauty bright, and ending every verse with what I gathered was supposed to be the three wise men presenting their gifts to the infant Jesus. The fact that the two Dingles had gone back to standing dead center at the top of the steps, right behind where their imaginary manger would have been located, added a delightful note of weirdness to the situation. Clearly neither Dingle could quite grasp what was going on.

Meanwhile, the Dingles in question appeared to be having some kind of not-altogether-friendly discussion. Neither was paying the least bit of attention to what might be happening inside the station.

On impulse I reached out and threw the dead bolt.

"Delaney," I said into the radio. "Do you have enough video recorded to pull off the switch?"

"Think so. I started recording as soon as I found the feed, so I've got at least twenty minutes' worth. It's kind of boring to watch—they move enough to show it's not a still photo, but not much more than that. And I haven't seen any of them do anything really memorable that would stick out if someone were watching, so that's good."

"Switch it over, then," I said. "And let me know when it's done."

"Done. You're going to let them out?"

"It occurs to me that it might be a good idea to have them out of the cells and ready to run if the chance comes." I strode over to the reception desk and grabbed the keys from the drawer.

"Good thinking."

I checked to make sure there weren't any other doors into the reception area. There was one, actually—a side door, with a small, utilitarian window made of chicken wire-reinforced glass. It appeared to be locked on the outside, though easily opened with a push bar from inside. I nodded with satisfaction. I liked having options. From what I could see through the smeared little window, anyone exiting from this door would be in full sight of everyone in the street, including all those gaping locals. But we might be able to do something about that.

I also found what seemed to be a small conference room that had been turned into a storage room. It was full of metal utility shelves, and every single shelf was covered with red plastic gasoline cans. Hundreds of them.

"Good grief." I tried to remember what I'd learned about gasoline safety. The vapor was more dangerous than the liquid gasoline itself—I remembered that much. And neither was dangerous without a spark to set it off. But still—this many gallons. Surely it was a bad thing. And—yikes! One of the cans had sprung a leak. A small puddle peeked out from under one of the metal shelves.

But curiously enough, I couldn't detect the telltale odor of gasoline. But there was a faint odor of . . . alcohol?

I bent down beside the nearest can and unscrewed the top. The fumes made my eyes water. Definitely alcohol, and pretty high proof. Probably the Dingles' equivalent of Everclear. And the red gas cans were their equivalent of Uncle Hiram Shiffley's cobalt blue bottles.

I wiped where I'd touched the gasoline can. If the chief succeeded in sending in the Feds, I didn't want them to find my prints on the moonshine. I took a picture of the storage room. Then I remembered that cell reception in Clay County was almost nonexistent at the best of times. I radioed Delaney.

"Can you get a message to the chief?"

"Sure. What's up?"

"If he ever manages to talk the Feds into making that raid, he might want to tell them that there are several hundred gallons of moonshine stored in the storage room here in the jail in red plastic gasoline cans."

"Roger. I'll tell him." She was giggling. Okay, it was a little funny.

I located the door between the reception area and the jail proper. It took me a few tries to figure out which of the dozen or so keys opened it. When I finally pulled open the door and peered in, I found myself staring down a short corridor with two barred cells on either side. The eleven prisoners were all standing by the bars, peering out, with anxious expressions that suggested that their interactions with the jail personnel had not been entirely pleasant.

"Oh, no!" Rob exclaimed.

"That's a fine way to greet someone who came all this

way to rescue you," I said. "If you're having a wonderful time here I can just go away again."

"I think Rob was assuming the Dingles had captured you the way they did us," Randall said. "But you don't seem to be accompanied by a deputy."

"I knew we could count on Meg!" Dad was almost dancing in place behind the bars of his cell.

"How soon are we leaving?" Grandfather asked. "The accommodations here are lousy, and I bet the breakfast would be inedible."

"I'm going to unlock your cells." I started with the first one on my left, which contained Dad and Grandfather. "But I want you to stay here in the cell block, for the time being. We're not home free yet. Get ready to move on a moment's notice, but stay out of sight."

Chapter 35

"So what's the plan for getting us out?" Randall asked when I'd unlocked all their cells.

"Don't have one yet," I said. "Originally we were just planning to create a distraction until the chief could arrange state or federal intervention."

"Who's 'we'?" Randall asked.

"Distraction from what?" Rob asked.

"And is the chief making any progress?" Vern asked.

"'We' would take too long to explain, and I have no idea how the chief is doing, although I might check on that soon," I said. "Normally, I'd have just sat back and trusted him, but the Dingles have a mole in the ATF who's sabotaging his efforts. And even though you idiots probably deserve to spend Christmas in jail, your families will be a lot happier if we can get you home. And there's also the fact that the Dingles still might have it in for Mr. Caverly. Now that we've been able to get you out of the cells, I'll be working on a plan to get you all the way back to Caerphilly even if the Feds take longer than we'd like. I'd explain at greater length, but I should probably get back out into the reception area, in case Sheriff Dingle figures out I've locked him out of his own jail."

I could tell they wanted to ask a lot more questions, but just then I opened up the door between the cell block and the reception room, and as if on cue, the singers burst into their next number

"DING DONG MERRILY ON HIGH

"IN HEAV'N THE BELLS ARE RINGING!"

"Is that the New Life Baptist choir?" one of Randall's cousins asked.

"Yup," I said. "We've weaponized Christmas carols."

I left the cell block, making sure the connecting door was unlocked. Then I stuffed the keys into my pocket and was about to see what was happening outside when I heard a gentle knock on the side door. Rose Noire was peering through the window.

I went over and opened the door for her.

"What's up?" I asked.

"I thought I'd bring the sheep in here," she said. "If that's okay. They're a bit unsettled with all the noise."

I'd always found Seth Early's sheep to be pretty imperturbable, but far be it from me to second guess Rose Noire, who was so much more in tune with the ovine psyche. So I flung open the door.

"Good dog, Laddie," Rose Noire called.

Apparently she'd borrowed Lad, Seth's Border collie, along with the sheep. With brisk efficiency, he herded the two dozen or so sheep into the reception room. Rose Noire held the door open until Lad had double-checked that his entire flock was present. Then he looked at Rose Noire and gave a brisk bark, as if to say, "So? What are you waiting for, silly human?" Rose Noire closed the door and pushed past the sheep to join me near the main door.

"There—now isn't that much nicer?" Did she mean nicer for the sheep, or was she of the peculiar opinion that the décor of any room would be improved with the addition of a few ruminants?

Lad trotted over to where we stood. He looked up at me as if to say, "Don't worry—I've got this." Then he laid down, carefully choosing a position in which he could keep one eye on the sheep and one on the door. Or maybe on us.

"Have you found them?" she asked, in a low voice.

"If you mean the prisoners, they're all fine," I said. "And hiding behind that door back there until we figure out a way to sneak them out of here. A pity you didn't bring the sheep costumes from the Christmas pageant. We could smuggle them out with the flock that way."

"Not unless this year's costumes are a great deal more realistic than last year's," Rose Noire said.

To my surprise, my phone rang. Apparently I was in one of Clay County's random pockets of cell phone coverage. I pulled the phone out of my pocket and glanced down at the caller ID. Then I braced myself and answered it anyway.

"Good morning, Chief," I said.

"What in blue blazes are you people doing over there?" he shouted.

"Bringing a little much-needed Christmas cheer to Clay County," I said. "We figure maybe if we sing a little Christmas spirit into them, the Dingles might let themselves be convinced to empty their jail for the holidays."

"And what happens if you're all still there singing 'in excelsis deo' when the state troopers and the FBI want to start their raid?"

Aha! Clearly he'd found his way to our video feed.

"Do they want to start their raid now?" I asked. "Because you'd be amazed how fast I could have everyone back on the road to Caerphilly if you give the word."

"It's coming together," he said. "I think it was your information about where the moonshine was stored that did the trick. Although even the Feds need a little time to pull a raid together. I saw you coming out of the jail—do you know who they've got locked up in there?"

"Randall's party, Grandfather's party, and Mark Caverly," I said. "All present and accounted for."

"Good," he said. "Fodder for the kidnapping charges I've

been telling the FBI about. At least—have you actually seen them? You could testify that they were there?"

"Even better," I said. "We've got video. Would you like me to have Delaney send it to you?"

He was silent for a moment.

"Why, yes," he said. "I think the FBI would find that highly useful. And may I tell them that all you innocent civilians will be out from underfoot in, say, an hour's time?"

"I think we can manage that," I said. "Should give the ladies time to sing enough carols to make the trip seem worthwhile and then load them on the buses."

"Oh, look!" Rose Noire exclaimed. "How lovely!"

Since her definition of lovely sometimes collided with my definition of looming disaster, I moved a little closer to the door so I could see what was going on.

Minerva, with ferocious energy, was directing the choir in a rousing rendition of "The First Noel." And right on cue, as the singers warbled "Three wise men came from country far," three of the zoo's camels strode majestically out between the choir and the jail steps, each bearing a brightly costumed wise person. Definitely all wise persons here—I recognized Caroline Willner, Rabbi Grossman's wife, Joyce, and Viola Wilson, the wife of New Life Baptist's minister. After a brief transit in front of the jail, they began circling around in back of the choir, pulling handfuls of foil-wrapped candy out of their saddlebags and flinging them at the Clay County onlookers.

"Lord have mercy," the chief muttered over the phone. Evidently he was watching the video feed.

The camels were nice, but I was more focused on what I had spotted over their heads—a small mechanical object flying around near one of the huge oak trees. Presumably Ekaterina's drone. As I watched, it slowly settled down on one of the oak's large, nearly horizontal branches, twitched a little as if adjusting its position, and then grew still.

"Look, if we're going to get out of the FBI's way in an hour, I should go do a few things," I said. "I'll keep you posted."

"You do that," he said, and hung up.

First, I called Delaney.

"Do we have a reasonable number of people watching all this?" I asked.

"More than reasonable," she said. "I wouldn't exactly say it's gone viral yet, but there's an impressive number of people watching the live feed, and a lot of people are posting clips on Facebook, so the numbers are growing steadily."

"Can you send Chief Burke a link to the feed from the cell block cameras?" I asked.

"Not a live feed anymore, remember?"

"He'll find the canned feed just as interesting," I said. "As will a few other law enforcement types, I hope."

"Funny you should mention that—I won't bore you by telling you how we use IP addresses and such to figure it out, but I'm pretty sure there's reasonably high level of law enforcement interest in our webcast."

"State or federal interest?"

"Yes."

"Great," I said. "Once you get the chief the link—"

"Already done."

"—we may be changing over to the drone camera."

"That's drone cameras. We have two in place. You're thinking of starting a strategic withdrawal? Does that mean you've figured out how to rescue the prisoners?"

"Maybe," I said. "Just keep the feed going, and do what you can to expand our audience."

I hung up and thought for a moment.

"Meg?" Rose Noire looked worried. "What's wrong?"

"Nothing's wrong," I said. "I'm just thinking. This is what it looks like."

"Sorry."

I called Ekaterina.

"Can you load up and pull out?" I asked. "With everything except the video and broadcasting equipment. And all the people, if they can possibly set the equipment up to keep running untended for an hour or so. And take the back way, the alleyway behind the buildings, as far as you can."

"Affirmative," she said, and hung up.

"Go open that door and get the guys out here," I told Rose Noire, pointing to the door that led to the cells. "We're going to try something."

She scurried through the flock and disappeared into the cell block.

I peered out through the front doors.

"Watch your step," I heard Rose Noire saying. "We fed the sheep rather heavily on the way over to keep them calm."

"The First Noel" gave way to "Deck the Hall (with Boughs of Holly)." As that was drawing to a close, I saw the two Dominion Energy trucks, real and faux, emerge onto the road at the far side of the Clayville Market and speed off homeward. A small compact car followed them—presumably Rachel.

"Meg?" Rob appeared at my elbow. "Are we leaving now?"

"Pretty soon, I hope," I said. "Stay out of sight for the time being."

He slipped back among the sheep.

"When I give the cue, start sending them out," I told Rose Noire.

"The prisoners?" she asked. "Or the sheep?"

"Why not both?" I asked. "And before you ask, the cue is . . . let's see . . . how about 'lost lambs.'"

"Got it," she said.

The choir began "It Came upon the Midnight Clear." I

hoped the denizens of Clay County were taking to heart the part about "peace on earth, goodwill to men." An encouraging number of them were singing along, at any rate. As the choir sang the final strains of the fourth verse, I unlocked the doors, pushed them open, and stepped out to stand by Minerva's side.

"I'm going to try to make a speech," I said in an undertone to her, while the bystanders were applauding and the singers were shuffling their carol books.

"Here." She handed me a battery-powered microphone. "This should make it easier."

I turned on the microphone and held up one hand to ask for everyone's attention.

Chapter 36

"Thank you so much, ladies, for the beautiful concert so far," I began. "And thank you all for getting up so early to bring this gift of music to our neighbors here in Clay County. How about it, Clay County—have you got the Christmas spirit yet?"

To my delight, many of the onlookers clapped and cheered. It was pretty feeble compared to the awesome combined might of the choirs, but it sounded happy and welcoming.

"And a special thanks to our hosts today," I went on. "Mayor Dingle? Sheriff Dingle? Come and take a bow."

The two Dingles, looking as if they'd rather eat ground glass, shuffled over somewhat closer and stood awkwardly and uncomfortably as the Caerphillians clapped and cheered. I noticed with interest that the locals' response was rather perfunctory. When the applause died down I went on.

"And I've just found out that we have another reason to be grateful to Clay County. As many of you know, my grandfather went missing last night while leading a nature walk. My father, my brother, and Clarence Rutledge, our local veterinarian, were in his party."

Both of the Dingles had snapped to attention and were watching me suspiciously.

"We were afraid they might have perished in last night's terrible storm," I went on. "And to compound the tragedy, so fierce were the weather conditions that a party of skilled local trackers, who set out to find and rescue Grandfather's group, became lost in the storm themselves. I know I'm not the only person who feared the worst. But we have good news!"

Everyone took that as a cue to clap and cheer—Clay County onlookers and Caerphilly visitors in equal measure.

"We've learned that some of Sheriff Dingle's deputies were able to locate and rescue both missing parties," I continued when the noise diminished. "And brought them here to the town where they could find food, warmth, and a bed for the night."

More cheering, and all the singers waved their carol books so the pages flapped noisily.

"Mayor Dingle, and Sheriff Dingle—I hope you know that we'll never forget what you've done." Their faces showed that they understood the double meaning in this very well. "And now—citizens of Caerphilly! Our lost lambs!"

Rose Noire flung open the door, releasing several annoyed-looking sheep, followed by Grandfather. The crowd cheered wildly, and Grandfather raised both fists above his head like Rocky entering the ring. He strode over to where I stood beside the Dingles, shook first Mayor Dingle's hand, then Sheriff Dingle's, and then continued briskly down the steps. A couple of the Ladies of St. Clotilda stepped forward to usher him into a waiting bus.

As if we'd rehearsed it, the New Life Baptist choir members struck up the hymn "There Were Ninety and Nine That Safely Lay." Those who knew the words joined in; the rest either hummed along or joined arms and swayed in time to the music—except for a couple dozen of the Ladies of St. Clotilda, who hurried up the stairs to embrace the rescued Caerphillians as soon as they emerged from the front door of the jail and hustle them past the Dingles to the safety of the bus. I glanced over to see that Mother was coordinating this last effort. Thank goodness. It was one thing for Grandfather to dash over and shake the Dingles' hands—being both well-known and widely considered a harmless if amusing eccentric gave him some protection. And if he'd given them his usual bone-crushing grip, with any luck at least one of them would have emerged from the handshake with a sprained tendon or two. But it would probably have been a bad idea for Mark Caverly or even the Shiffleys to give the Dingles a chance to intercept them. I tried to pretend that I was absorbed in the music while the front door of the jail emitted sheep in twos and threes, interspersed with liberated prisoners. Both Dingles looked ready to blow a gasket when they saw Mark Caverly being led to the bus, but they didn't try to interfere. They were probably planning to demand the prisoners' return in the morning. I was relieved to see the last of the prisoners disappear through the door of the school bus just as the choir belted out "Rejoice! I have found My sheep!" I had a feeling "There Were Ninety and Nine That Safely Lay" was going to become a popular favorite in Caerphilly churches from now on.

And that was also the moment when Rose Noire gave Lad permission to follow his sheep. He bounded down the steps and began diligently working to round them all up.

"The chief wants us to wrap this up and hit the road before the FBI arrives," I said to Minerva in an undertone. She nodded, and then made a gesture. A murmur ran through the New Life Baptist choir members, and then Minerva led them in "Hark! The Herald Angels Sing."

Clearly this was some sort of prearranged signal. All the singers fell to with a will, but I could tell that everyone was preparing for their exit. Caroline and the other two camel riders turned their mounts toward the zoo truck, which was parked beyond the buses. People who had brought things seemed to be surreptitiously gathering them up.

The bus drivers took their seats. They didn't start the engines, but they were clearly ready to do so. Rose Noire emerged from the side door of the jail and went over to the ancient farm truck in time to let down the loading ramp when Lad arrived, driving Seth Early's sheep before him. Mother was standing by one of the Caerphilly County school buses waving to catch my attention. When I waved back she pointed at me and then at the bus door.

When the final refrain of "Glory to the newborn king" rang out, I expected to see everyone bolt for the buses. Instead Minerva took the portable microphone.

"Thank you for having us, neighbors," she said. "We'd like to invite you to join our community carol sing tomorrow night. Seven P.M. in the Caerphilly town square. Dress warmly, and enjoy the free hot chocolate! And from all of us to all of you, we hope you have a merry and very blessed Christmas."

At that, the assembled singers broke out in "We Wish You a Merry Christmas" and began heading for the buses in a brisk, orderly fashion. Their progress was slowed a little by the fact that first a few and then more and more Clay County onlookers were coming up to shake the carolers hands and wish them a Merry Christmas.

I was surprised to see that the Dingles appeared to be standing there just observing the impending departure. My first impulse was to feel relieved, but that gave way to deep suspicion. Were they really going to let Mark Caverly go? Were they plotting some way to steal him back? Or worse, were they planning some kind of ambush between here and the county line?

I pulled out my phone and called Chief Burke.

"We're taking off soon," I said.

"Yes, I see," he said. "Please tell me you're not going to do something quixotic and stupid, like staying behind to play rear guard."

"No, I plan to leave with the rest. Mother's saving me a seat on one of the school buses."

"Good. Don't let anyone linger. You want to be out of there when the SWAT team arrives."

"Oooh, there's a SWAT team coming?"

"I think the Feds have some other high-falutin' name for it, but that's what it is. Not sure how much longer they're going to be content to cool their heels in the zoo parking lot. So make tracks."

"To hear is to obey."

He snorted at that and hung up.

The trucks and buses had started their engines, and the last of the visitors from Caerphilly were climbing aboard the buses. Most of the Clay County residents were watching from the sidewalks on both sides of the street, waving at the buses, many of them sucking on candy canes.

About the only sour faces I could see were those of the mayor and the sheriff. Both of them were glowering at the buses—and occasionally at me. Probably a very good thing I was leaving with the rest. The several deputies standing in a clump near their boss didn't look hostile—just confused, and maybe a little anxious, as if it had begun to dawn on them that they'd be the ones around to take the heat when the sheriff decided it was safe to let his hair down.

Time to board the bus. If this were a movie, I'd pause just long enough to utter a final devastating witticism—something that would cut both Dingles to the quick and make them realize what utter scum they were. Of course, if this were a movie, a team of expert screenwriters would have been working for months to perfect that witticism. I decided to settle for a cheerful wave.

Probably wiser. It also dawned on me that if this were a movie, it might be one of those ones where the arch villain comes back for one more crack, just when you think he's dead and buried. I was under no illusion that we'd defanged the Dingles. We'd just gotten the better of them for the time being. They'd be back.

Unless the waiting SWAT team got enough evidence to put them away. Now there was a cheerful thought.

I strode down the steps toward the Caerphilly school bus where Mother was standing in the door, tapping her foot. I was the last to board.

"Take a seat, or I'm not going anywhere," the bus driver said. Since the bus driver was Ginnie Shiffley, who actually did drive for the Caerphilly school system, she probably had a lot of experience saying that. I plopped into the seat Mother had been saving for me, and Ginnie took off.

"You did it!" Dad was sitting just behind me. "I knew we could count on you!"

"Well done!" Grandfather said, from the seat behind Dad.

"Now if you can just convince Delaney I'm not the scum of the earth." Rob, sitting across the aisle from Dad, was probably the only person on the bus who didn't look overjoyed. Well, except for me.

"Delaney helped with your rescue, you know," I said. "She would have been here with us if I hadn't convinced her that she'd be much more valuable at a keyboard, using her tech skills. If I were her I'd refuse to speak to you for at least a week, to pay you back for coming so close to getting yourself killed. But she might not be as hardhearted as I am."

"Oh, she is." Rob sounded surprisingly cheerful. "But if she helped you rescue me, she can't be all that mad, can she?"

He sat back beaming happily, leaving me the only sane, sensible, worried person on the bus. Well, with the possible exception of Mark Caverly, who was craning his neck to see out of the window, clearly keeping a watchful eye on the Dingles. He glanced over and saw me watching him.

"I'll feel a lot better when we put some distance between us and that jail," he said. Although he sounded curiously calm for a mild-mannered accountant who'd just been rescued from dire peril.

I leaned forward so I could talk to Ginnie without being overheard.

"If you hear sirens, keep going," I said. "I wouldn't put it past Sheriff Dingle to try to stop us before we get to the county line."

She nodded.

"And don't be startled if you hear helicopters overhead," I added. "That will be the FBI. Or possibly the ATF."

"After thirty-seven years driving this bus it takes a lot to startle me," she said.

We were halfway to the county line when we met a caravan of law enforcement vehicles heading toward Clayville. I wondered if Chief Burke had briefed them in enough detail that they knew why there were busloads of people speeding away from Clayville, cheering wildly and serenading them with "The Battle Hymn of the Republic."

"We'll be going straight to church, dear," Mother said, from where she was sitting with Dad. She said this as if it were a given, and a good thing in the bargain.

"Straight to church? Why?" I hoped I didn't sound testy, but I'd only had a couple of hours of sleep all night—so while I would be the first to admit that our rescue effort owed an enormous debt to the combined Caerphilly churches and I wouldn't be averse to a nice ceremony of thanksgiving eventually, or whatever was appropriate—I didn't think The Book of Occasional Services included anything like a Ceremony of Discreet Gloating, which was what I craved right now. But what I really wanted more than anything at the moment was go straight home, kiss Michael and the boys, and fall into bed.

"It's Sunday morning, dear—remember?" Mother said. "And besides, all the men will be waiting for us there. They're under the impression that we were out all night cleaning and painting the new shelter—at least they were until the video began appearing on the internet. But we just sent out messages to everyone that we're on our way, and we should get there only a little late for the ten o'clock service."

Mother sat back as if this settled everything. I looked around at my family. Dad, Rob, and Grandfather were still dressed as ninjas, and quite obviously ninjas who had been up all night and possibly dragged through at least one stable. I was still wearing the badly fitting stolen Dominion Energy uniform and had sheep droppings on one shoe. But Mother was beaming at us just as proudly as if we were wearing our Sunday best.

"Okay, ten o'clock service it is." I'd beg Robyn to keep her sermon short. "How about some carols on the way?"

"A lovely idea," Mother said.

So we all joined in on "Angels We Have Heard on High" and trilled "Glo-o-o-o-ria!" in four-part harmony all the way back to town.

Chapter 37

"Mom! Elijah took my staff!"

"Mom! All the glitter is coming off my halo!"

"Mrs. Waterston! Colin spilled my myrrh!"

I took a deep, calming breath and reminded myself that I only had to survive the next hour and the Christmas pageant would be over for the year. And I'd have at least ten months to find someone I could sucker into running it next Christmas.

"Elijah! If you don't give Josh back his staff, I will take away your crook and promote Kyle to head shepherd! You can go sit out in the pews and watch the pageant! Colin! I want all the myrrh back in the box in five minutes or I'll make you eat it!"

The latter threat seemed to make a profound impression on Colin, who scurried to obey. In fact, a profound impression on the whole Christmas pageant cast, probably because they were unaware that the myrrh we were using for the performance was actually lumps of rock candy made from brown sugar. I'd been planning to share it out among the cast members after the pageant. Probably not a good idea if it had been rolling around on the floor of the parish hall. I turned to my son Jamie, aka the Angel Gabriel, who was almost tearful over his diminished halo.

"There's still a lot of glitter left," I said. "And you know, having less glitter might actually be a good thing. Before, it was so shiny that the reflection made it hard to see your face. This will look much more effective—especially in the cast photos. But if you really want more glitter, go ask your dad if he can find some."

Jamie looked thoughtful, and I was relieved to see that he didn't run over to demand glitter when Michael returned, accompanied by the smallest of the sheep, who had become overstimulated in the exciting backstage atmosphere and had to be escorted to his mother for a short time-out and some remedial cuddling. I was also relieved to see that the little sheep was calm again.

"How much longer?" Michael asked.

I glanced up at the clock.

"Half an hour! Whatever possessed us to get them ready so early? How can we possibly keep them distracted for a whole half hour?"

"Relax. I will lead the cast in a pre-performance relaxation and focusing routine. You will go out and fetch our missing cast member."

"Missing cast member? Who—"

"Lark."

"Whose real name is Andrea, you know. And yes, I can do that."

"Take your time," he said. "I've got this."

I wasn't going to argue with him. I was still running short on sleep after yesterday morning's adventures. And I had to admit, he was great with the cast.

So I slipped out of the parish hall, and the wave of sound hit me. Trinity's vestibule was packed full of people, here early either to drop off their kids or to get a good seat, and they were all talking a mile a minute.

I checked one of the side doors into the sanctuary—yes, that was filling up as well.

Then I spotted a familiar face—familiar, but slightly out of place.

"Chief," I said. "Don't tell me you're defecting from New Life Baptist."

"Hardly," he said. "But we don't have any services until evening, and Adam wanted to see Josh and Jamie in their pageant."

He pointed through the side door to where his grandson was sitting, front and center in the first pew. Probably planning to see if he could break the twins' concentration and make them giggle.

"I'm glad you were able to get away from the station," I said. "I trust that means things are going well."

"That's one of the advantages of having crimes in adjacent counties instead of our own," he said. "So much less red tape to deal with. In case you were wondering, the particular batch of red tape required to liberate your car from Clay County is pretty much taken care of. If it's not in your driveway when you get home, then it will be before much longer."

"I'm glad you managed to rescue it before they had a chance to chop it up for parts."

"There wasn't really as much danger of that as you'd think," he said. "Cy Whicker may talk a good game, but his chop shop operation moves about as efficiently as everything else in Clay County, which means hardly at all. The state troopers found stolen cars from six or eight months back still languishing there."

"Oooh," I said. "Please tell me he's going to do time for that."

"One to five years per stolen vehicle, in theory," the chief said. "And his operation is a big one, even though it is inefficient. If the judge makes those sentences consecutive instead of concurrent, we taxpayers could be footing the bill for his room and board for decades."

"I'd consider it money well spent," I said. "And what about the Dingles?"

"It will take a while to sort out who gets them first. The FBI wants them for the kidnapping charges and the public corruption, the ATF for the moonshine, the DEA for the marijuana farm, and the Virginia State Police has overlapping jurisdiction for most of it. But they're doing all that wrangling over in Clayville at the moment, so all I have to do is look sympathetic when they drop by to vent about how unbelievable it all is and how annoying the other agencies are. Look sympathetic and bite my tongue, because it's really a bad idea to say 'I told you so' to a Fed. Oh, and in case you were wondering what happened to that woman who was pretending to be Lark's mother—"

"Valerie Peters," I said.

"That's her. The Suffolk police called to say that she's safely in rehab and they send their thanks for the part you played in helping them apprehend her."

"I didn't do much," I said. "It was Horace's uniform that chased her away."

"If you hadn't had the brains to suspect her and the gumption to act on your suspicions, she'd have been gone before she had a chance to see Horace, taking poor little Lark with her. From where I sit, that's a lot. And now, about the only case I have to deal with is the one involving Urisha Peebles and Tyler Whicker."

"The two thugs who tried to invade the Women's Shelter, right?"

"Right. They're not going anywhere for the time being, and while the Feds haven't actually come out and said so, I think they will be rather happy if I drag my feet on the shelter invasion case. They're probably hoping to cut a deal—a break on sentencing if Peebles and Whicker testify against bigger fry."

"As in the Dingles?"

He nodded.

"The thug Josefina whacked with the frying pan is going to be okay, then?"

"Peebles. Yes, thanks to your dad. He'll live to stand trial.

Or testify, if the Feds can convince him it's in his best interest."

"What about Inman, the crooked Fed?"

"In it up to his eyeballs with the Dingles. He was lying to his own agency, the FBI, and everyone else. Claiming he was in touch with Mark, and that Mark said it was too soon to send in agents. But apparently someone hacked his phone records and sent them to the right people. When the FBI saw all those calls from Inman to various Dingles, they couldn't wait to go in."

"Please tell me they'll be able to convict him of something."

"Oh, he'll do time, all right." The chief smiled grimly.

"And did I get Brianna in very much trouble for borrowing the Dominion Energy truck?"

He chuckled.

"Luckily, she managed to get it back to their work yard before anyone noticed it was gone," he said. "And the trucks didn't actually appear on camera, so if Dominion does hear a rumor that one of their trucks might have been involved in the Clayville concert, Ekaterina can probably convince them that she also did her logo forging on a Shifley Construction bucket lift truck. Since I have no official knowledge of unauthorized use of a Dominion truck, that's what I've chosen to assume."

"That's a relief. I hate to hurry off—"

"But you have a pageant to get on the road." He smiled. "Good luck."

I turned to go. Then I stopped, and peered out into the sanctuary again.

"Something wrong?" the chief asked.

"That guy's one of the FBI agents," I said. "I saw him on television last night, in one of the news reports about the raid. The extremely buff guy with the short-back-and-sides haircut in the third pew from the back. He's sort of hiding his face behind the order of service. Don't stare!"

"I see him."

"What's he doing here?"

"He appears to be perusing the order of service, if that's what you call it. I'd have said the program, but what do I know? Maybe he's an Episcopalian FBI agent."

Maybe. Still, I stood there for few moments, watching him. Yes, he did seem to be reading the order of service. Eventually he opened the hymnal. And when he grabbed a couple of offering envelopes from the rack on the back of the pew in front of him and used them to bookmark the hymns to be sung, I gave up watching. Either he was a genuine Episcopalian, or his impersonation was too good for me to find fault with it.

I hurried off and began threading through the crowd in the vestibule, saying hello to friends and promising them I'd tell them all the news after the pageant.

"Hello, Meg."

I turned to see Rachel standing nearby.

"Greetings," I said. "Come here to watch Lark—sorry, Andrea—in the Christmas pageant?"

"Partly," she said. "But there's something else—could you introduce me to your minister?"

"Of course." I led her into Robyn's office. For once, I didn't see Noah. Since I couldn't hear him, either, I wondered if she'd left him at home with a babysitter. No, probably not. Although he wasn't in sight, he'd left his mark in the form of a tiny still-damp spot of milky spit-up on Robyn's vestments.

"Let me clean that up," I said, reaching into my pocket for a tissue so I could dab at the spot. "And have you met Rachel Plunket, who helped us out with the raid on Clay County?"

"Thank you," Robyn said. "And delighted, Rachel."

"Actually, it's Rachel *Driver* Plunket," Rachel said as they shook hands. "Soon to be just Rachel Driver. I'm planning on dropping the Plunket bit as soon as I figure out how you do that. Driver's my mother's maiden name. I haven't quite forgiven Mom for marrying a Plunket, but I still think her name's an improvement."

"Judge Jane would know how to get that done, wouldn't she?" I asked Robyn, who nodded. "Judge Jane Shiffley," I added to Rachel. "Four of the guys you helped rescue are her kin, so I suspect she'd be more than happy to help you out in return."

"I think a name change has to be done in whatever jurisdiction you're resident in," Robyn said. "Are you staying around here?"

"I am now," Rachel said. "I was going to run away as fast and as far as I could—but you know what? After yesterday, meeting all y'all, I figured out I don't really want to leave this part of the country altogether and lose touch with all the friends I grew up with—I just want to get out of Clay County. So yesterday I went in and asked Muriel at the diner if she had any openings, and she took me on. And then Delaney put me in touch with her landlord, who has an efficiency apartment opening up any day now. So meet the newest resident of the beautiful county of Caerphilly." She beamed at us.

"We're very glad to have you," I said.

"Welcome!" Robyn exclaimed.

"And I have something I wanted to ask you," Rachel said, turning to Robyn. "Could you do the funeral for my brother? I know he wasn't a member of your congregation, but I don't want Reverend Dingle to do his funeral and—"

"Absolutely," Robyn said. "We can start arranging it now if you'd like."

"After Christmas will do," Rachel said. "Chief Burke tells

me it will be at least a few days before they release the body, so there's no big hurry."

"Come in Wednesday, then," Robyn said. "We won't be able to set the date until we know when they're releasing him, but we can work out all the other details. And if you'd like, I can go over to the funeral home with you and see that they take care of everything properly."

Which meant, I knew, that Robyn would talk Maudie Morton at the funeral home into giving Rachel very good service at a rock-bottom price. Not that Maudie wouldn't be a soft touch anyway for someone in Rachel's situation.

"Thanks—I'll do that."

"Tell me," Robyn said. "Janet says you sometimes look after her daughter. You wouldn't happen to be interested in earning a little extra money by babysitting for my son, would you?"

Rachel's eyes lit up.

"I'd be very interested," she said. "I need to save up all the money I can for college."

I made a mental note to ask Michael if he'd had a chance to speak to the Caerphilly College financial aid office about Rachel. If there wasn't already a scholarship she was eligible for, I knew plenty of people in town who'd be happy to help create one.

But that was a project for later. Right now I had a pageant to manage.

"I hate to interrupt," I said. "But where are Lark—sorry, Andrea—and Noah? Time for me to collect whichever one's in a good mood to play his or her part in the pageant."

"Janet and Mark are watching them both," Robyn said. "In the overflow room."

I left Robyn and Rachel to plan an introduction to Noah.

In the overflow room someone had set up a playpen. Andrea/Lark was lying in it, fast asleep, with her parents standing over her, arms around each other's waists, gazing down as if they couldn't get enough of seeing her. They looked up and murmured soft hellos.

Nearby, in an old easy chair, Josefina was holding Noah on her lap, cooing nonsense syllables at him. And while Noah wasn't exactly silent, his fussing wasn't very loud, and had a perfunctory air, as if he was only doing it because he had his reputation to think of.

"The ladies at the shelter asked me to say hello," Josefina said. "And to thank you for talking your grandmother into letting us all stay at her house."

"I didn't have to talk her into it," I said. "She offered before I could even ask. And I think she's hoping they'll still be there when she goes home after Christmas."

"Lilly also says hello," Josefina added. "The little one who was so suspicious of Santa Claus. When she heard I might see you, she asked me to bring you this."

She handed me a picture. A pretty good drawing for a child of maybe eight or nine years old. Two large and rather scary monsters occupied the left side of the page, hulking and bearded, with long teeth, both holding oversized guns. On the right side were a cluster of women and children, huddled together, with terrified eyes and mouths opened wide as if screaming. And in the middle, and larger than all the others, were a short, squat figure wielding a frying pan and a tall, wild-haired figure holding an enormous claw hammer.

"She used to draw only monsters," Josefina said. "But for the last few days, more and more she also draws people defeating the monsters. I think it is progress."

"I think so, too," I said. "Tell her thank you. I'll hang it in my office."

She smiled, and went back to playing with Noah. I turned to Mark and Janet.

"So it looks as if La—as if Andrea is the better choice for playing baby Jesus—if that's still all right with you."

"Fine with us," Mark said.

"And you can call her Lark if you like," Janet added. "I have to admit—the name's kind of growing on me."

"I like it," Mark said. "I think we should use it."

"A special nickname from the first big adventure of her life," Janet said, nodding.

"That's good," I said. "Because it could be hard for people around here to get used to calling her Andrea. Of course, maybe that's not a big worry—have you decided where you're going to go?"

"Not really." Janet was picking up Lark, who to my relief only sighed slightly and didn't awaken.

"Your brother has offered me a job in his financial department, if I want it," Mark said. "And I'm tempted."

Was he serious? Or was he saying that as part of his cover? Because while I couldn't prove it, I had a theory that Mark Caverly wasn't actually an accountant but an undercover ATF agent who'd deliberately taken the job in Clay County to bring down the Dingles' moonshine enterprise. I didn't have any hard evidence to back up the theory—just the memory of how calm he'd been during our escape from Clay County and the sneaking feeling that some of the ATF and FBI agents were only pretending to not know him. And my nagging feeling that Janet had been holding something back.

"Caerphilly is exactly the sort of place we thought we were going to when Mark took the job with Clay County." Janet carefully handed Lark to me.

"But we need to decide whether we'd feel safer putting a little distance between us and the Dingles," Mark said. "And see how the Dingles' trial goes. If there is a trial—with any luck they'll plead out and save the taxpayers a lot of money. I get the feeling that's what the FBI guys are hoping," he added, perhaps realizing that he was starting to sound more like a Fed than a witness.

"Understood," I said. "I'm sure Rob will understand if you take a little time to decide." And given the generous salaries Rob tended to offer his staff, if Mark did turn down the job, I'd be almost positive he was a Fed.

"Are things okay between Rob and Delaney?" Janet asked.

"Better than okay," I said. "If you come into the sanctuary to watch Lark's stage debut—"

"Wouldn't miss it for anything," Mark said.

"Then you will have a hard time missing the honking big diamond ring Delaney is wearing on her left hand," I said. "I'm giving serious thought to borrowing it to represent the Star of the East in the pageant."

They both chuckled.

"See you in the pageant." I lifted Lark's chubby, limp hand and waved it at them.

Then I hurried out into the vestibule with her fast asleep on my shoulder.

And speak of the devil, Rob and Delaney were there, with Mother and Dad and Caroline and Cordelia and Rose Noire and Grandfather gathered around them, all beaming.

I waved and hurried on.

As I passed the side door to the sanctuary, I glanced in and saw Chief Burke standing just inside, talking to the FBI agent. When the chief saw me, he waved for me to come over.

"Meg, this is Special Agent Durham. He was expressing his appreciation for your diversionary tactics."

"I admit, I got a little hot under the collar when I first saw the video feed," Durham said. "Not a big fan of vigilantism or civilian interference or whatever you'd call that stunt you pulled. But I have to admit, the raid went a whole lot more smoothly than I'd been expecting. Took us half an hour to convince them that we really were law enforcement instead of another batch of nosy parkers from Caerphilly bent on making them look like idiots. And the video's going to prove useful—pretty hard for an arrestee to prove excessive force when you've got him down on video throwing sheep—um, sheep manure at the arresting officers. So all's well that ends well this time."

"Happy to be of service," I said. "I should go—we can't start the pageant without a baby for the manger."

"Looking forward to it," Durham said.

I ducked back into the parish hall. Michael was sitting in a folding chair facing a delta of sheep, shepherds, wise persons, angels, camel parts, and members of the Holy Family. They were sitting cross-legged on the floor with their eyes closed and were taking deep breaths. And they all looked calm and eager—even the smallest and most excitable of the sheep.

Michael opened his eyes when he heard me come in.

"And here's our final cast member," he said. "Okay, it's show time, folks! Let's do our huddle!"

As I placed the still-sleeping Lark in the manger, ready for the trustworthy Josh to wheel into the sanctuary, I saw Michael and the rest of the cast clumped together in a tight knot—it looked rather like the team-spirit-building ritual with which the boys' baseball team always began its games.

"On three," he said. "Ready?"

"One! Two! Three!" they all chanted. "MERRY CHRISTMAS!"